APRIL JACKS

Mercedes' Closet :

KEEPING
DEADLY
Secrets

Dedication

This book is dedicated to my babies and grandbabies: Vania Jackson, Cardell Beasley, Dayja Beasley, Angel Martinez, Seiji Beasley, William Jackson, and Jin-Lewis Beasley. My children have watched me suffer so much over the years. They have wiped away many tears from their mother's face. I just want you all to know my strength comes from each and every one of you. The best thing God could have done was to bless me with children as wonderful as the ones he placed into my life.

This journey was a long and very trying one, so many stops along the way. I would like to give thanks to my longtime friends Vernetia Moore and Cathy Blash for always being a shoulder when the road grew weary. A special thanks to my friends Ileana Sierra, Briona Griffin-Atwater, and Brandon Enis, for listening, caring, and the countless rides around when I had nothing or nobody.

I also would like to take time to thank Mrs. Lisa Malone for all the pages she read, all the errands she ran, and the countless tears she wiped away. Ms. Robyn Robbins of Robyn Robbins Enterprises for pushing me to not give up on myself and for being my writing coach and book midwife.

To the love of my life Tami Jackson-Hunter, thanks for not taking no for an answer. If it wasn't for your stubbornness I wouldn't have known that love still existed in my heart. Thanks for not letting me give up on me. Words can't express the gratitude and love that fill my heart for you.

My mother, grandmothers, and aunties for showing me where my strength within lies.

Last but not least, thanks to my entire family for just being them, the memories of great times got me through the bad nights. Couldn't have completed this journey without any of you, really can't say thank you enough.

Contents

Dedication iii

Acknowledgments ix

1. Nightmares and Secrets 1

2. Innocence Lost 17

3. Love or Lust 23

4. More Skeletons in The Closet 31

5. Perfect Stranger 37

6. Lover and Friends 43

7. Gay or Straight? That's the Question 51

8. A Wolf in Sheep's Clothing 65

9. Shattered Glass 73

10. Love is Not Always Enough 81

11. She Loves Me Not 91

12. Side Chick or Main Squeeze 107

13. Once The Closet Door Opens 113

14. When I Love You Never Come 119

15. Ticking Time Bomb 129

16. The Quiet Before the Storm 137

17. Desperately Seeking Answers..143

18. Running Scared..149

19. Blood on Your Hands..155

20. What Nightmares Are Made Of.....................................161

21. The Enemy of My Enemy is My Friend.........................167

22. When the Smoke Clears..175

23. Why Does Love Hurt? 183

24. I Love You to Death 191

25. Predator or Prey 197

About the Author...205

In Loving Memory Of

Ronald A. Jackson

Father, Best Friend, and Super Hero

Love you to infinity and beyond

Acknowledgments

Everyone has a closet filled with secrets that they hide from the world. These secrets or skeletons as some may call them, build up over a lifetime and began to occupy space in your heart and mind. This occupancy makes a person unable to live, love, or even grow. Know the signs, Domestic Violence comes in many forms and has many different faces.

According to the National Domestic Violence Hotline (http://www.thehotline.org/is-this-abuse/abuse-defined/) Domestic violence can be defined as a pattern of behavior which involves the abuse by one person against another.

According to the National Institute of Justice (https://www.nij.gov/topics/-crime/intimate-partner-violence/Pages/welcome.aspx) Partner violence in lesbian (and gay) relationships recently has been identified as a growing social problem. Partner or domestic violence can consist of physical, sexual and psychological abuse.

It's never ok for someone to do things that you don't want to happen. It doesn't matter if you're gay or straight, abuse whether it's sexual, physical, verbal, or mental is never ok. If you or anybody you know is being abused get out and seek help.

Not everyone is lucky enough to walk away from domestic violence. I was one of the lucky ones, but there are plenty of faces and names that flash across the television of those who weren't. This book is also dedicated to them.

1

Nightmares and Secrets

Mercedes

The blaring of the phone ringing snapped Mercedes out of the dream world and back into reality. Without thinking twice or checking the caller ID, she answered with a groggy hello. "Yea bitch you thought you were gonna get away from me!" "I'll see you soon!" The call ended as fast as it started.

Mercedes sat straight up in bed, clicked on the light, checked the time on her phone. 2:45 she said to herself. Grabbing her notebook off the stand she wrote down the time the call came in, what was said along with the other calls that had come in earlier.

The calls had started up again a few days ago. Mercedes thought she had done everything right, never taking the same way twice and always looking over her shoulder. She was just always being extra cautious. Despite months of being careful and hiding, her ex had found a way to contact her again.

In her mind she had already started packing up and moving yet another time, but something inside her began to grow stone and callous. The word NO screamed so forcefully in her mind that it bellowed out her mouth into the darkness of the room. I'm tired of uprooting my life, and my kids. The tears were falling soaking her night gown within minutes.

After letting herself cry for a moment Mercedes dried her face with her hands and got out of bed. She stopped for a brief moment to check the baggage under her eyes in the mirror on the dresser before she went down the hall to check on the kids. They were perfectly sound asleep tucked tight under the covers, not affected by the madness and she wanted to keep it that way. Mercedes checked the windows, under beds, and in the closet before leaving each room. She then made her way around the rest of the house making sure every nook and cranny was the way she left it. After checking her fortress from top to bottom Mercedes climbed back into bed. "Lord I ask you to protect us in our troubled times. Let us come to no hurt, harm, or danger. In Jesus name I do pray, Amen." Mercedes snuggled into her pillows and let sleep take over,

Mercedes met her ex when she was 16 years old. At that point in her life Mercedes felt like a pawn in a custody battle between her parents. The constant war between them and the never ending moving from house to house left her confused. She felt misunderstood, lonely, and that fueled with raging hormones turned her into an out of control teenager. To cover her pain, she turned to alcohol and sex. She would constantly run away and get in trouble at school. Mercedes was on a whirlwind path to a troubled life.

Until one day while she was visiting her sister Michelle for the summer she met a tall light skinned brother named Hakeem. He walked by her sister's porch, he most definitely caught her eye, but she wasn't sure if she caught his. "Mmm mmm mmm!" Mercedes said to herself as she watched the light skinned cutie turn the corner and disappear. After taking a sip of the forty of Ole English she had just popped open Mercedes bent down to finish painting her toes.

"What you doing drinking that?" an unfamiliar voice said above her head. Mercedes quickly sat up and was looking right into the brown eyes of the handsome stranger that had passed by earlier. "I guess I had caught his eye after all." Mercedes said to herself. They exchanged pleasantries, he sat down, she poured him a cup, and they began to talk. By the end of the night they felt like they had known each other forever.

Over the next few weeks Mercedes began sneaking Hakeem into her sister's house at night while everyone was upstairs sleeping. They would have sex all night and she would sneak him back out in the morning before everyone got up. Mercedes just knew she was in love. But at 16 who really knows what love is. She was about to get a rude awakening.

The smell of chicken frying awoke Mercedes and she got up and headed to the kitchen. "Man, that food smell so good that woke me out my sleep!" Mercedes said as she peeped inside pots on the stove. Her sister shooed her away and she went upstairs to relieve her bladder, wash her face, and brush her teeth. Moments later Mercedes came back to the kitchen and sat at the table. While waiting on her sister to finish cooking Mercedes ate two lunchables and three oranges. "Dude I'm starving." Mercedes said to her sister as she began rummaging through the fridge for food. She found some left over food from the night before. Mercedes warmed up the food ate it but was still in search of more food. It felt like the more she ate the hungrier she became.

After watching her sister devour what seemed like an endless array of food, Michelle turned around, put her hand on her hips, and said "Mercedes you pregnant?" "What! No!" Mercedes responded. She played back the amount of food she had just consumed and thought to herself, "I can't be pregnant? Can I?"

Mercedes got up from the table, dumped her plate in the trash, and went back downstairs to her makeshift bedroom. The words swam through her head like a swarm of hornets nesting in the flesh under her skull. She spent the next few days pondering the question in her head. It wasn't until her friend Charity confided in her that she thought she was pregnant and she was going to the free clinic to take a test, that she decided that she should do the same. They two girls had been friends for some time and over the summer became practically inseparable. Charity had already become a mother last year to a beautiful little girl that Mercedes just adored. However, looking at her friend with a baby on her hip and listening to her talk about thinking she could be expecting another scared the life out of Mercedes. "I don't know if I'm ready to become a mother." Mercedes thought to herself. Despite her uneasy feeling Mercedes quickly agreed to go with her but she didn't disclose her own reason for going.

Charity and Mercedes arrived at the clinic late one evening. Mercedes hadn't told anybody in her family what she was going to the clinic for. She had finally broken down and told Charity that she thought she was pregnant too. They both signed in but when they were called up to the counter the receptionist said that since they were under age they had to have an adult consent for them to be seen. There was no way Mercedes was calling anybody that she knew to get permission. There would be too many questions asked. Finally, Charity called her mom, and she agreed to consent for both of them. The walk to the back rooms was like a walk of death for Mercedes. Her heart was beating out her chest so loudly that she could hear it thumping in her ears. The nurse came into the room asked her a few questions about her period and gave her a cup to take to the bathroom to give a sample for the test. Mercedes was so nervous that she was trembling so bad she almost dropped the cup in the toilet while she was peeing in it. After she finished she wiped the cup off, put it inside the little window, washed her hands, and went back outside to the waiting room like she was instructed to do.

It felt like an eternity as they sat in the waiting room to hear their names called again to learn their fate. "Charity Adams and Mercedes Jackson" the nurse at the door called them both at the same time. The two friends stared at each other as they stood up and walked to the door. The nurse led them towards two separate rooms, placed the chart on the door and walked away.

Several moments passed and then there was a light knock at the door. "Come in!" Mercedes called out to the faceless knocker. "Hey Mercedes, I'm Dr. Anderson," the doctor stated as he came to stand next to Mercedes. "Congratulations"! he spoke to her. Mercedes sat there like a deer trapped in some headlights. "Looks like you're having a baby" the doctor. tried again to get a response from her. "I know you're young and scared. You want some help telling your parents?" Dr. Anderson spoke as he grabbed hold of Mercedes hand. The gesture woke Mercedes from her trance and she started to cry. "Thank you, but no I'll do it myself" the weeping teenager spoke as she wiped tears with the back of her hand. "Well from the info that you are giving us it seems like you're about six weeks along. We made you an appointment, so we can check the baby and be for sure," Dr. Anderson said as he stood up and handed her the paperwork. Mercedes took the papers in her hand, but as soon as she did the tears fell like gigantic rain drops from heaven and she collapsed in Dr. Anderson's arms.

The sound of the alarm blaring snapped Mercedes back into reality. She sat on the edge of the bed and rubbed her face with her hand. At first, she couldn't tell the difference from dream or reality, and she sat there for a moment trying to gather her thoughts. Finally, Mercedes stood to her feet and made her way to the shower. After the shower Mercedes woke up the kids and went to start breakfast while they got ready for school. While her children ate their breakfast, Mercedes cleaned up the kitchen and placed the chicken from the freezer in the fridge to thaw out for dinner. She finished just as the school bus pulled to a stop. "Bus!" she yelled out and hustled everyone out the door. "I love you guys!" she yelled as they boarded the bus.

After checking the house and making sure everything was locked down Mercedes quickly finished her morning routine and hurried back to the room to get dressed for work. Mercedes gave herself a once over in the mirror before going thru the house again to check things one last time. Feeling secure with everything she grabbed her keys and darted out the door. Once in her car she drove the twenty minutes it took to get to work in Atlanta traffic. Once at work Mercedes circled the parking lot to make sure she wasn't being followed. Feeling satisfied she parked her car in the usual spot backed in and facing to see the entire lot. Since she's always early she leaned the seat back and fired up a Newport to kill some time.

Letting her mind wonder again Mercedes thought about all the things that were happening. It brought sadness to her heart that things had changed and become so bleak and unhappy. However, deep down inside Mercedes knew she could never truly be happy unless she stopped running from Hakeem.

The alarm on her phone signaled that it was time to go inside. After gathering her things Mercedes checked her reflection in the mirror. Letting out a short breath of air, she got out the car and headed inside, where the kids of Washington high school awaited her arrival to cook and serve them their meals. Being a cafeteria lady wasn't her ideal job, but hey it pays the bills.

As soon as Mercedes walked into the building her stomach turned and she thought to herself. "Could my day get any worse?" Shunta, the district manager for not only the school where Mercedes works but 20 other schools in the district was there and on a war path. Normally the day runs smoothly, but when she's around everyone's scared that if they inhale wrong they'll get fired. "Why is she here today? I hate that bitch!" Mercedes mumbled to herself. "She's always talking to people like they were beneath her. I'm definitely not in the mood for her shit today." Mercedes said and walked thru the kitchen as fast as she could. Holding her head down desperately trying not to draw attention to herself Mercedes quietly walked toward the locker room. "Good morning Mrs. Jackson!" Mercedes heard Shunta's annoying voice say from behind her. "Morning!" Mercedes managed and walked on to the locker room.

Mercedes took as much time as she could getting ready to work. She knew her day was going to be hell. Walking out the locker room door Mercedes felt like she was walking into Satan's den and there she was, Lady Satan herself, waiting on her first kill which was to be Mercedes.

Mercedes couldn't get out the locker room fast enough before Shunta started calling her name. "Mercedes if you would please pull all the old milk out the fridge and check the dates on the open products as well." Shunta said as she stood there with her hands on her hips. "You know you guys will be having inspection soon; we have to make sure everything is correct." Without saying a word Mercedes walked past Shunta and into cooler. Every time Shunta called Mercedes' name she could feel her blood boil more and more. Mercedes thought she would erupt before too long. Being in the cooler gave her some time to think and the coolness relaxed her.

The rest of the morning was spent trying to keep out of Shunta's sight, but every chance that woman got to fuck with Mercedes she did just that. Mercedes was standing in the corner on break trying to regain some of her sanity, when into the cafeteria walked the temptress of Mercedes' desire. Mrs. Monea Daniels the school counselor and damn she was looking HOT today. She was hot every day in Mercedes' eyes. From where Mercedes was standing she could watch her safely without having to disguise the fact that she was looking at her. Mercedes was brought up by her grandmother in a very religious family. Women are supposed to be with men and vice versa. Mercedes was still very feminine, so people couldn't readily tell she was gay. So, her secret was well kept.

Today Ms. Daniels had on a tan business dress complete with jacket that stops just above the knees. The dress looked like it was tailor made to fit every curve on her body. Her outfit was accompanied by a slightly lighter shade of tan open toed stiletto heel. Heels which made her legs look like long waterfalls of caramel that cascaded from under her dress. Silky black shoulder length hair that was never out of place swayed every time she took a step. "Damn that woman is fine," she said more to herself than anything. Mercedes stood there until she was out of sight, then she leaned back against the wall and daydreamed of what Monea would look like naked. That woman drove her crazy, seeing her made Mercedes' insides melt. After several attempts of trying to regain her composure, she finally shook it off and headed for the bathroom. She had to wipe away some of the wetness that had accumulated between her thighs.

The rest of the day passed by without a hitch, because no matter what was going on all she could see was Ms. Daniels standing in front of her with nothing on but those heels. Having been so immersed in her daydreams, 2:30 came in no time. Mercedes hit the locker room, changed and headed for the door. She was five inches from freedom when Shunta's annoying ass starts calling her name from the manager's office around the corner. "Fuck her!" Mercedes thought to herself and went out the door as if she hadn't even heard her. No sooner as she was out the door her eyes caught sight of Ms. Daniels heading for her car. Not wanting to seem like a stalker and break out into a full run. Mercedes speed up her pace slightly. Thanking her lucky stars when Mercedes realized her car was three cars down from hers. "Thank you for small favors!" Mercedes said under her breath. "Good afternoon Monea" Mercedes spoke as she came up behind her. Having actually been caught up with her, she took a moment before speaking to watch the gorgeous counselor's voluptuous bottom bounce as she walked.

"Hey Mercedes girl!" "How you doing today?" The words from Monea's mouth soaked Mercedes' panties instantly. "Why haven't you been up to the office to see us?" she asked. Mercedes use to make up reasons to go to her office in the afternoons, but she couldn't very well say that. "Well you know we've been getting ready for inspections and I haven't had the time," she replied. Monea just stood there listening to Mercedes go on and on about things in the kitchen. It proved to be very tricky for Monea because the whole time she was focusing on Mercedes' lips and how she wanted them on hers. Having to do something to break the trance Monea randomly spoke out. "Oh, by the way I'm having a party next weekend. I thought maybe you and some of the other ladies in the kitchen may want to attend," she said as she opened her car door. "I'll come down to the cafeteria tomorrow with the invitations." "That a work!" Mercedes said way too loud. "So, I guess see you tomorrow." And with that Monea closed the door and started her car. Mercedes stood there watching as she began to pull off. Monea stopped and rolled down her window. It looked like she wanted to ask something but advised against. "Never mind see you later." Monea spoke out and drove off. That brief encounter with her had Mercedes' whole body bubbly, bad enough to make her quiver as she traveled the short distance to her car. Once inside behind the safety of her smoky gray tinted windows, Mercedes let her mind wonder away. She wondered what her life would be like if she lived as a lesbian woman. The thought of her enjoying life with the lovely Monea had her contemplating coming out the closet.

The phone rang scaring the shit outta her. Mercedes looked at the number on the phone, it was an unknown caller. Reluctantly she clicked the button and answered it. "Yes!" Mercedes said into the phone. "Oh, you think you safe at work, don't you?" The sound of his voice was like nails being dragged down a chalkboard. Breath caught inside Mercedes lungs and she sat there frozen in time. He held the phone for unknown reasons for what seemed like eons to Mercedes. She could hear him inhaling and exhaling oxygen. Finally, she was able to vocalize words though her mouth. "Leave me the hell alone!" Mercedes yelled into the phone and hung up before she heard a response. Mercedes just wanted for this nightmare to be over. Placing her head in her hands she sat there sobbing uncontrollably. One thing she learned in therapy is that crying is not a show of weakness, sometimes your body is using that moment of tears as a form of release. After letting herself have her moment Mercedes fixed herself in the seat, started her car, and drove off. On the way home she stopped at the liquor store, because from the sound of Hakeem's voice she knew there would be more calls again tonight.

Mercedes arrived at home, her beautiful children that she had with her crazy ex Hakeem had not arrived home from school yet. Evon, Desmond, and Marie were the reason she kept moving forward. They alone were the reason she packed up and left her abusive ex-husband. They would be the reason she would stand her ground and not leave again. She was tired of uprooting her family because Hakeem wouldn't let go. Mercedes made her way inside as quickly as she could. She did her normal routine of checking the house making sure everything was as she left it. Satisfied with her rounds she put the small bottle of vodka and the six pack of beer in the fridge and headed for the room.

She turned the music on but not too loud, so she can still hear the sounds in the house. She began to undress but the song on the radio Vivian Green's Emotional Rollercoaster, caused her mind to leave her body. She could see herself walking to the door of the old house she shared with Hakeem. She opens the door to enter as though she was coming home from work. Hakeem didn't even give her a chance to shut the door before he started with his shit. Not wanting to be bothered Mercedes side stepped him and headed for the room. "Where the fuck are you going?" He yelled behind her as she kept walking. "To shower and change so that I can cook dinner." Mercedes replied. "So, I guess you been fucking or something!" he yelled. Grabbing her clothes and things so she could take a shower seemed like a normal thing to do, but that only made things worst. "You really have been fucking, haven't you?" "I know how you are." Hakeem's words came out like fire as he stood there blocking her path making Mercedes have to maneuver to get around him. The silence from her was only adding fuel to his fire. "Bitch I know you hear me talking to you!" he yelled as he pushed her against the wall and thrust his forearm into her throat. Hakeem lowered his head and whispered in her ear. "Yeah you been fucking, haven't you?" "Man leave me alone, nobody been doing shit!" Mercedes tried to push him off, but he put more force on her throat. He slid his free hand inside the front of her pants and parted her lips. He inserted two fingers and removed them as quickly as he had put them there. He put the fingers to his nose and sniffed. "Oh, you ain't been fucking huh?" He asked. "Is that why your ass running for the shower?" "I try to show you love and this how you repay me, sucking some other nigga's dick!" "I know how you are, you're a fucking slut!" He yelled at her.

The words felt like frozen hard daggers piercing every part of Mercedes to her soul. She knew what was coming next. Mercedes tried to reason with him, but the rage had already consumed him and there was no talking to Mr. Hyde. "You like sucking dick, don't you?" He whispered in her ear. Hakeem let the silence from her become an automatic admission of guilt. "Oh, you don't hear me, ok!" He grabbed her by the hair, twisting it in his hand as he dragged Mercedes to the edge of the bed. He held her hair so tight, Mercedes felt as though he would ring her neck like a chicken.

Hakeem undid his pants and pulled his already swollen penis out. Mercedes burst out into a full-on cry. She knew that with Hakeem angry sex was gonna be harsh and painful. "Please I'm tired, I wasn't doing anything!" "Please I don't wanna have sex!" Mercedes pleaded. "You think I'll fuck you!" Hakeem angrily snapped. "Ain't no telling who you done been with." He yanked her hair and pulled her face toward his erection. She tried to fight but the more she struggles the harder he turned her neck. Mercedes resisted for as long as she could, but her neck was so twisted that she had no choice but to give up. The fatigue from her hectic work day was catching up to her. She collapsed onto the floor in front of him. Mercedes tried to close her mind on what was about to happen. She closed her eyes and focused on Vivian Green as she ironically sang out Emotional Rollercoaster to her.

Seeing he had won the battle, Hakeem grabbed her hair with both hands and pushed his harden shaft inside Mercedes' mouth. If you bite me I swear you'll regret it. Holding her head with both hands he began pounding her mouth as if she was one of those plastic blowup dolls, Hakeem showed no signs of remorse. At the slightest feel of teeth, he yanked Mercedes' hair again. Mercedes felt as though her hair was ripping and thought he might pull it out from the roots.

As his orgasm grew closer Hakeem started thrusting inside her mouth deeper and harder causing gaging and choking at the same time from her. With one final thrust semen exploded in her mouth like hot lava from a volcano. Mercedes tried to move but he still had her hair in a death grip. She could feel thick hot release sliding down the back of her throat. The sensation was too much for her. With one last gag the contents of Mercedes' stomach spewed from her mouth. Hakeem jumped back, and she threw up all on the floor and the edge of the bed. "Get up and get your ass in the shower!" He barked at her.

Still whimpering like the cowardly dog, she felt she was, Mercedes gathered up her clothes and headed toward the bathroom. Turning on the water she stepped in and let the water take her away. She stood under the hot scalding water of the shower oblivious to the world around her. Time stood still as Mercedes tried to get her thoughts together. She finally came to her senses and began scrubbing the filth from her body. When she was done Mercedes wrapped herself in a towel and grabbed her toothbrush. She aggressively brushed her teeth, then gargling with mouthwash several times after that.

She didn't want to leave the safety of the bathroom but then Mercedes heard her younger daughter Marie calling for her from beyond the door. As she reached for the bathroom door knob her daughter burst thru the door jarring Mercedes back into the real world. She had lost all track of time and the kids had arrived home from school. "I'm here." Mercedes said as she emerged from the depths of her past. She looked down at her hands and she was gripping her house dress so tightly that her hands had started to turn colors. Running her hand over her face to completely break the trance she stood up to finish getting dressed. Mercedes checked her appearance in the mirror, and then left the confines of her bedroom to join her offspring in the kitchen. Mercedes greeted her children with a hug before she washed her hands to start cooking dinner.

She stood there at the sink trying to gain her composure, but her hands were trembling severely. She could feel a panic attack coming on like a massive wave. She didn't want the kids to witness her breakdown, so she told them to take a break from homework and go watch some T.V. She fought against the wave as much as she could. She could still hear the sound of his voice. Mercedes' skin crawled and her stomach contents lurched but she managed to keep her composure. Mercedes quickly grabbed a glass out the cabinet she filed it with Vodka and chugged the clear liquid without hesitation. It took her to repeat this two times before she had the power in her to force a smile on her face. Once the vodka set in a sense of calm began to take over. She chugged one more for good measure. She could feel the cold fluid going down, but the burn felt like relief to her. Within moments the mask was back on and like nothing ever happened, she went to work finishing dinner.

Mercedes served everybody, but she didn't eat. While they ate she went into the room and sat on the edge of the bed. No sooner as her butt hit the bed did her phone start ringing. She looked down at her phone and Unknown caller glowed up at her. Mercedes hit the reject button on the phone sending the call to the voicemail. She wrote down that call as well as the call from earlier in her notebook. Ten minutes had passed, and she thought maybe he had gotten the picture and she would have a goodnight. Breathing a sigh of relief Mercedes left the room to rustle everybody for bath time and bed.

Two hours had passed by the time Mercedes was able to clean the kitchen and get everybody in bed. She got up in the bed, grabbed the remote and flicked the T.V. on. On instinct, she grabbed her phone to check it. Mercedes starred at the phone shockingly. Hakeem had called over thirty times and left more than fifteen messages. Mercedes clicked on the button to listen to one. "Bitch you think not answering the phone is gonna stop me!" "Your dead when I get hold to you!" the message ended just as abruptly as it started. She listened to each message and they all said the same. She already had a restraining order against him, but Mercedes thought that wasn't going to be enough.

Her mind was going in every direction and her hands had started shaking again. Mercedes jumped out of bed to check the house to make sure everything was secure. After she did her rounds she made her way to the kitchen. Mercedes grabbed a glass out the cabinet and filled it half way with vodka. Tilting her head back she tossed the chilled liquor in her mouth. She refilled her glass and grabbed a beer out the box. Taking her hand, she twisted the cap of the bottle and tossed in the trash. Without hesitating the bottle met her lips and she let the cool bitter taste of Bud Light Platinum overtake her mouth.

Once she had regained her nerves, she refilled her glass and grabbed another beer. Grabbing her two drinks she headed back to her room. Mercedes stood next to the bed and lifted the bottle to her lips again. She then set the drinks down on the nightstand. Reluctantly Mercedes picked up the phone and click the on button. Just in the short time she was in the kitchen Hakeem had called ten more times and left three more messages. Tears formed in her eyes as she shut the phone off completely. Mercedes set the small alarm clock on her stand, picked up the glass, popped a Zoloft and got in bed. The mixture of alcohol and pills engulfed her, and she drifted off to sleep.

Once asleep Mercedes found herself back in time again. Mercedes sat on the bed with tears streaming down her face. She had just told Hakeem she was pregnant. In her mind, she thought he would be happy. He always told her he loved her, and she knew she loved him. Reality set in quickly when he gave her the "It's not mines!" line of a scared boy of seventeen before he walked off and she didn't hear from him again. The sting of the memory was too much for sleep and tears ran down her cheeks as she slept. Mercedes found herself seventeen, pregnant, and alone. She packed up her stuff and went back home to her mom.

The dream switched, and she was back home, the months flew by with her stomach growing by leaps and bounds. Soon she saw herself nine months pregnant and as big as a house. The dream changed again, now she was in labor giving birth to her beautiful daughter Evon. The nurse walked over with the baby. Mercedes was about to meet the person that tortured her insides for months. Mercedes looked up at her mom, but the face was not a face of joy. "She looks just like him!" Mercedes said as she handed the baby back to the nurse. Mercedes rolled over on her side and balled her eyes out. Wasn't it enough that he left her to deal with being pregnant alone? Now she had to look at his face every day for the rest of her life.

Her mom pulled a chair up to the bed and sat down in front of Mercedes. "Baby you have to deal with this now." "That's the same baby you sang too and bonded with for nine months." "Your gonna have to look past all that and find the love you felt for her then." Mercedes laid there not moving, unwilling to listen to her mother. "Ok." Her mother said. She moved hair from Mercedes' forehead before she leaned over and kissed it. "I'm going home to shower and eat" She said as she stood up to leave the room. Standing there for a moment to see if there was gonna be a response, she turned and walked toward the door. "Be back later." With that she was gone, and Mercedes was left with her own thoughts.

Mercedes laid there as she waited for her recovery room to be ready for her. She watched as the nurses came in and out of the room. She made no attempt to hold her new bundle of joy. The pediatric nurse came to take the baby to the nursery to get cleaned and checked out. She asked Mercedes if she wanted to hold the baby before she took her away. Mercedes sat up in the bed stretched her arms out to hold her new baby. This new being she had created was so tiny and fragile. Something inside Mercedes erupted and the tears came forth. She pressed her cheek to her daughter's cheek. She kissed her tiny nose, counted her fingers, and toes, whispered in her ear "I will love you forever." Then she handed the baby back to the nurse.

The dream shifted again, and she saw herself standing at Hakeem's cousin's door with her older sister Toya who was holding tight her newborn baby girl. It was winter time and they were all bundled up. Even though it was a dream, Mercedes could feel her fingers getting numb. Her sister had been dragging her by the hand thru the entire complex. Once she reached their door Toya pounded the door with the hill of her hand. "Who is it?" Hakeem's cousin Tracy popped her head out the door. "Hey Toya girl" she said as she pushed open the door to let them in. Toya had lived in that neighborhood for a while and knew just about everybody that lived there. "I came down here cause I had something for y'all." Toya said as she came in dragging Mercedes by the hand. Tracy close the door behind them and stood there with her hand on her hips. "What you got girl?" Toya threw the blanket off the baby's face and handed her to Tracy. "Y'all baby!"

Tracy looked at the tiny bundle, looked at Mercedes, then back to the baby. Without one word she walked over to the table and picked up the phone. "Hakeem what you doing?" they couldn't hear the response from the other side. "Somebody just dropped a package over here for you. I don't know! You need to come right now." Tracy hung up the phone as quickly as she had picked it up. "Make y'all self at home" she said to them. "He'll be here in a minute."

They all sat there while Tracy played and cooed with her new-found cousin. The sudden knock at the door startled the three women. "Who is it?" Tracy yelled to the back of the door. "Tracy it's me!" The familiar voice came back in response. "It's open!" Tracy yelled back at the door. The door swung open and in walked Hakeem. Mercedes hadn't seen him since she told him about the pregnancy. Tracy walked over to her cousin and placed his daughter in his hands. "What is this?" he asked looking confused. "Your package." Tracy replied. "You can't deny that one boy, she looks just like you." As Hakeem stood there staring at his daughter Tracy and Toya got up and left the room. At that moment it was like ice had melted, he lowered his head toward the tiny baby and kissed her tan little cherub cheeks. With tears in his eyes he glanced over at Mercedes, "I'm sorry!"

The sound of the alarm clock jarred Mercedes back into the real world. She laid there starring at the ceiling. Those were the times when things between her and Hakeem were good. He had fallen in love with his daughter that day and had vowed to never leave her side. At first, he stuck to his words. The young couple would run away and elope, and before long be expecting their second child. The memories stung like fresh cuts doused in alcohol.

Mercedes sat on the edge of the bed for a minute, and then got up to go wake the kids. The dreams had seemed so real that even after the alarm clock woke her she could still smell the milk on her baby's breath. She rounded up the kids and had them dressed and fed right before the school bus came to a screeching halt. Mercedes got dressed quickly and was out the door in a flash. Leaving extra early she beat the traffic and got to work super early. She sat in her car for a moment to clear her head Mercedes lit a Newport and wiped the tears from her eyes.

Knock! Knock! The sound scared her making Mercedes jump straight up in the seat and turn toward the sound. Damn! It was Monea! She checked her face in the rearview and rolled down the window! "Hey girl didn't mean to scare you! You alright?" She asked. "Yea sure, what's up?" Mercedes asked. "Well I just wanted to give you the invitation to my party. The address is on the front, would love to see you there." The smile on her face was enough for Mercedes to plunge herself face first into hot lava for her. "I'm not making any promise but I'm a see what I can do. You know its short notice and all." Mercedes said trying not to sound too anxious. There was no way in hell she was missing a chance to see her in something other than work attire. Mercedes thanked her for the invitation and Monea walked off. Mercedes watch her walk across the parking lot and into the building. She had on pants today and they hugged her body perfectly. Her magnificent body moved to the sound of Mercedes's heart every time she took a step. "Cut it out!" she said to herself, with everything that's going on with Hakeem she had to stay focused.

After smoking half of the cigarette, she put it out and exited the car. She walked to the building slowly, dreading the day ahead. While ringing the doorbell Mercedes silently prayed that Shunta's ass wasn't here. After she was buzzed in Mercedes walked in the building said her good mornings and walked into the locker room. "No Shunta today, thank you lord for small favors." She said under her breath.

The morning went by smoothly and quickly without Shunta there nagging everybody. All the morning tasks were complete before Mercedes knew it, and it was time for break. Mercedes told the others about Monea's party while everyone sat in the break room. Nobody was sure they were gonna make it, which was definitely fine with her. She was all smiles from then on out. The rest of the day was just as smooth as the first half. They served the kids, cleaned up the kitchen, and prepped everything for the next day. Just as quickly as it started Mercedes found herself back in her ride rolling home. She hit the mp3 player on the phone and jammed all the way home.

2

Innocence Lost

Nashunta

The alarm goes off and scares the crap outta Nashunta! Rolling her eyes, she reaches over to hit the snooze button. Before she could get a chance to shut her eyes again there is a Boom Boom Boom at the room door. "Nashunta I know you heard that alarm" her mom screams through the door. "Get your butt up girl! I'm not taking you to school today!" "I'm up momma!" she yells back at the door. "Ugh! Damn, she gets on my nerves," Nashunta huffs and rolls out of bed. She sits on the side of the bed gathering her bearings not really wanting to get up. Her mind starts to wonder and the events from the night before came into view. The fight she had with Lameka yesterday was a massive one and Nashunta was struggling with herself. After gathering her stuff to head to the bathroom, Nashunta walked past the mirror and seeing the purplish bruise that had formed on her cheek brought anger and hurt flooding back with blinding fury.

Lameka had gotten mad because she was walking down the hall to class with one of her male classmates. She knew Lameka was upset by the look on her face when she turned the corner. Despite the look she never mentioned it at school so Nashunta dropped the uneasy feeling she was having. After school they headed to Lameka's house like usual, her parents work late so they always had time to be alone. Before they even got in the house good and shut the door, Nashunta was broadsided with a horrendous slap across the face. Wham!!! The sheer force of the hit knocked her off balanced and sent Nashunta tumbling across the kitchen floor. "Bitch you disrespect me like that in front of the whole school!" Lameka yelled as she stood over Nashunta.

Remembering the pain of hitting the floor brought reality back. Nashunta wished the fight had all been a horrible dream. She wanted everything to be the same as it was before. After seeing the bruise on her face, feeling what had to be other bruises on her back and legs, that wasn't a thought worth entertaining.

"Damn why does the bathroom have to be so far from my room." Nashunta thought as she peeked out the door. She wanted to see if her mom was still insight before she emerged from her room. Seeing the coast being clear she darted out and ran toward the bathroom. Just before Nashunta could safely make it behind the door she spotted her little sister trying to go in. Without a second thought she pushed her aside, shut the door, and locked it before she could protest. "Mom!" she yelled "Nashunta just ran me over trying to beat me to the bathroom!" "C'mon Kimmie please I'm running late!" Nashunta begged. Kimmie reluctantly agreed with one last punch of the door. "Hurry up!" She yelled.

Nashunta appeared 20 minutes later from the bathroom fully dressed, hair, and makeup done. She made sure to comb her hair toward her face and she also used an ample amount of foundation and concealer on that side to cover the bruise. She made her bed, put her clothes away, and headed downstairs to leave. "Man! Why does everyone have to be in the kitchen already?" She asked herself as she stood just outside the entrance to the kitchen. Grabbing her stuff off the back cabinet Nashunta headed for the door. Before she could make it, her mom stepped into her path. Despite knowing that she had covered the bruise well enough she knew her mom was a bloodhound. "Yes mother, what is it?" Nashunta snapped not wanting her mom to get too close. "You don't want to eat something before you leave sweetheart?" "No!" She snapped again. "I don't wanna miss the bus remember!" And with that she stepped around her mother and shot out the door. Nashunta practically ran across the yard trying to get away before her mom came to the door behind her. Halfway to the bus stop she looked up and saw Lameka leaning on the hood of her car. If my parents were as understanding as Lameka's they would have already known about me being a lesbian. Lameka had been out the closet for years. Feeling regretful about keeping secrets from her folks Nashunta put her head down and tears formed in her eyes. She knew she would never find the courage to come clean to her parents.

"Hey baby girl, I got up early today and decided to come pick you up." Lameka spoke as Nashunta got close to her. God knows how pissed off she was at her, but Nashunta didn't want to deal with her mom either so in she jumped and they sped away.

Jessica Jones stood by the front door of her home dumbfounded by what just happened. By the time reality set in and she ran after her child, Nashunta was nowhere in sight. "What the hell is wrong with her?" "I know she was going thru a rebellious stage but never had she been blatantly disrespectful to me." Nashunta Jones and her mother Jessica Jones where thinking the same thing at the same time. "How did I get here?"

"You know I'm really sorry about yesterday?" Lameka's voice cut through the silence of the car. "I love you so much that I just get so jealous seeing you talking to boys." "If I wanted to be with a man Meka I would be! How many times I gotta say that? I know you've had girls leave you for guys before, but I'm gay I don't want to be with guys! If I wasn't with you I would be with another woman." Seemingly satisfied by Nashunta's answer Lameka turned up the radio and focused on the road. Nashunta was glad to have the music on to drown out some of the thoughts she had in her head. Without the distraction of their talking Nashunta let herself drift deep into her thoughts and she was asleep in no time.

Sensing something wasn't right, feeling the uneasiness in her stomach she snapped back to reality. "Where are we? Where are you taking me?" she asked. "I wanna try to make it up to you!" Lameka said grabbing a hold of Nashunta's hand.

They were riding down a heavily wooded area, where there were no houses insight. Nashunta felt very scared and she could feel her heart in her throat. "Lameka, what are we doing here? I want you to take me to school!" "I got you baby girl! This is some old property that my grandfather inherited, but never did anything with. It looks creepy, but I use to come out here with him when he wanted to get away from my grandma." She smirked and drove on. Ten minutes later she turned the corner and there stood this raggedy shed of a house. It looked like it should have been condemned, the house was a dirty rustic white color and the widows in front were broken out. The grass looked as though it hadn't been cut in years and bags of trash could be seen for miles up and down the road. She pulled the car to a stop and got out. "I'm not going in there!" Nashunta protested. Lameka walked around to the passenger side of the car and opened the door. She grabbed for Nashunta's hand to guide her out. "It's ok I promise." Reluctantly Nashunta took her hand and got out. They walked around the broke down shack and behind it stood what looks like a work shed of some sort. Lameka let go of her hand momentarily to unlock the door. Once the door was opened she pushed Nashunta inside and followed close behind.

It took Nashunta's eyes a minute to adjust to the darkness, but when they did she could see that the room was setup for their arrival. There were rose petals, a radio, candles, and food all waiting for her. While she stood dumbfounded Lameka busied herself lighting the candles and turning on the radio. Once Lameka was finished with everything she came and stood in front of her awaiting lover. Taking Nashunta's hand Lameka knelt and looked up into the most gorgeous brown eyes she knew. "I'm so sorry for what I did, hitting you I mean. I know I've promised before that it would never happen again, I don't know what's wrong with me. I've never had a girl make me feel the way you make me feel. You have all the right to be mad and want to leave me, but before you make your decision know that I love you more than myself and I can't live without you in my life." The words she heard from her lover moved Nashunta to tears. Her emotions over powered her and her knees buckled. With unsure words she spoke. "I love you so much Lameka. I never dreamed of leaving you, I just can't understand how you could get so angry at me." Looking around at the room again Nashunta was overcome by her girlfriend's romantic gesture. "I never had somebody do this for me before." She looked down into her partner's eyes as she spoke and saw tears forming in Lameka's eyes. "I've never done this for anybody before." Lameka stood and met her lover's lips with a deep and passionate kiss.

The kiss was deep and warming heating them both to their core. Nashunta stood dreamingly as she watched her clothes hit the floor piece but piece. Lameka picked her up, pushing the food to the side and placing her on the table. "This is the only thing I'm hungry for at the moment." Lameka whispered as anticipation bubbled inside her and she lowered her body into position. Placing her face between Nashunta's legs she could smell the longing and anticipation from her love as well. Lameka had been experimenting with her sexuality since she was ten. Now at nineteen she was a very experienced lover compared to the naïve Nashunta.

Lameka tasted and teased her lover with her tongue. Leaving Nashunta breathless as huge gasps for air escaped her lips. Nashunta was shaking, quivering and begging to be taken by the time Lameka was ready to enter her. Pulling herself up Lameka wiped the wetness from her mouth as she repositioned herself between Nashunta's legs, "I'm gonna to make sure you never want to leave me." She spoke as she stared down at her quivering lover. She touched and rubbed Nashunta's center with vigorous movements feeling the heat as it radiated from Nashunta's body. The feel of her lover beneath her drove her wild with longing. "I want to feel you inside of me!" Nashunta said breathless. Lameka was all too willing to oblige her. She inserted one finger to loosen her up and then inserted a seconded. Nashunta's juices ran down her hand and she pulled back her hand and licked at her fingers to taste her. Lameka pleased her lover continuously until she had her on the verge of boiling over. She felt her lover's climax was near and she inserted a third finger to push her over the edge. Lameka made love to her body with such force, Nashunta never felt from her before. Nashunta felt fire rising from the pit of her stomach. Just as she was about to explode she felt Lameka insert another finger and pure bliss ran from her core. "I'm cuming!" She screamed and held on to Lameka for the ride. Hearing the words she was waiting for escape her lover's lips she bucked wildly, giving her all she had. "Look at me!" she told Nashunta, "Do you love me?" "Yes!" Nashunta screamed. "Say you'll never leave me!" "I'll never leave!" "I promise" Came the breathless response. "I love you Nashunta!" "I love you too Lameka!"

Nashunta pulsated from her climax at the same moment Lameka's body giving way to the excitement around her; she spontaneously climaxed on her own. They both held on to each other as the massive tidal wave overcame them. They collapsed against the table making a magnificent centerpiece for the food that lay scattered around them.

"I'm not done with you yet!" Lameka Yelled. They had never made love like this before, but this was a no holds barred moment. Lameka wanted her to know exactly what she could do to her body. She removed the rest of her clothing and tightened the strap she had adorned for this occasion. Nashunta eyed the lightly tanned dildo hanging from her lover's harness and smiled with anticipation. Lameka grabbed Nashunta by the waist and flipped her over pulling her towards her fate. Once she had her at the right angle she grabbed the back of her neck and slid the plastic appendage into her warm saturated mound. The sounds escaping her lips were that of delight and passion mixed. The more Lameka dug deeper into her milky center the more Nashunta bucked her hips to gladly accept the gift that was being given. Lameka felt her lover tighten as her body prepared for her climax. She vigorously picked up speed, and just when she thought she could take no more Lameka pushed further inside Nashunta. Her body exploded with an orgasm so powerful that her vagina exploded sending cascading gushes of nectar all over the table and floor. Feeling the wetness of her lover release and the rubbing of the strap against her center Lameka gave way to her own climax, she bucked and rode Nashunta's plump round backside. Nashunta arched her back allowing her lover to go as deep as she wanted. Lameka grabbed Nashunta's hair and dove inside her as deep and as hard as her body would allow until she too released cascading rivers of nectar from her core. With the last bit of her strength she lifted her lover up and carried her to the sofa. She laid her down and planted her body beside hers. They both let their bodies succumb to the passion induced coma that awaited them.

3

Love or Lust

Mercedes

Mercedes was so excited about going to Monea's party that she was watching the clock all day. Mercedes read the invitation for the directions. What! She yelled after reading the reverse side of the invitation. She was having one of those purple passion party's which Mercedes already knew about. The one thing that failed to catch her attention was that it was a pajamas party. Damn it! "I'm going to the store" Mercedes told Evon as she grabbed her purse. Mercedes didn't wait to hear what the response was; she shut the door and bounced down the steps to the car.

Mercedes was at the Wal-Mart in ten minutes flat. The invite said prizes for the sexiest and the best nighty. Mercedes was not trying to win any prizes, she just wanted to blend into the crowd. Mercedes raced through Wal-Mart as fast as she could to find the perfect sleep attire to fit her voluptuous and curvy size 18 frame. Mercedes had a black girl country booty complete with nice thick thighs. Her 40DD bra size and curvy hips gave her a perfect hourglass figure. All this accompanied by her natural curly hair and grey eyes made Mercedes a picture of beauty. She was often told she was cute for a big girl, whatever the hell that means.

Mercedes couldn't make up her mind, there were so many things to choose from. Settling for two pieces, one was a snoopy t-shirt complete with matching boy shorts that showed off the tattoo on her upper left thigh. The other was a t-shirt that had Oscar the grouch on it that read Get Lost in large green letters that were accompanied with panties that made her bottom look

23

eatable. She paid for her things and headed toward the car. On the way home Mercedes stopped by the liquor store to renew her stash because it had gotten low. After gathering her favorites Mercedes paid the cashier and was out the door. Mercedes jammed all the way home she was in a great mood. She pulled up to her apartment, cut off the car, and got out. She opened up the passenger side door to retrieve bags, when she heard her name being called. She was reluctant to answer because she didn't know anyone since she was new to the area.

Taking a deep breath, Mercedes turned around to face the person that was calling from behind. Mercedes found herself face to face with Tracy, Hakeem's cousin. "Girl how you doing?" Tracy asked as she grabbed Mercedes holding her tight. Mercedes stood there with a look of pure shock. "Hey." Mercedes managed to respond. It wasn't a secret as to why she and Hakeem separated. Even though Hakeem's family knew about the abuse, she hadn't talked to any of them to see if they knew what he was recently up to. Tracy went through the formalities of asking how Mercedes and the kids were before asking if she'd talked to her cousin. Mercedes looked down at the time. "Sorry I'm running late." Mercedes said cutting the chat short. Tracy gave Mercedes her number and told her to call her if she needed anything. "Tracy can you do me a huge favor?" Mercedes asked as she stood next to her vehicle. "Sure girl." Tracy replied. "Can you please not tell your cousin where me and the kids are." Tracy agreed hugged Mercedes once more and walked off.

Mercedes watched Tracy disappear before she opened the door to get her bags. Mercedes left the bag of clothes in the back under the seat and went into the house.

Mercedes fixed herself a drink and headed to the room. Gathering the outfit, she had laid out. a pair of skinny leg jeans, a black and red Falcon t-shirt. A shirt that she had cut up and tied to show off her deliciously caramel rack, which was accentuated by a black widow she had tattooed on her left breast and went to the bathroom. The time ticked endless away but once she emerged from the bathroom Mercedes looked like a new person. Her hair pulled back into a ponytail that grazed the top of her butt when she walked, a pair of large hoop earrings, and some black air force ones.

Mercedes sat in the living room drinking her second drink, while she waited for the sitter to come. It had been two days since Hakeem had called and she was hoping he was over the games. She was praying she could just enjoy the evening without incident. The sitter arrived just in time. Mercedes checked the house, kissed her children and darted out the door.

Mercedes got to Monea's house really early, the purple passion ladies had just gotten there and were setting their stuff up. "Hey girl!" Monea said greeting her. "I didn't tell you it was a pajama party?" "No!" Mercedes said with amusement in her tone. "Thank goodness I read it before I got here and stopped and pick something up." Monea looked amazing; Mercedes thought to herself. She had on a French maid outfit complete with push-up bra, ruffled boy shorts, garter, thigh high stockings, and black stiletto heels. "You have anywhere I can change?" Mercedes asked Monea. "Sure," she said and led her toward a room in the back. "This is my room you can change in here." The house had people everywhere trying to get ready. She closed the door and Mercedes started getting changed.

Mercedes had just removed her bra to put on the snoopy shirt she chose to wear, when Monea walked in on her. If she wasn't crazy she would have thought she timed it just perfect like she was waiting when she knew she would have something off. "I'm sorry! Girl I forgot to get the gift bags I had in the closet." She said as she came in and shut the door behind her. Mercedes was standing there like a deer caught in headlights, in underwear with no bra and her standing there in that outfit. She felt like it was something out of her dreams. Monea's voice broke the silence, "damn Mercedes you have a really nice body." "Umm! Thanks, I think!" Mercedes said. "No for real, I never saw a girl of your size naked before. The world have you thinking big girls look sloppy or something. You have a really sexy body. Very voluptuous and curvy and your breasts are so gorgeous!"

Monea just stood there watching her for a moment, then finally she spoke. "Oh, I'm sorry girl did I make you uncomfortable?" She asked still unable to take her eyes off her house guest. "Who me?" Mercedes asked surprised at the question. "Hell naw! I'm very comfortable with my body!" "So, you are, are you?" The question made the hair on Mercedes arm stand on end. "So, give me a show then!" Monea said. "What kind of show?" Mercedes shot back. "Move that sexy body and dance for me. Come on let me see!" Monea replied as she slowly swiveled her hips. "Girl I can't dance you crazy!" Mercedes yelled. Mercedes thought Monea might have taken that answer as her being scared. She started heading for the door. "Wait I thought you wanted a show!" Mercedes spoke. "I can't dance but how about you just watch me change." That caught her attention and Monea slowly turned around and sat on the bed. Mercedes was already damn near naked, she just closed her eyes and went with the flow. Mercedes started rubbing her breasts until her pierced nipples stood erect. She could tell Monea was enjoying this, from the way she started licking her lips. Mercedes couldn't tell whether this was real or another one of her many fantasies about Monea. Either way she was going to give her the show she asked for. Mercedes let her hand glide across the lavender lace low cut panties she had on. Even through the delicate fabric she could feel the wetness seeping through. She wanted Monea so bad. Mercedes had dreamed of this moment since she first laid eyes on this lady. As Mercedes moved her hands slowly over her body, she kept her eyes focused on Monea's eyes. The air in the room was so thick with anticipation she could tell Monea was getting turned on by what she was doing. Just as Mercedes was about to slip her hand under the edge of her panties, they heard Monea's name being called from down the hall. Both of them jumped back to reality. "I'm here! I'll be out in a minute." They both had forgotten about the party that was about to commence just outside the closed door.

Monea got up from the bed and walked over to Mercedes. She picked up the snoopy t-shirt Mercedes had pulled out the bag to wear. She rubbed Mercedes's right breast with her hand, caressing the nipple with her soft fingers. She bent down and whispered in her ear, I enjoyed the show. She slipped the shirt over her head, then kissed Mercedes' forehead. "You should really wear it like that." she said. "Like what?" Mercedes asked dumfounded. "With just the shirt and the panties, wear it like that." Mercedes agreed, despite her better judgment. Monea assured she would be fine and she packed Mercedes's stuff up in the bags and put them away in her closet while Mercedes gave her hair a once over in the mirror. Walking back over, Monea gave Mercedes a quick up and down look and they headed out the door.

Mercedes felt uneasy standing around in her underwear in front of strangers. She guessed Monea sensed her pain because she came over and handed her a cup. "Here drink this, it should help" Monea said. Mercedes gratefully took the cup and drank as much down as she could in one swallow.

After about an hour the house started getting crowded. All you could see was half naked women. You would have thought it was a college dorm slumber party. By the time intermission and the food was ready to be served Mercedes had drank five cups of spiked punch. Needless to say, she no longer cared about being in her underwear.

Mercedes had gotten some food and was sitting alone, because she didn't know anybody. She was grateful none of the other coworkers changed their mind about coming. Mercedes could relax a little and be herself. She sat quietly eating and watching the surrounding cliques of women. "Is this seat taken?" Mercedes heard from over her shoulder. She turned around, and Monea was standing in front of her with a plate full of hot wings and meatballs. "No, there's no one sitting there." Mercedes said with unsteady lips. "So how are you enjoying the party?" Monea asked. "It's great, thanks for the drinks they really helped." Mercedes responded. "Is this your first lesbian party?" Monea's question shocked Mercedes. "What?" She asked. "This is a lesbian party? So why did you invite me?" Mercedes asked looking confused. "Because I was right about you." Monea said smiling. "Tell me what you mean by that!" Mercedes said. As if she didn't already know what she was gonna say. "I know you watch me. Do you like what you see?" Monea asked. "I secretly hoped you would come alone" Monea continued. "Are you serious?" Mercedes asked. "Why would I lie?" came her response. Monea and Mercedes talked all the way through the intermission. Before they knew it, the ladies were ready to start the show again. "Ok ladies let's give away some prizes," the lady in the nurse's uniform yelled. "When the party's over hang around a bit," Monea said. She got up walked over to where the lady was standing to start handing out door prizes. The party went on for about another hour and then it was over. Mercedes walked away with a prize that Monea gave her personally herself. She said it was for being the first guest to arrive. When Monea handed Mercedes the bag she whispered, "open it before you leave."

There were lots of ladies still standing around waiting to get a turn to place orders for items they saw demonstrated at the party. Monea was so busy trying to talk to all her guest that damn near forty-five minutes had passed. Mercedes was sitting in the same chair watching her work the room. Monea must have felt Mercedes watching her because she turned her attention toward her. "Open the bag" she mouths and gave Mercedes the thumbs up gesture. Mercedes leaned down and picked up the purple passion bag and opened it. Inside was one of those outfits made out of fishnet material and a note. The note read: "I'm so glad you came! I hope you like it. Go upstairs and try it on for me, because you still owe me a finale." Mercedes looked up at her, but she was gone. She got up from her chair and walked back toward the room Monea said was her bedroom.

Mercedes opened the door and saw that the room was empty except for a light beyond a door in back. Fearing someone was in the room she walked over to the door. "Hello!" Mercedes said as she opened the door and looked in. There Mercedes saw another note which read: "relax enjoy the bath and try on your gift." She couldn't help but smile. Mercedes undressed and slide into the tub. The water was perfect, and she could smell the hint of cucumber melon. I loved that fragrance, damn she good! Mercedes thought to herself as she laid back and immersed herself in the steaming liquid.

Not knowing how long she was in there made Mercedes uneasy, she jumped back to reality. She had to get home she hoped it wasn't too late. Mercedes jumped out the tub and reached for her clothes. "My clothes! Where the hell are my clothes!" Mercedes gasped. Instead of finding what she had removed before entering the tub she found the outfit Monea had giving her and a bottle of Strawberry Champaign body spray. Much to Mercedes's surprise the digital clock on the bathroom wall read 9:20. She was doing great on the time, so she relaxed a little and toweled off. As Mercedes was pulling the barely there outfit over my freshly toweled skin she could hear soft music began to bellow from the other side of the door. She quickly sprayed herself down and headed for the sounds of seductive jazz that was hypnotizing her from beyond the door.

When Mercedes opened the bathroom door Monea was standing there in a lavender see thru negligée and matching bottoms. Everything about her was beautiful. From her deep caramel skin tone all the way down to the soft peach paint she had on her toes. Mercedes felt like an innocent virgin on her wedding night. She was unsteady on her feet, and her heart was racing. Monea walked over and took Mercedes' hand and led her to the center of the room. "This is your stage I want you to dance for me." Monea turned up the music, and then walked over to the dresser to pick up a cup she had waiting there. After taking a quick sip Monea lowered the cup and brought it back to Mercedes. Mercedes took a long deep drink and set the cup down. Monea kissed Mercedes's lips so softly before she turned and sat down on the bed.

Mercedes listened to the music coming from the stereo. At first, she was just moving stiffly to the beat but after a couple minutes the drinks started coming down on her. Mercedes closed her eyes and let go. She let the music consume her and started really dancing, moving her body along with the beat, and licking her lips. Monea came over to Mercedes and started dancing with her. She lifted Mercedes arms up over her head and told her to hold them there. The excitement of it all drove her to the brink of madness. Everything in Mercedes wanted to do whatever Monea wanted her to do without hesitation. All Mercedes could think about was all the dreams she'd had of this very moment.

Monea started kissing Mercedes, first starting at her forehead, then her lips. She kissed Mercedes so passionately that she felt it in the pit of her stomach. She kissed down Mercedes's neck and then her breasts. One after the other making each one jealous that she had taken her lips from it. She left Mercedes harden nipples and traced her tongue down her stomach. She kissed her navel and continued on. Right when she was about to go further Mercedes phone began ringing. The sound of it jolted her out of her trance. "I'm sorry!" Mercedes apologized as she grabbed Monea's beautiful face. "My kids are with a sitter I gotta get this." By the time she made it to the phone the ringing had stopped. She flipped and unknown caller shined back her heart sank into her stomach.

"Damn it I gotta go!" Mercedes yelled mostly to herself than anything. "I'm sorry I have to go," Mercedes said apologetically. Monea set up on her elbows and looked at Mercedes. Her eyes so sexy, the fires inside Mercedes started growing again. "Damn I don't wanna have to leave." "I understand" Monea replied and she kissed her lips.

Mercedes changed her clothes quickly and grabbed her bags and headed for the door. "Hey!" Monea yelled and grabbed Mercedes' arm and pulled her back, she kissed Mercedes so gently that she wanted to stay right there forever. "See you at work," Monea smiled and released her. Monea stood in the door until Mercedes drove away.

Thank goodness the roads were empty, and Mercedes booked it all the way home doing about 90. She drove in the parking lot of her apartment complex about twenty minutes later. Mercedes dimmed the lights and turned into her normal parking space. She gathered her bags and quickly exited her car. Once up the steps she hurried to the back door and peeked in the window. The lights were out, and she started getting nervous. Mercedes opened the door and walked in. The house was quiet except for the television that was softly playing in the living room just beyond the kitchen. As soon as she walked through the threshold of the living room Kennedi popped her head up from the sofa. Each one scaring the crap out of the other one. Mercedes dropped her bags and Kennedi threw the covers over her head as they screamed out loud. "Girl you scared the mess outta me" Mercedes said to the young sitter as she regained her composure. "I'm sorry! I didn't hear you come in. I guess I must have falling asleep." "It's fine." Mercedes said in an effort to reassure the frightened teenager. "How was everything?" Mercedes asked. "It was cool" Kennedi replied. "We ate, watched some T.V., and they crashed out. Easy peasy!" "Cool" Mercedes replied. Hearing everything went smoothly she paid Kennedi and watched her walk to her car. After she left Mercedes made sure the house was secure before she went in and checked on the kids. everyone was asleep, tiptoeing to her room she opened the door and went inside. Mercedes breathed a sigh of relief as she put away her bags in the closet. Mercedes jumped in the shower quickly and headed to bed. She fell asleep dreaming about Monea's lips on her. The sound of the phone jolted Mercedes awake making her jump clean off the bed. She grabbed the clock to see what time it was, and she noticed there were six missed calls and even more texts all from Hakeem. Just knowing that he was out there somewhere calling her made her very uneasy. There was no way she was gonna be able to get back to sleep. She grabbed a pillow and went to go watch T.V. in the living room. Her mind fluttered with thoughts of Monea that would be overcome by visions of Hakeem and his nonsense. By the time she finally did get to sleep the kids were getting up. She sat up on the sofa and fired up a Newport, she already knew it was gonna be a bad day.

4

More Skeletons in The Closet

Mercedes

The rest of the weekend went by quickly without problem. The only thing that was on Mercedes' mind all weekend was what happened between her and Monea. When she pulled up at the job on Monday she could hardly keep her cool. Mercedes found herself looking for Monea's car. "You have got to get it together!" she said to herself trying to keep her composure. Mercedes went into the building and got straight to work. Thoughts of Monea consumed Mercedes mind completely. She tried everything she could to keep her mind busy. Shunta was onsite and fussing about any and everything, but Mercedes was so consumed with her thoughts she didn't hear anything she was saying. The lunch period went by smoothly. Mercedes had a good pace going; she was moving the kids thru the line faster than ever.

During the break between lunch periods Mercedes was restocking her steam table to get ready for the next set of kids when out of nowhere. "Hey Mercedes!" she heard from over her shoulder. The sound of Monea's voice melted Mercedes' insides instantly. She drew in her breath and turned around to face her dream girl. "Hey Monea." Mercedes said as calmly as she could manage. Monea looked magnificent, Mercedes wanted to wrap her arms around those perfect hips and kiss her plush lightly glossed lips. "I just wanted to say thanks again for coming to my party. I hoped you enjoyed yourself." Monea whispered. "Yes, ma'am I did, and thank you for inviting me." Mercedes said. They stood there for a second lost for words and then she turned to go.

"Oh, by the way" Monea started to say but she slightly brushed up against Mercedes and a spark of sexual energy passed between them. Both ladies jumped back and stared at each other. If everyone wasn't so busy doing their own thing they would have given themselves away. "The stuff you ordered from the party arrived at my house by mistake. If you want, you can come by my office and pick them up before you leave today." Mercedes looked at Monea puzzled because she knew she hadn't ordered anything. However, she agreed anyway. "Well, let me go" Monea said. "I know you have tons to do before the kids come down. Talk to you later" she said. Monea turned to leave. It took everything in Mercedes not to watch her walk away.

The rest of the lunch periods took forever to end. Finally, after all the kids were feed Mercedes quickly counted down her money and cleaned her area. She was moving so fast that she finished a whole hour ahead of time. "Shunta I need to fax some papers down town to the head office." Mercedes said from the doorway of the office. Shunta was so busy trying to finish her own paper work she just waved her hand up in response. Rushing into the locker room Mercedes hurried to the bathroom to check her face and hair. Once she assured herself everything was as it should be, she grabbed some gum out of her bag and headed to the elevator.

Mercedes reached Monea's office and knocked on the door. "Come in!" came the response from the other side. "Hey Mercedes, you can have a seat, I'll be with you in a moment." Monea said turning her attention back to the phone. Mercedes felt like a child sitting in front of the principal waiting for him to get off the phone with her mother.

After what felt like forever Monea completed her call, returned the phone to its place, and turned to face Mercedes. "Hey baby doll I've been thinking about you since I woke up on Sunday." She said getting up and walking over to where Mercedes sat.

Monea came to stand directly in front of Mercedes. She stood so close that her navel was inches from her face and Mercedes could smell the body spray radiating off her perfect frame. Monea grabbed the back of Mercedes' head pulling her face toward her body. The smell of her enveloped Mercedes and she encircled her arms around her lover. Monea leaned down and kissed Mercedes' awaiting lips; Monea's lips tasted like the cotton candy lip gloss she always kept stash in her purse. Their kissing sessions left them both panting and out of breath. Monea pulled Mercedes face closer to her body again. This time Mercedes could smell the scent of her femininity and she forgot they were in a school building. Mercedes hands followed the trail of Monea's legs up to the center of her universe. She ran her fingers along the lace material of her panties and could feel her wetness. Mercedes slipped her fingers underneath the edge of the lace and across her soft lips. She wanted her so bad and from the look in her eyes Monea wanted her too. Please forgive me Mercedes said and ripped her panties letting them fall to the floor. Before Monea could respond to what had been done Mercedes was face deep between her thighs and all she could do was hold on for the ride. She grabbed Mercedes hair pushing her further into her. Yes, right there Monea whimpered. Mercedes gave her what she asked for, she licked and tasted her like she was starving and Monea was her last meal. Mercedes lifted her up on the desk. Not once letting her lips leave their place. Mercedes could tell by the way Monea was bucking against her that she was ready to climax. Mercedes pushed her fingers inside Monea as she continued to please her lover. The sensation was so overcoming that she let out a small gasp as her sweet juices saturated Mercedes fingers. Mercedes removed her fingers and tasted the juices that ran down them. Inhaling her intoxicating aroma Mercedes kissed the inside of Monea's quivering thigh sealing the completion of their escapade.

"Mercedes are you listening to me?" The question awakened Mercedes from her trance. "where did you go just then?"

Mercedes stood there for a moment lost for words; she could not believe what had just happened. Coming back fully to reality she realized everything that had transpired was a day dream. Mercedes didn't know what she should do next, her mind told me to leave but her body wouldn't cooperate. She was just standing there like a lost puppy. Then in the proverbial words of Zack Morris, she was Saved By The Bell. The bell rang, and the halls filled with teenagers racing to get out of the school building. "I guess I better go," Mercedes said breaking the awkward trance they were caught in. "When can I see you again" Monea asked? "I don't know" Mercedes replied. She lowered her head and walked out the door. Instead of getting on the elevator Mercedes hit the stairs. 'What the fuck am I doing?' she asked herself. This can't possibly go anywhere. Mercedes wanted her in the worst way, but she faced two problems. One was Hakeem's ass, she didn't want to bring anyone into the madness that she lived. The other was she wasn't sure is she was ready to come out the closet.

When Mercedes got back down stairs the kitchen was dark. Shunta was the only person left. Girl I thought you were gone she said. You came right on time I was finna lock everything up and leave for the day. Mercedes could tell Shunta wanted to talk but she didn't want to get near her. So, she quickly ducked into the locker room grabbed her things and while Shunta was locking the fridge she darted out the door. Got to her car, turned on her phone and…. Fuck five missed calls from an unknown number! Damn, this is not gonna end well. Fuck it! She lit a cigarette, turns the music up and headed for home.

When Mercedes walked in the door the kids were sitting in the living room watching the Cartoon Network. Speaking to everyone as she made her way around the living room then she turned and headed straight to the bedroom. She quickly changed her clothes and then darted to the kitchen. She got dinner started and sat down at the table. Mercedes let the day's events run thru her mind. She wanted nothing more but to start a life with Monea. She felt lost not knowing which direction to go, she poured a drink and finished cooking.

At the end of the night the kids were feed and were sound asleep in bed. Mercedes had cleaned up the house and headed off to bed herself. She was so exhausted that as soon as she changed her clothes and laid across the bed she quickly drifted off to dreamland. Suddenly her door opened and in comes Hakeem. It was like she was locked in a dream state. She was standing there out of her body looking at herself. She saw the younger version of herself laying sleep on the bed with her newborn son. She remembered this night like it was yesterday, this was at the time Hakeem was always high on something. Hakeem got on the bed and started kissing on her. She knew what he wanted but she just recently delivered a baby and wasn't able to oblige him. She thought maybe he would be intoxicated enough to just wanna go to bed and sleep it off. There was not a chance in hell of that happening. Mercedes must have resisted a little too long because the next thing she knew he was on top of her pounding the shit out of her face. Mercedes was laying there in a state of shock. When her mind finally caught up with reality he had ripped her pants off and was trying to position himself, so he could enter her.

Something inside Mercedes just snapped. She balled her fist and with all the might she could muster she punched Hakeem right in the face. Hakeem was stunned by the fact that Mercedes had hit him, and he jumped up. Mercedes took that opportunity to get off the bed. She jumped up grabbing the now crying newborn. They were face to face, she wanted to run but he was blocking the door. All of a sudden WHOMP! He slapped her cross the face knocking her up against the wall. Without thinking Mercedes brought her knee up between Hakeem's legs with all the strength she had in her. As soon as he dropped to the ground she darted out the room. Quickly running into the kids room. She dropped Desmond into his car seat and snatched up Evon out of bed and ran for the door. Mercedes was so busy tryna make it out the door that she didn't notice Hakeem was no longer on the floor. The barefooted Mercedes busted out the door carrying her week old newborn son and her fifteen-month old daughter at 2 o'clock in the morning. Before she could make it to the car she heard Hakeem as he came off the porch behind her. He blindsided her across the back with his fist knocking her off balance. She dropped the car seat as she fell forward still cradling Evon in her hands. Despite the fact that his two babies were now screaming at the top of their lungs, Hakeem grabbed Mercedes by her hair and punched her in the chest. "Where the fuck do you think you're going!" The tears were streaming down her face, but she sat there holding on to her kids for dear life.

Her strength was gone, so Mercedes did the only thing she had left to do. She started screaming at the top of her lungs. "Help me!" "Please somebody help me!" Nothing happened. Nobody came to her rescue, not even a porchlight flicked on. Hakeem stood over her and laughed. "You're mines to do whatever I want to!" "Nobody's gonna help you!" Hakeem said as he stood over her. "Give me my son!" he taunted as he kicked her in her side. The sharp pain shot through Mercedes causing her to ball up releasing the hold she had on the carrier holding the crying newborn. Hakeem snatched up the baby and carried him into the house. "No!" Mercedes screamed but her battered exhausted body refused to move. Again, Hakeem stood over her as she still laid balled up on the front lawn. Without warning he slapped her across the face several times causing blood to trickle down the front of her face. He then grabbed the sobbing toddler right out of Mercedes hands. Mercedes laid there not knowing what to expect next. She no longer heard the kids cries. That in itself gave her motivation to make her body move. But before she could get off the ground another blow came from nowhere knocking her face forward to the ground. Grabbing her by the hair Hakeem forced Mercedes upward as he leaned closer to her. "Nobody will help you!" "If you ever think about calling the cops! Once I get out and trust I will get out! I will kill you, make no mistake about it!" He punched her again causing her body to go limp. Still holding her hair, he half dragged half carried the barefooted limp Mercedes into the house.

Once inside the house he dropped his wife on the floor. She couldn't tell where or what part of the house she was in. It was so eerily silent that it made the hair on the back of her neck stand on end. Moments later she heard the door close and footsteps coming towards her. He was there somewhere in the darkness standing watching her. Mercedes heard him unzip his pants and then she could hear his clothes as they hit the floor. He kicked her legs open as he got down on the floor between them. "No, you can't!" Mercedes started to protest. Without saying a word, he slapped her across the mouth. "I can do with you what the fuck I want." He said low and calm in her ear. Mercedes didn't know what to do, she had to think fast. "Please baby!" She spoke back just as calmly as he had spoken to her. "I just gave birth to your son." If you do this now you're gonna hurt me." "Baby please don't." despite the calmness in her voice the tears were streaming down her face. The wetness crept over her cheeks causing the mixture of tears and blood to flow into her mouth. There was nothing, no movement, no noise, just nothing.

Apparently, Hakeem had a conscience and he knew his wife was right. He let out a long breath and started to get up. Mercedes couldn't believe what was happening, but she knew all too well not to trust him, so she kept her guard up. He sat there on his knees for a second, then the monster in him won out and he grabbed her by her hair and punched her in the side of the face knocking her out instantly. He dropped her back down to the floor but that wasn't enough for him. He stood up pulled out his penis and masturbated, letting his ejaculation cover the face of his unconscious wife.

The phone rang snapping Mercedes back to reality. She jumped up rubbing her hand across her face in an effort to wipe away the essences of her bad dream. Grabbing the phone, she sat up in the bed. Unknown number again, it was like he knew what had happened in her dream and was calling to torture her again. There was no escaping him, sleep or awake! She didn't know what to do. Mercedes covered her face with the pillow and cried until she fell back to sleep.

5

Perfect Stranger

Raven

Raven Alexander thought she had her life together. At 36 she was lead teller at Wells Fargo where she's worked for the last 6 years. She had two beautiful kids Omari and Kelly that were the center of her universe. She had met the woman of her dreams and their relationship was blossoming into something promising. Ms. Tonya Hakeem with her hazel eyes and chiseled abs had walked out of a Jet Magazine right into her heart. She had met Tonya one afternoon when she came into the bank to open up a checking account. When she approached the counter, it felt like time stood still and Raven couldn't keep her eyes off the gorgeous beauty.

"Can I help you?" Raven asked with more sizzle then she normally used. "Yes," Tonya said still looking down at the papers in her hand. When she looked up they locked gazes, the sight of her greenish hazel eyes took her breath away. "Umm yea, I just opened an account the other day and wanted to add some money to it." "Yes, ma'am I would be happy to help you with that. Can I have your account number please?" After helping her with her transaction, Raven stared her in the eyes and asked "is there anything else I can help you with today Mrs. Hakeem?" "No, thanks that will be it;" she said and turned to leave. "Oh, by the way I think you gave me this by accident." She handed Raven a piece of paper that looked like her deposit receipt and walked off. Raven looked at what she had handed her; the paper had her name and number on it. When did she write it? She laughed and stuffed the paper in my bra. That was the beginning of a wonderful connection in Raven's eye.

Tonya Hakeem was a 40-year-old correctional officer from Miami Florida. She has always had a reputation as a player back home, but she recently transferred to The Fulton County Jail in Atlanta Georgia. She'd been on a couple of dates since she been here, but nothing had made a dent in her heart. That was until walking in the Wells Fargo bank to open up an account and seeing the sexiest thing on earth. She played it cool handled her business and bounced, seeing her was one of the reasons she opened the account there. Tonya waited all weekend before she came back to the bank. Tonya made sure to dress the part. She wore ashy black skinny leg jeans, a white button down with a black blazer, and a white and black Borsalino hat. In order to go to her window, Tonya let everyone go up until her window was clear. She had already writing down her info, her plan was to play it cool and just slide it to the beautiful teller before she walked off. When Tonya looked up at her and saw Raven gasp she knew she had it in the bag. So instead of sliding the info to her she did a Mack move and gave it to her, so she knew Tonya was coming at her.

Tonya waited so anxiously for Raven to call, but by the third day without a call she thought her player card had been revoked. She chopped it up to her having somebody already and let it go. Just about a week later, it was one of those really horrible days at work, she was sitting back at home with her feet up, glass of vodka and O.J., and some old Brian McKnight playing. Tonya's phone goes off in the room, but she really doesn't wanna leave her comfortable position. "Fuck it, I need a refill anyway," she thought. "Hello," she said in the most irritating voice she could muster, she wanted the caller to sense her mood. With the day she was having I hated for it to be a telemarketer Tonya thought to herself. "I'm sorry did I catch you at a bad time," the seductive voice said on the other end of the phone. When she realized who owed the voice Tonya damn near dropped the glass out of my hand. "No ma'am, I thought you were someone else" Tonya halfheartedly said. This girl was good she had turned the tables on her. So, Tonya had to get back in the lead of the chase. "So, Ms. Jones what can I help you with today?" Tonya asked putting a little jazz in her voice to sweeten the deal. "Oh, so now it's your turn to help me?" "You help so many people, when's the last time somebody took the time out to help you?" Tonya asked. Raven paused and nothing but silence came thru the phone, Tonya knew she had stunned her with the question. "I'm not sure, never really had anybody care about how my time was being spent," came her response. "So why don't you let me change that for you?" "What are you doing tomorrow night?" Tonya proceeded in questioning Raven. "If I'm not free I'm sure I can make room for you in my busy schedule," Raven said. Tonya seeing that as her moment and she went for it. "So how about we meet for dinner at Chili's by the bank at 8'oclock tomorrow night. That way we can get to know each other because I really don't like talking to you over the phone, it's so impersonal." "That will be great," Raven said "8'oclock it is. I can't wait to see you then," was the last thing Raven said before the line clicked off.

Tonya went through her day so fast that it was a blur. She punched the clock and was back in her car just as quick as ever. Tonya arrived at the restaurant about a half hour ahead of time as, so she could already be seated and waiting on Raven. When Raven walked in the door Tonya knew she was the one she had been dreaming of. Damn she was fine, the dress she was wearing hugged every curve of her luscious frame. Watching her sashay her way to the table made Tonya's mouth water and she longed to taste her. "Hey Beautiful," Tonya said rising to greet her lovely dinner date with a kiss of her dainty hand. I have to have her, Tonya thought. She wanted to own Raven's body, to punish it, to worship it, devour it. Tonya needed Raven in her world, to bathe in her essence always. "Hey handsome!" Raven responded, but it was barely heard over the sound of Tonya own heart beating. Raven sat down, and their enchanted love affair began its waltz. By the end of the night Raven was as mesmerized by Tonya as she was by her. Neither of them wanted to leave but they knew it was getting late. They kissed each other good night and parted ways.

The passion of the memory made Tonya's heart flutter and she stared at the ceiling with tears running down her cheek. She didn't know why she treated Raven so badly, she had put her hands on her queen. At the exact same moment Tonya was feeling sorry for herself Raven, was in the bathroom at work crying in the stall. They were now entering their 2nd year and Tonya's possessive behavior was getting out of hand. At first it was excessive questioning or and angry stare. Now Tonya had become physical with her, she had grabbed her arm digging into it with her nails. Raven looked down at the phone vibrating in her hand. Flipping over the phone to see the caller, speak of the devil Raven thought then hit the accept button. "Yes Tonya!" she barked in the phone. "Babe, I'm so sorry please forgive me! You know how much you mean to me. I don't know why I got so angry. Baby let me make it up to you; I promise it won't happen again." she sounded so pitiful, and her pleading melted Raven's heart. Even though Raven had decided to forgive her she wasn't gonna let her off that easy. "Look Tonya I'm at work, we can discuss this further when I get home." Before she could agree Raven slammed the phone shut and the call ended.

Raven's day went by extremely slow, but despite her emotional state she still showed no sign of turmoil. At the end of the day she didn't wanna go straight home because she knew Tonya would be at home and she didn't want to deal with her right now. She called ahead and asked for the babysitter to keep the kids an extra couple of hours. Raven pulled into the first bar parking lot she came upon and planted herself at the bar.

After a multitude of vodka cranberries and about three hours later Raven slips into her car and reclines the seat back. Tonya had started blowing up her phone an hour ago. She had been sending her to voicemail every time her name appeared on the caller ID. She closed her eyes and finally let the tears rolled down her cheeks. After the moment of feeling sorry for herself had ended she checked her face in the mirror. Starting her car, put it in gear and drove home.

Raven arrived home to find Tonya asleep on the sofa. Putting on a brave face she tried to walk pass the living room without stopping. She made it as far as the hall when the floor creaked giving her away. Damn creaky floor she screamed to herself and held her breath hoping Tonya hadn't heard it.

"So, you were just gonna walk past and not acknowledge me sitting here waiting up for you?" Tonya said jumping to her feet. Raven was feeling so good from all those vodka and cranberries she didn't want to fight. She merely waved her hand as to gesture leave me alone. As she turned to walk away Tonya grabbed her arm. "Baby I love you, please don't push me away." Tonya screamed as she spun Raven around to face her. Tonya's face was so close to Raven's the she could smell the scent of Patron on her breath. When Tonya looked up at Raven there was so much pain and sorrow that it brought tears to her own eyes. Raven's head was so clouded from the vodka and from the pure emotions flowing from her lover. She was suddenly overwhelmed by the need to have Tonya take possession of her body.

Without warning Tonya wrapped her arms around Raven and kissed her forehead. Raven was enveloped by her lover's arms and femininely hard body. She gave in and collapsed against her lover's chest, Tonya knew she had her right where she wanted her. She lowered her head and kissed Raven's perfectly full lips. "I love you so much babe," Tonya said to Raven. "If you love me then you gonna have to show me," Raven responded. Tonya kissed Raven so passionately and deep that she fell back against the wall. "Sorry baby for all this," Tonya whispered and with that said reached down and removed Raven's favorite peach lace embroidered Victoria Secret's panties. Before she had a chance to protest her legs were wrapped around Tonya's neck and her lover was devouring her savory center.

Raven bucked against Tonya's face like a wild beast. Increasing heat radiated from Raven's creamy center. A gasp escaped Raven's lips and she clasped her legs around Tonya's neck. Raven's nectar filled Tonya's mouth and ran down the sides of her face. Tonya lowered her lover into her arms and carried her to the bedroom where she made love to her until the sun began peeking through the mini-blinds.

6

Lover and Friends

Mercedes

"Good morning Crawford Long High School cafeteria Shunta speaking how can I help you." "Good morning Shunta, this is Mercedes I'm not feeling well I don't think I'm going to make it in today." Mercedes spoke into the phone trying to keep the tremble out of her voice. "Ok thank you for calling but you do know if you're out longer than three days you will need a doctor excuse upon your return to work." "Yes, I know" Mercedes said and then she slammed the phone on her. She dropped the phone on the bed, rolled over and closed her eyes.

Mercedes awoke to the sound of the phone ringing in her ear. She had rolled on top of it while she slept; her head was positioned like she had fallen asleep talking on it. She checked the caller ID, unknown caller. "I can't deal with him right now." Mercedes thought. I have to get up and get myself together. Mercedes got up walked down the hallway first stopping at the kids' room to check on them. She opened the door and the room was empty. Her heart sank, and she began to grow hysterical. Pausing for a second, she laughed at herself she had forgotten that it was a school day. They had gotten up and went to school by themselves. Her emotions were running on high again, she started crying. She paced back and forth up and down the hall, chain smoking as she went. An hour had passed before Mercedes had gotten herself under control.

Mercedes walked into the kitchen, taking a deep breath, she clicked on Pandora, and pour herself a drink. After the warm concoction began moving through her body, she let the music take over her and began to clean the house. By the time the kids came home from school Mercedes had enough liquid courage in her system to stop a heard of charging elephants. She already had dinner done and the house was spotless. The kids were happy to see her in a better mood. They all came in one by one kissed her then bolted for the door. She guessed they felt comfortable leaving her for the hordes of friends they had waiting for them outside. Which was fine by Mercedes because she refilled her glass, popped in a DVD, then plopped on the couch. Just when she was about to immerse herself in the comedic antics of Tyler Perry's Medea Goes To Jail, her phone rang. Mercedes figured it was just Hakeem calling again. She grabbed the phone ready to ignore the call, but when she looked at the caller ID she didn't recognize the number. Mercedes really didn't feel like dealing with telemarketers at the moment, but she answered it anyway.

"Hey beautiful!" The tantalizing voice she'd heard numerous times before caught her completely off guard. The voice belonged to Nikeya. Mercedes had known her for about five years now. She would satisfy her fix when she wanted a woman. Despite her gigantic personality, Nikeya was only 5'3", with long flowing dreads, perfect pearly whites, and a toasted almond caramel complexion. "Hey beautiful yourself, what you up to today and why you calling me from another number?" Mercedes asked. "Oh man you won't believe what happened to me,: Nikeya said changing the sexy Mack daddy tone she used at first. "What the hell have you done now," Mercedes asked. "What you doing right now," Nikeya shot back. "Nothing! why?" "I'm in your area, just wanted to see if you could get out the house for a while." "I have a date with Tyler Perry," Mercedes laughed through the phone. "So that means you're free tonight I guess" Nikeya said with a laugh. "Get dressed let's go out." Mercedes agreed, hung up, and ran like crazy to the shower. Nikeya's ass was closer than she thought; Mercedes barely had time to lotion and slip into her black lace boy short set before Nikeya was knocking at the door. Mercedes opened the door wearing only her underwear. "Damn I'm right on time I see," Nikeya said standing there with a Kool-Aid grin on her face. "Get your ass in here before the neighbors see me." Mercedes turned to head back to the room to finish getting dressed while Nikeya made herself at home on the couch.

Twenty minutes later Mercedes stood in front of Nikeya with black leggings; a low cut sleeveless mini dress that was held together with chains and large safety pins, Black sandals, large hoop earrings, and her favorite ponytail. Mercedes grabbed the phone and texted Evon for her to round up her sibling and head home. Mercedes and Nikeya sat and had a drink waiting for the kids to come in. Mercedes fixed the kids' plates, gave Evon instructions on what she expected to be done upon her return, kissed them all and hit the door.

Nikeya and Mercedes ended up at JR Crickets lounge on Cascade road. After a couple margaritas and some wings Nikeya finally started talking about why her number had been changed. "I met this fine ass yellow boned chick at the club last month," Nikeya started off. "Man, shawty was fine, she had ass for days." Mercedes looked over at her with the spare me the details look. Even though they weren't a couple Mercedes, still got jealous of the other girls in Nikeya's life. "Ok ok!" She got Mercedes' point and moved on. "Well we talked for about a week and I invited her over for drinks." Mercedes knew what that meant, in laymen terms she got her drunk and they had sex." The next day she called me at like 7 in the morning and every hour after that, I was like what the fuck! She didn't even want shit. Talking about she just wanted to hear my voice. I finally cursed the bitch out and told her to lose my number. She then called at 2am crying saying she was in love with me. I said fuck it and had my number changed. Trey told me that her ass had been at the club every night since looking for me." Trey was Nikeya brother slash road dawg. They called each other brothers even though they were both girls. Mercedes just looked at her laughing, "that's what you get for trying to be a Mack." Mercedes said to Nikeya unable to contain her humor. Mercedes thought about telling her about Monea. On second thought decided to keep that a secret.

After a few more drinks they were on the dance floor. The mixture of tequila and friction of Nikeya's body had Mercedes' libido raging. "When are you gonna let go of the men in your life and let me take care of you?" Nikeya whispered in her ear. "You're not ready for any form of relationship" Mercedes whispered back. Mercedes would have totally become Nikeya's girl if she wasn't such a player. Everyone could tell Nikeya was a lesbian from a mile away. She dressed like a man from her Haynes boxers to the Curve cologne. Her only turn off was that she thought she was God's gift to all women in the world. On the upside when she's with Mercedes she made her feel like she was the only girl in the world. Nikeya always has, that's the main reason Mercedes became a pawn in Nikeya's chess game. "You know I only have eyes for you" Nikeya said whispering in Mercedes ear. She encircled Mercedes with her arms and kissed her slow and deep. "I missed you" Mercedes said to her, having forgotten they were on the dance floor. When they looked up they had a wide variety of spectators and she released Mercedes. That's not uncommon being a lesbian couple in a straight environment. The men look at you with excitement whereas the women look at you down their noses. Mercedes didn't really care no one here knew her so she could be open and free. Nikeya took her by the hand and led her back to their table. This time Nikeya sat beside Mercedes instead of across from her. Nikeya was in full Mack mode she touched and kissed Mercedes until she was ready to jump on her right there. Knowing she had Mercedes right where she wanted her Nikeya waved for the waitress to pay their tab. While she did this Mercedes went to freshen up and check her appearance. When she returned Nikeya was standing by the door like the perfect gentleman she portrayed herself to be. Mercedes walked up to her grabbed her hand letting her lead the way.

The wonderful brisk early night was a welcomed change from the smoke-filled dungeon of the bar. They strolled hand and hand until they reached the car. Instead of getting in Nikeya leaned against the hood a pulled Mercedes to rest in between her legs. Wrapping her arms around Mercedes Nikeya kissed her on the side of her head. "I didn't want to ask but What's going on with you? You seem out there sometimes, what's on your mind?" Just having someone ask was enough to break the damn. She told her about everything that was going on with Hakeem. Nikeya was fuming mad. "What the fuck the police think a goddamn piece of paper gonna do! I got something for that." Nikeya said. "Let's go!" Nikeya lit a Newport handed it to Mercedes and lit another one for herself. She started the car and they drove off.

The only sound made on the ride was the mellow tones of the quiet storm on V103. The music was slow and seductive and made Mercedes feel infatuated with the idea of being in love. Mercedes didn't want her uncapped raw emotion and the way Nikeya was making her feel to infect her grip on reality. Mercedes never saw Nikeya look so serious before. "Where we going?" Mercedes asked "No worries I got you" Nikeya said without taking her focus off the road. Mercedes grew nervous, she had no clue of what Nikeya had in store. Nikeya parked the car, sit tight I'll be right back. She grabbed her bag from the trunk and entered a house in back of them.

Mercedes could feel the anxiety building from her core. Seconds felt like hours, minutes like days. To ease her nerves, she lit a Newport. Too afraid to roll the window down she cracked it just enough the let the smoke drift out. Finally, what felt like eons ago Nikeya jumped back in the car, place the bag behind her seat, and drove off.

The house was silent the kids were all in bed asleep. They went straight to the bedroom Mercedes turned on the radio while Nikeya set down her bag. "Would you like a drink?" Mercedes asked. "Sure," Nikeya responded. Mercedes exited the room and ventured to the kitchen to get some drinks. Upon returning she saw that Nikeya had made herself at home in the room. She was down to her sports bra and boxers. Nikeya looked magnificent with her muscular arms and sexy abs. Mercedes thought to herself, there was a man somewhere mad as hell because she had his mentality and his body. The thought made Mercedes laugh, Nikeya turned around catching Mercedes looking at her. "So, you like what you see," she asked. "Always" Mercedes said. The smile on Nikeya's face brightened the dimly lit room.

"Come here." Nikeya said so Mercedes sat the drinks down and made her way over to where Nikeya was sitting. Nikeya took her hand a pulled her down to where she was sitting. "I've never said this to a woman that wasn't in my family before. I love you girl; I don't want to see anything happen to you." The way Nikeya was looking told Mercedes she was dead serious. Reaching into her duffel bag Nikeya pulled out something wrapped in a towel and place it on her lap. "I got this from my homeboy." Nikeya said. "he owed me a favor." Nikeya opened and their laid the biggest chrome handgun Mercedes had ever seen in her life. "This is a Desert Eagle, it's very heavy and has one hell of kick when you fire it. Make sure you hold it with both hands and keep your arms firm when you pull the trigger." Nikeya took out the clip and made sure the chamber was empty before she handed the gun to Mercedes. The gun was a lot heavier then she anticipated. The feel of the cold hard steel in her hands felt amazing. Nikeya got up behind Mercedes showing her exactly how to hold the gun. Nikeya also showed her how to load the clip, insert it, how to remove the safety, as well as disarm it.

"You know what? Come on." Nikeya said grabbing her hand. She opened the back door and they stepped out on the back porch. It was very dark, and no one was out. "Have you ever fired a gun before?" Nikeya asked checking the gun before she handed it to Mercedes. "Yes, but nothing this large." It's fine take it in your hands like I showed you." "What am I aiming at?" "Just shoot in the air." Mercedes stood there for a second getting her thoughts together. She let a long sigh, then she grabbed the gun in both hands, raised it over her head and squeezed. "BOW!" You could hear the sound radiating thru the night. "Damn girl, You a lil soldier!" Nikeya said as she grabbed the gun and quickly led Mercedes back in the house. "Now close the door before one of your neighbors call the fucking cops." The shot was louder then Mercedes expected it sounded like a canon being fired. The kick back was mad crazy, if she hadn't held her arms tight it would've definitely jerked her back.

Into the bathroom they went. Nikeya placed the gun on a towel on the back of the toilet. She turned the shower on then turned to face her follower. Slowly she undressed Mercedes touching teasing her body along the way. After Nikeya finished Mercedes stood there in the nude while she undressed herself. Nikeya stepped in the shower turned, reached for Mercedes' hand grasped it then pulled her in the shower. "Stand here!" Nikeya commanded, Mercedes obliged because she was intrigued by Nikeya's intention. Picking up the loofa she then filled it with body wash. Nikeya washed every inch of Mercedes' body slowly and seductively. After she had successfully accomplished her task she pushed Mercedes under the running shower to rinse off. Mercedes then returned the favor deliberately taking extra-long on her lower region. By the time Mercedes finished rinsing Nikeya off, her once straight hair was all in curls. Damn she looked good wet! Mercedes thought to herself. Her muscular body now looked femininely soft with her breast and perfectly trimmed treasure exposed.

Once back in the room Mercedes wrapped the gun in the towel and placed it in the back of her closet on the shelf. They laid back on the bed and started talking. The next thing she knew the sun was coming up and the alarm clock went off they were still in each other's arms talking. Mercedes made sure the kids were up and off to school. Then she called while it was still early left a message on Shunta's answering machine about her still being sick. Nikeya made a few calls and then they crashed on the bed and slept well into the afternoon.

Mercedes jumped straight up in the bed having forgotten where she was. Damn! The dreams were all too real. She looked around the room trying to catch her bearings. Reassuring herself that she was safe, she went to lie back down and caught a glimpse of Nikeya's half naked frame. "You ok?"

Nikeya asked as she laid there with her arm folded behind her head. "I'm tryna be."

Nikeya sat up on the edge of the bed and lit a cigarette, while Mercedes sat in the chair doing the same. "What are you doing later tonight?" Nikeya asked. "I'm not sure. Why what's up?" "When was the last time someone treated you to a nice dinner?" Nikeya asked. They both laughed in unison. "Don't do the whole I'm a good boyfriend routine!" Mercedes said in return. Having Nikeya there really eased her nerves.

About an hour later they were both showered and dressed. Mercedes walked Nikeya to the door kissed her like a husband leaving for work. They said their goodbyes and Mercedes watched Nikeya bound the steps and enter her car. She waved at Mercedes as she pulled off. Mercedes waved back then shut the door. Mercedes thought about Monea, she wanted to call her but advised against it since she had called out from work. Mercedes cleaned up her house, started dinner, and waited for the arrival of her brigade.

7

Gay or Straight? That's the Question

Nashunta

Things between Lameka and Nashunta were great for a while after that evening. Nashunta had even decided to come out of the closet to her parents and tell them about the love of her life. She thought long and hard on how best to tell them. So, she came up with the idea to do it over dinner. As the day of the dinner approached the knots in her stomach grew. She wanted to cancel; several times she came damn near close.

Her family had agreed to stay away from the house until that evening. After the dinner was prepared and the table set, Nashunta sat on her bed and downed one of the little miniature bottles of vodka she kept hidden in the hole in the side of her mattress. She sat there for the longest going over what she'd say in her head. When her father called her name from downstairs she felt nausea sweep over her. She gathered herself, said a small prayer, and headed for her door. Here goes nothing she said and down the stairs she went.

Nashunta served everyone then she took the seat farthest from her parents. The family ate in silence everyone wondering what this meeting was about. Nashunta cleared her throat letting her family know she was ready to start.

"First off mom and dad I just want you guys to know that I love you. I know I've been going through something and hope this brings some clarity toward my actions. I've been consumed lately, and I didn't know how to tell you." "What is it baby?" Mrs. Jones said interrupting her. "Baby if you're pregnant just tell us we'll figure it out". "What! You're pregnant!" yelled Kimmie. "Who is he? I'll kill em!" Yelled Mr. Jones. There was so much commotion about her being pregnant that they wouldn't let her finish talking. "I'm gay!" Nashunta screamed at the top of her lungs. The room abruptly went silent and everyone was staring at her. "What!" Her parents said simultaneously. "We didn't raise you like that!" Her father yelled. "You're not gay; I won't have no child of mines going against God in that way." "I won't have any faggots in my family!" Her father yelled. "I would have rather you told me you were pregnant then to have said that." Mr. Jones barked as he stood and walked away from the table.

"Honey, how do you know you're gay? You just need to meet the right guy. I'll talk to your father and calm him down. Honey you just shouldn't say such things." "But mom," Nashunta tried to speak. "I've met someone I want you to meet." Mrs. Jones turned to face her daughter. "You're not gay! We're not gonna have this discussion anymore! I have to go talk to your father." Mrs. Jones turned and left Nashunta and Kimmie standing in the dining room alone. Kimmie feeling sorry for her sister put her arms around and held her as she cried.

Nashunta stayed locked in her room for the duration of the weekend. It was only when her parents went to bed did she venture out to eat. She was angry; she didn't even want to set eyes on them. She gathered what she could and dashed back to her room. She didn't come out again until it was time to go to school Monday morning.

Damn I hate being late Nashunta thought to herself as she ran down the steps of her home. She makes it to the top of the hill just in time to catch the bus going to the school. She settles back against the seat to catch her breath when she realizes that she had left her phone. "Oh my God! Wait!" she yells to the bus driver! "Sorry Miss you'll have to wait until the next stop to get off," he yelled back. Damn if she got off she'd miss her final and fail her sociology class. The driver pulled up to the next stop and asked if she wanted off, reluctantly she said no, and he proceeded on. At school, she started toward class but stopped in the bathroom first to check her appearance. She looked haggard, her red swollen eyes with her teardrop stained face. The sight of her face brought back the memories of the weekend's events. She dried her face and left the bathroom making it to class seconds before the tardy bell rang . After she took her seat she saw Lameka standing at the door. "What's up?" She was motioning with her mouth. "I'll talk to you after class" Nashunta mouthed back. Just then the teacher noticed her and shut the door.

As soon as the bell rung for class to be dismissed Nashunta was outta her seat and through the door. She didn't have to look far because Lameka was standing just outside in the hall. So, what happened to you? Why you haven't called me or nothing? Nashunta told Lameka what happened and what her parents had said. Before she could help herself, she was balling right there in the hallway. "Aww! Babe it's alright we'll just have to keep low key and when you're ready to tell them again we'll both tell them together." Nashunta couldn't have been more in love with Lameka than she was now. She wrapped her arms around her girlfriend and kissed her as if they were the only people in the hall.

Months after the dinner Nashunta and her parents still weren't on proper speaking terms. The customary greetings and the mandatory I love you's were the only forms of communication. Nashunta lay across her bed in deep thought. Keeping her relationship from her parents was becoming a strain. Knock knock! The unwanted knock on the door frustrated her. "Who is it?" Nashunta said agitated. "It's mommy honey, may I come in?" "It's your house, do whatever you want." She replied. Ever since Lameka started sneaking in her window and spending the night she started locking her door. She quickly set up on the bed and unlocked the door.

Mrs. Jones entered her daughter's room which was a rare occasion lately. "Nashunta you've been so cut off from the world and I think you should get out and have fun. I know I had no right to do this, but my friend Yolanda's son is home from college and I suggested you two hang out." "Mom! I'm not hanging out with no one!" Nashunta snapped. "Yes you are! I've never asked you for much." Her mom said. "This nonsense among this family has gone on for long enough. If you what your father to loosen up a little, then you'll go." Mrs. Jones grabbed her daughter's hand, "you've spoken I've heard you, but you have to do this. Ok." With that being said Nashunta could sense her mom was coming to terms with her sexuality.

Nashunta let out her last defiant breath, "fine mom I'll go." Mrs. Jones smiling big. "Well get dressed he'll be here within the hour" and dashed out the door before Nashunta realized she had been tricked. "What?" Nashunta ran behind her mom. "You didn't say he was coming today." "Hurry honey" Mrs. Jones yelled over her shoulder. "You don't have much time." Exactly 45 minutes later Yolanda's son Nathan was at the door.

Nashunta wanted to dress casual but didn't know where she was going. She had on black skinny leg jeans, a silver off the shoulder sweater that was cut so you could see her teal green belly ring, and her favorite black and silver open toed stilettos. She pulled her long mane up into a ponytail. She did her make up as to appear she wasn't wearing any, glossed her lips and headed for the stairs. Nathan was handsome he had dark brown skin and sexy bedroom light brown eyes. He wore black jeans, a white V-neck polo tee, a black polo blazer, and some dressed up polo boots. He accented his ensemble with polo cologne. He looked like a magazine model for polo. He looked magnificent, but it was something about him that Nashunta couldn't put her finger on.

Mrs. Jones introduced him to the family, making sure her husband saw his daughter going out with a boy for a change. Then she pushed the both of them toward the door. Right before she shut the door she snatched Nashunta's phone from her hand. "You won't be needing that tonight." She turned it off and dropped it in her pocket. Seeing the concerned look on her daughter's face she said "don't worry I won't go thru it, it'll be in your room when you get home." Nashunta was still holding her breath when Mrs. Jones shut the door on them. She hadn't had time to call Lameka and explain all of this. She wanted to beat down the door, she knew Lameka would be pissed. "I know the feeling." Nathan spoke to her for the first time. "My mom did the same to me, I think they planned it." She'll just have to try and explain everything to Lameka when she gets back and pray she'll understand.

Just as Nathan and Nashunta were leaving the porch Lameka was pulling up. What the fuck, she said under her breath as she saw her lady being escorted to a laid-out baby blue SS Monte Carlo. Lameka grew so angry that it felt like flames would shoot out her eye sockets. She waited for the car to pull off and she followed behind them.

"So where are we going?" Nashunta asked breaking the silence of the ride. "Have you eaten? Would you like to have dinner or coffee and dessert?" Nathan asked with a voice that would make the average girl swoon. "How about dinner, then coffee and dessert?" Nashunta cheered. "Your wish is my command! I know the perfect place we can have both." Nathan said in return. "So, do you mind if I ask you a question?" Nathan asked as he turned the radio off. "Sure, be my guess." Nashunta replied. "Why would a beautiful girl such as yourself need help from her mother to find a date? Let me guess you bring home the typical pants sagging, gold chain wearing, Plies wannabe's that all parents despise, and your parents are on a mission from God to save their family line." Nashunta looked at Nathan and they both burst out laughing.

"I would ask you the same question" she turned the tables on the conversation. "You don't look like you should be having any problems finding beautiful women to bed out in college," Nashunta sarcastically stated. "To be honest, I don't have a problem getting people in my bed it's the people I choose that my mom has a problem with," Nathan said more to himself then anything. He really didn't want to speak the truth in fear that she would want to end the date. He had already made a promise to his mom to at least try to make it to dinner before he started running his mouth and ruin everything. Nashunta was stunned by the reply and turned completely in her seat to face Nathan. Nathan took this as hostile behavior and prepared himself for the question he knew was coming. Here we go, he breathes as he tried to preoccupy himself with the road.

Lameka tried to stay far enough behind that Nashunta wouldn't recognized her car. She could see them laughing and talking in the car as they rode along. The way he looked at her infuriated Lameka and before she realized it she had dug her nails into her palm and she was bleeding. Let me see what lie she'll say explain this. Reaching for her phone she dialed Nashunta's number. No ringing just went straight to voice mail. This bitch has her phone off, O she's gonna pay for this. She wants to play, game on! Lameka thought to herself. She grabbed her phone and dials her ex Montana's number. Montana was a 26-year-old dental assistant, her and Lameka had started messing around when Lameka was only 16. They had met one day when Lameka and her mom had gone in for Lameka's yearly checkup, Montana was new to the office. She had playfully joked with Lameka the entire time. Once Lameka was in the chair and her mom nowhere in sight she continuously rubbed her voluptuous backside across Lameka's hands. Lameka got the message and they exchanged numbers. A few days later Lameka went into the office for a fake toothache and ended up with Montana in the storage closet of the dental office. They secretly messed around for a year until Lameka came out to her parents. After that they found out about Montana and threatened to sue the dentist office if she didn't leave their child alone. Montana backed off, but she and Lameka never really stopped messing around, until Nashunta came in and stole the spot light. Lameka knew she could always get whatever she wanted from Montana and she used that power whenever she saw fit. Nashunta knew who Montana was and they completely despised one another.

Montana didn't give Lameka a chance to even speak; I'll be waiting on you when you pull up. I have on that favorite nighty you like. I'll be there in 10 minutes she said and shut the phone tossing it into the passenger seat. She followed Nashunta until they reached the restaurant, she turned right and speed off toward Montana's place.

Nathan and Nashunta rode to the restaurant in silence the air between them was thick and heavy. When they arrived at the place, before Nathan had a chance to exit the car Nashunta grabbed his hand. "Nathan are you gay?" She asked looking as sympathetic as she could. Nathan turned to face Nashunta, "before I answer your question you have to promise to at least have dinner with me for our mom's sake." Nashunta agreed. "Yes, Nashunta I'm gay." Nashunta smiled at him and said "Nathan I'm gay too." They both looked at each other and burst out laughing again. Nathan felt more relaxed about the evening; a weight had been removed from his chest. Nathan got out and walked to open Nashunta's door. She took this time to refresh her make up in the mirror. Wait is that! She took a double take in the mirror, she could have sworn she had just saw Lameka's car. She shook the thought from her head and took Nathan's waiting arm and they walked into the restaurant.

Once they were seated and the food ordered, the conversation picked up between them. "So, I guess both of our parents are on a mission from God to save their bloodline." Nathan candidly joked. "My mom found out about me when she dropped in to check on me last year and caught me in bed with my ex-boyfriend. I thought me giving her a key to my college apartment would be a good idea since we weren't in the same state. But her having no man and no life leaves her with a lot of time on her hands. The only good thing about it was we had already finished having sex and we were only laying there sleep holding each other. She didn't really over react as I thought she would have. She dropped the bags on the floor that's what woke us. Lord Jesus! is all she said. She turned left and drove back home. We didn't speak for a week after that. I don't know why she didn't call me, but I was afraid to call her. She finally called the next week and acted as if nothing had happened. I went along with it but when I came home for the holidays she had started tryna set me up on dates. That's my life, so what's the story with you?" Nathan asked his dinner guest. "Well I made dinner for my parents and told them I was gay, only to have my father tell me he would have preferred me to have told him I was pregnant than to have said I was gay. I didn't even get a chance to introduce my girlfriend to them. I'm kind of getting the feeling my mother may be coming around but I don't know. I've been locking myself in my room since it happened. I guess my mom told your mom about me and your mom suggested this date." Nashunta stated. Nathan shook his head. "We better be careful, or they'll have us married off pretty soon." "That wouldn't be a bad idea come to think of it;" Nashunta said finishing up the last of her fruit punch she had spiked herself. "What's not a bad idea?" Nathan asked puzzled. "Us getting married! We could get married, move away, and we would be free to live our live like we want." "So basically, you're saying you wanna use me as a cover?" Nathan asked laughing whimsically. "I'm pretty sure if we come home tonight proclaiming we wanna marry our parents would suspect something. Look if you really wanna do this then we'll gradually date for a minute, then right after you graduate I'll confess my undying love and ask you to marry me. You can apply to some colleges out there where I'm living and before you leave for college we can get hitched." Nashunta agreed excitedly, all she heard was the sound of freedom ringing in her ears. They spent the rest of the evening getting to know each other just in case their parents decided to question them about the date.

Lameka pulled up at Montana's house within 10 minutes flat. She had smoked a blunt of loud before she pulled up, so she was ready. Montana opened the door wearing a purple lingerie set that barley left anything to the imagination. Lameka was pissed and Montana was gonna feel all of her aggression tonight. Montana could take whatever Lameka threw at her and tonight she would put her into a coma. Lameka didn't waste time talking as soon as the door was shut she push Montana forcefully against the wall and ripped her nighty right off. "You wanna be my naughty tonight?" Lameka whispered in Montana's ear as she removed her clothes. "Yes!" Montana breathlessly whispered back. "Then get on your knees!" Lameka order her lover. "I want you to make me cum and swallow all of me before I can consider giving you what you want." Lameka leaned against the wall as Montana lowered herself to her knees and began orally pleasing her lover. Montana wrapped her pulsating tongue around Lameka's long clit and insistently devoured it. Montana knew exactly how to please Lameka. She could feel the bulge growing inside of Lameka and she knew she was about to explode. "You wanna taste my juices!" Lameka spoke to Montana. "Umm

Hmm!" Came the response. "Uhh! I'm finna come!" Lameka yelled out. She grabbed Montana by the hair holding her head in place Lameka released herself inside Montana's mouth. Montana happily accepted the gift drinking all Lameka had to offer.

Montana rose to her feet awaiting her next instructions, she was so aroused by Lameka that she had cum on her own and it was running down her leg. Look at you! Lameka said to her. Montana kept the strap that her and Lameka used stating that she didn't want anyone else using it. Montana hurried and grabbed the 12in strap that they use together. She watched excitedly as her lover adorned the appendage. "Bend your ass over that chair," she commanded Montana. Lameka wasn't in a gentle mood tonight she wanted to beat her up in the worst way. As soon as she slid inside of Montana she went to work. She showed Montana no mercy, she drove every single inch of it inside her. Montana enjoyed when Nashunta made Lameka mad, she knew Lameka would call her. Within seconds she had Montana cumming but Lameka showed no signs of stopping. "Turnover I wanna see your eyes" Lameka told Montana. She wasn't being her usual aggressive self this was something different Montana could see it inside her eyes. She was really being forceful and after Montana told her to stop she became enraged. She grabbed Montana by the throat choking her as she forcefully thrust the plastic appendage inside her. Montana became afraid and tried to fight but the more she fought the tighter Lameka squeezed her throat. Her air supply was restricted, and she felt she would blackout. Her eye started to roll in the back of her head. Lameka stared down at Montana as she struggled against her. Knowing the power, she had in her hands aroused her. The fear in her face as her eyes began to roll back was enough to send Lameka over the edge. Just when Montana thought for sure Lameka would kill her, she let out a loud sigh as she reached her climax. Her body shuddered, and she released her grip on Montana's neck. She grasped for air between coughs. Montana wanted desperately to get Lameka off of her, but she was too afraid to move. Without a word Lameka stood up got dressed and left. Montana lay frozen on the chair she was so afraid Lameka would be there is she moved and kill her. 20 minutes had passed before she realized, and she made a desperate dash to lock the door. Once she had the door securely locked she sank to the floor and balled like a baby.

By the time dinner was done Nathan and Nashunta felt like old friends. They had agreed that if their parents continued on this path of trying to match them up they would put operation get hitched in to play. They ordered dessert to go and then headed home. They laughed and talked all the way back to Nashunta's house. Nathan walked her to the door they made plans to meet up again before he headed back off, they hugged and Nashunta headed inside. She hurried to her room to get her phone but before she could make it half way up the stairs her mother was coming full steam behind her. "So how was the date? Did you like him? He was cute, wasn't he?" "Mom! Let me get my phone and I'll come downstairs and talk to you about my evening." Mrs. Jones excitedly agreed and turned and rushed back down the steps.

Nashunta made it to her room grabbed her phone and pressed the power button. Her phone turned on and blinking light indicated she had a message she knew it was Lameka and her stomach started turning in knots. She tried to call Lameka, but the call kept going straight to voicemail, this was never a good sign. She knew her mom was waiting for her downstairs and if she didn't show she would be up knocking at her door. Nashunta quickly dialed her voicemail and entered her password but instead of Lameka voice she heard Montana's. What the fuck does she want? She said to herself. Nashunta couldn't make out what she was saying, and she sounded like she was crying. Nashunta had to turn the volume on her phone up just so she could try to make out what she was saying. "Nashunta something happened tonight I'm afraid for myself, I'm afraid for you!" Montana spoke thru sobs. "Please call me as soon as you get this message. Oh God I pray you call me! Please call!" And with that the call ended. That bitch was up to her tricks again or maybe Lameka put her up to it just because she was mad. Either way Montana was way too old for the games she played. She decided she would call her back at another time she didn't feel up to her games tonight. Nashunta removed her shoes and changed her clothes.

When she finally made it downstairs dessert in hand her mother was waiting with cups of tea ready for the juicy gossip of the night. "Mom, Nathan is a great guy and we've made plans to go out again before he leaves next week." "Yes!" Her mother cheered. "So, what happened? Come honey, you know nothing exciting ever happens to me anymore, amuse your dear old mother." "Nothing really happened, we went to the Cheesecake Factory. We talked, come to find out we have a lot of things in common." As Nashunta replayed the evening for her mom, her phone was buzzing in her pocket. As soon as her mom went to refill her cup she checked it. Montana again, this girl was not giving up tonight. Nashunta rolled her eyes and quickly texted Montana. What do you want? I'm having a talk with my mom. I don't feel like your bullshit games tonight. Just leave me alone, ok! Nashunta quickly stuffed the phone back in her pocket before her mom returned from the kitchen. Nashunta and her mom talked like old friends, it had been awhile since they've talked. It was well pass 12am before they called it a night. Luckily it was the weekend and they could both sleep in.

By the time Nashunta made it upstairs she had three more texts from Montana. One by one Nashunta opened the texts and read them. Nashunta I know we have our differences but please call me, I'm afraid for your safety. Nashunta call me please! I really need to talk to you! This is not any game please call me. Nashunta decided she was too tired to deal with Montana. She tried dialing Lameka again, straight to voicemail. Well I guess I know why she wants me to call her. Hope you enjoy yourself tonight because it's gonna be a long time before you touch me again. She closed her phone and turned over and drifted off to sleep.

Nashunta jumped out her sleep her phone was ringing nonstop in her ear. This better be good she told herself. Looking at the time it was 11:45 in the morning, damn I was sleeping good. She checked the caller ID and saw that Lameka had called twice and Nathan had called as well. She checked her voicemail Nathan wanted to go to the mall and wanted to know if she wanted to come with. Nashunta never missed an opportunity to go shopping. She thought about calling Nathan but decided she'd better deal with Lameka first. She reluctantly dialed Lameka's number, this time it rang. "Oh I see you've chosen to cut your phone back on this morning," Lameka words oozed with sarcasm. "Good morning to you too" Nashunta replied to the statement. "So, I spotted you with your little date last night. I know how easy you are to spread your legs for niggas, so did you fuck him?" "Lameka can you at least give me a chance to explain before you start accusing me of sleeping around." "No need to explain, did you fuck him!" Lameka yelled thru the phone. "That was your car I saw last night," Nashunta said more for her own revelation than anything else.

"Oh, so I guess you got jealous and went and gave your friend Montana another courtesy fuck!" Nashunta yelled thru the phone. "Is that why she keep calling and texting my phone?" Nashunta asked. "What?" Lameka yelled. "When did she call you? And what the fuck did she say?" Lameka demanded. "She just kept telling me to call her, but I didn't" Nashunta shot back. "I figured it had something to do with you." "You know what don't go nowhere today we need to talk I'll be over that way in a sec to get you." Lameka said thru the phone. "No way I've made other plan!" Nashunta protested. "Nashunta you're really starting to piss me off. I'll call you when I'm close." Lameka hung up before she had time to protest anymore.

Lameka jumped in her car and sped off, she quickly dialed Montana's number no answer. "Uggh! This dumb bitch I'll kill her" she said thru clenched teeth. Montana saw Lameka's number appear on her caller ID and she pressed ignore. She knew Nashunta would have called her and she would be heading for her. In a panic Montana threw some clothes on and ran for the door she had to get the hell away before she got there.

Lameka must have been breaking all sorts of traffic laws because just as Montana was turning to shut the door Lameka hit her from behind knocking her back into the house. "What the fuck you tryna do Montana? You got what you wanted!" Lameka yelled! "If you fuck things up between me and Nashunta I'll kill you! Do you understand me you filthy whore!" Lameka had Montana's face pressed against the wall so hard she thought her eye would pop out the socket. "Do you understand me?" Lameka spoke again this time she slowed down to make sure Montana heard her every word. "Yes Lameka, please you're hurting me!" Montana screamed. "If you keep your mouth shut I might come over and fuck you again like last night, I enjoyed myself." Lameka released Montana and turned to leave. "I don't want to have nothing else to do with you" Montana yelled at Lameka. Lameka walked back over toward Montana. "It's over when I say it's over bitch, and don't you ever forget that." Lameka slapped Montana so hard across the face that it knocked her into the wall. "I'll be back tonight for an instant replay of last night," she said and out the door she went.

Like hell she would be here when she came back, Montana locked her door and ran upstairs. She packed two suitcases and an overnight bag. She crammed everything inside her Nissan passport made sure the house was locked tight jumped in her car and speed off.

Nashunta was on the phone declining Nathan's invite to the mall when Lameka's picture flashed across the phone indicating she was calling. She said goodbye to her new friend and clicked over to answer the other line. "I'm about to pull up meet me around the corner," Lameka said and clicked the phone before Nashunta could speak. Nashunta grabbed her purse and headed out the door. She turned the corner just in time to see Lameka 's car coming down the street. "Get in the car" Lameka said. "Where are we going?" Nashunta asked. "Just get in the car Nashunta I don't have all day." Nashunta opened the door and got in and Lameka drove off. Lameka's parents were gone for the weekend so they ended up at her house.

"You never answered my question" Lameka said to Nashunta as she came back from the kitchen with two sodas. "What question was that?" Nashunta asked her. "Did you fuck him?" Lameka asked Nashunta. "No! Nathan is gay!" Nashunta yelled at her overreacting girlfriend. "You're a lying bitch you know that!" Lameka screamed and before Nashunta had a chance to react Lameka had attacked her. Grabbing her by the shirt she snatched her outta the chair. "You think I'm gonna let some nigga come in and take you away from me! I swear to God If you ever think about leaving me for a man I'll kill you!" Lameka spat the words outta her mouth like a rabid dog ready to attack. She slapped Nashunta's face so violently the blood ran from her nose. "Lameka stop please! I didn't do anything! What's wrong with you!"

She looked into her girlfriend's face, the eyes of her lover were gone. What she saw was anger, pure rage. At that moment Nashunta was afraid. Lameka saw the terrified look on Nashunta's face and the blood running down her cheek and she let her go. Nashunta ran in the bathroom and locked the door. Looking in the mirror she saw that her nose was bleeding and her lips were swollen. Wetting some tissue Nashunta cleaned the blood from her face. Nashunta had had enough; she had told Lameka that if she put her hands on her again it was over. She threw her bloody tissue in the garbage, grabbed her lipstick outta her purse, and wrote in large letters on the bathroom mirror IT'S OVER! Nashunta pushed the window up as quietly as she could. She then threw the things back in her bag and jumped out the bathroom window. She ran as fast as she could not knowing if Lameka was following her or not. She took out her phone and the first number she saw was Nathan.

"Nathan please I need you to come get me, I'll explain later! Please!" Nashunta screamed into the phone. Nashunta told Nathan where to meet her. She hung up the phone and walked the three blocks to the gas station. She practically had to beg the clerk to let her stay inside to wait on her ride.

By the time Nashunta was headed to the gas station Lameka was realizing that she had been in the bathroom way to long. At first, she knocked on the door lightly. "Come on baby, I'm sorry! You know I get jealous when I see men tryna put the moves on my girl." No response came back. "Come on Nashunta, if I have to kick my parent door in I'm gonna be pissed!" She yelled at the door, still no response. Lameka ran to the kitchen and grabbed a butter knife from the drawer. She came back to the door and with one swipe of the wrist the locked pop open. She threw open the door and was surprised to find Nashunta nowhere to be found. She darted to the open window and peered out, still no sign of Nashunta. As she turned to race out the door she caught sight of the red writing on the mirror. IT'S OVER! The words were like venom to Lameka. "That bitch!" Lameka yelled grabbed her keys and rushed out the door.

Nashunta waited impatiently for what seems like an eternity for Nathan to arrive. As soon as she saw that baby blue SS Monte Carlo she darted out the store right into Nathan's arms. Nathan took one look at Nashunta's face, "what in the world?" he yelled. "What the hell happened to you?" "Drive now, ask questions later" Nashunta cried and jumped into the car.

After driving around the neighborhood, Lameka stopped her car at the red light. "She couldn't have gone too far on foot." She thought to herself. Lameka turns the corner just in time to see Nashunta race from the store into Nathans arms, she jumped in his car and they raced off down the street. There are no words to describe the level of rage Lameka had coursing thru her veins. Lameka pulled into the gas station put her head on the steering wheel and sobbed. Everything that she knew and loved in the world was gone.

8

A Wolf in Sheep's Clothing

Raven

R aven's phone rung, this was the call she'd be waiting for. She jumped outta bed grabbed her phone and she tried to down play her excitement. Raven had been very pleased with Tonya lately and she wanted to show her appreciation. "Good morning Simon!" Raven said cheerfully as she answered the phone. "Good morning Raven!" I just called to let you know that everything is all set. Simon was one of Raven's good friends. He worked as a travel agent for some of the wealthiest people in Atlanta's LGBT community and got her the hook up on all her vacation getaways. "Oh, miss thang you're gonna knock Ms. Tonya's socks off with what I've put together. There will be a limo there to pick you guys up Friday morning," Simon started reading the itinerary. "A limo? How much did you charge to my credit card?" Raven asked. "The limo is courtesy of Teal and Simon," Simon replied. Teal Morgan was an aspiring model who had a moderate modeling contract with the Polo Company. He was Simon's flava of the month and with a caramel covered body like he had I could see why Simon's head was in the clouds about him. "I know a friend that knows a friend," Simon said. That's what Raven liked about Simon, he was so good at what he did for people that they were always giving him free stuff here and extra stuff there.

Simon continued talking without missing a beat. "I booked you at the Stone Mountain resort. I managed to get your room bumped up to a suite facing the lake. I took the liberty of having it stocked with your favorite food, beverages, and I threw in a giant gift bag filled with all the fun things you lesbians like to use. And before you ask Ms. Raven, all the extra stuff was courtesy of the resort, including the gift bag." "How did you manage that?" Raven asked. "Well if you must know, one of the co-owner of the resort just married his longtime lover and I was able to add four free nights on to their Brazilian honeymoon. After that girl, you know I was able to add him to my I got a friend who knows a friend list. Well I hope you ladies enjoy your weekend and call me with all the juicy gossip when you get back." "You know I will," Raven retorted. "Alright Ms. Diva smooches."

When Tonya heard the phone ring and saw the way Raven had jumped outta bed she felt the jealousy monster rising up in her. Despite of how she felt, Tonya continued to lay there in hopes that if Raven thought she was asleep she would slip up and say something. She couldn't quite make out what she was talking about, but it sounded like it had something to do with money or her credit card. Tonya wanted to question her but didn't want to let on that she was ease dropping.

Raven was so excited when she got off the phone she jumped in the bed and grabbed hold of Tonya. "I love you so much" she whispered in her ear. "I have a huge surprise for you this weekend." "Oh really," Tonya said. "So, what's the surprise?" "You have to what until Friday," Raven retorted. Raven jumped out of bed and ran to the shower. "What?" Tonya ran behind her. Their love making session put them behind in their morning schedule and Raven had to end up taking the kids to school because they missed the bus.

After dropping the kids off at school Raven decided to call her baby daddy to inquire about him picking the kids up a day early for his weekend visit. She opened her phone and dialed his number. Raven hated calling Stacey. He hated the fact that she'd left him and resented even more that she was gay. Raven had secretly been bisexual for years; the only guy she ever told was Stacey. After she told him he kept pressing her for a 3some. When Raven ran across Candice at her book club meeting with that flawless hourglass figure and chocolate skin she wanted to give it a try. After weeks of seducing Candice, she finally agreed to the 3some. However, the ladies were so into each other that they really didn't pay Stacey no mind. Subsequently Candice and Raven started messing around behind Stacey's back. Soon Stacey had become obsolete, and Raven left him behind. Candice was Raven coming out story.

"What do you want Raven?" Stacey asked immediately after picking up the phone. "Good Morning to you too Stacey." Raven said. "Are we all set for you to come get the kids this Thursday?" She asked. "Why should I give you a break to run off and fuck that so called manly ass bitch you have up in your house?" "I don't want to get into this with you Stacey!" Raven yelled in to the phone. "Raven I don't trust her, I hate the way she treats you, like you're an object or a possession." "Really so I guess the way you treated me was better?" she asked him. "Raven we were a family, I know I wasn't the best man, but you know I still love you!" "I love you too Stacey but not the way you want me to, and besides what's Ms. Monique gonna say about all this love you spreading around to me?" Stacey hated what had happened between them. He loved Raven so much that all the other women he dated afterwards failed in comparison. Monique was great in bed but wasn't someone he wanted a family with. Stacey wanted Raven back.

"I'll be there Thursday to pick them up after school, but when I get there can we talk," Stacey said sounding wounded as usual when he wanted to get his way with her. "Yes, we can talk briefly then. Stacey you're a good father why can't you just focus on that for now." Raven's statement drew silence from the other end of the phone. "Well I appreciate this a lot and I'll talk to you Thursday," she said into the phone. At first, she thought he wasn't gonna respond but he gave a dry "you're welcome" and hung up the phone.

Tonya's morning couldn't have been going any better. Her little rendezvous with the little lady this morning had her floating. She was in and out of the jail so fast she didn't remember interacting with the inmates at all. She was in her car getting ready to jump on I75 heading home when her phone rang. The name on the ID flashed Monique Campbell, what the hell did she want? Tonya and Monique had a few rumbles in the sheets before Tonya met Raven. Monique was the kind of person that had mastered the art of fucking. Whenever Tonya didn't have a main squeeze, Monique was always good for an excellent session. The thought of Tonya releasing in Monique's mouth moistened her boxers. She quickly dismissed the thought. Monique was now messing with Stacey Raven's ex. Tonya never told Raven that she knew Monique. She made Monique swear to keep her mouth quiet and in return she would do the same.

The fact that she was calling her now was puzzling.

"Yes Monique." Tonya said tryna sound as irritated as she could. "Damn that don't sound like you're happy to hear from me." Monique responded. "Well considering that you're fucking my girl's ex and now you're calling me, this would be a little hard to explain," Tonya nonchalantly replied. "I see your little wifey was calling my man this morning." "Well since they have kids together I would expect that from them," Tonya commented. "Well as you know I eavesdrop on most all his calls from the house." "Ok, can you get to the fucking point already!" Tonya barked. "Well they all on the phone saying I love you to each other and making plans to talk about them on Thursday when he come to get the kids." "He's getting the kids on Thursday? Why the day early?" Tonya asked. "Something about some plans she had." Monique returned. "You better not be bullshitting me Monique!" Tonya angrily screeched. "Would I ever lie to you sexy?" she asked. "Since our exes are tryna reconnect, then maybe you can come over and let me get reacquainted with your sexiness." Monique stated. Tonya wouldn't give her the satisfaction she knew Monique was only out for a payday. Without even giving a response she clicked the phone shut.

Monique couldn't get enough of Tonya, finding out that Stacey was Raven's ex couldn't have been better. She was gonna use every inch of her being to drive a wedge between them, so she could get back in Tonya's bed.

Tonya was pissed now, and she sped the whole way home. She couldn't even tell Raven why she had and attitude without giving away that she knew about her talking to Stacey. "Hey babe" Raven said as Tonya came in the door. "Dinner will be done in a minute, go jump in the shower and get relaxed. By the time you're done I should be finishing up." Tonya walked away but deep inside she wanted to confront Raven.

Tonya let the water run down her body, she didn't even know why she trusted what Monique had to say. Fuck it! She thought to herself. By the time she got out the shower she felt a little at ease. Raven had dinner on the table just like she promised. This is my family Tonya thought I will fight to keep it.

The rest of the week went by smoothly, Tonya had almost forgotten about what Monique had told her. That was until she came home and saw Stacey and Raven standing at the far end of the yard talking. Their body language telling her that they were in a heated discussion. They hadn't seemed to notice her. She pulled up slowly in front of the house, but she didn't get out right away.

"Raven you know we belong together. The kids deserve to have their mother and father raise them as a family." Stacey said grabbing hold to

Raven's arm. "We tried that Stacey and it didn't work out for us." Raven replied. "Please just give me another chance; I know I can make you happy." Stacey pleaded. "Stacey you can't make me happy! I'm gay!" Raven angrily shouted. Stacey pulled Raven toward him and hugged her tightly. "I love you and I won't give up on us." Raven let Stacey envelope her in his arms. She laid her head on his chest and she let the tears flow.

Tonya watched as Stacey and Raven embraced. The anger was so overwhelming that she could feel flames shooting from the top of her head. Raven really thought she was stupid. She wanted to kill them both, she couldn't breathe. She had to get her thoughts together or she was finna go to jail. She started her car and drove back up the street.

Hearing the tires screeching made Raven jump. She saw Tonya's car backing up and driving off. Oh no! She had seen them embracing and who knows what she could be thinking right now. Stacey had seen Tonya pull up and pulled Raven in his arms on cue. Raven looked up at Stacey, "you're a wonderful father but there can never be another us. I love you as my children's father but I'm in love with Tonya." "You're so in love with Tonya then why the hell is she talking to Monique on the phone!" The words slapped Raven across the face.

Stacey had found Tonya's picture and number in Monique's phone a while back and confronted her about it. Monique had told Stacey that she and Tonya had shared a one-night stand. She assured him it was nothing more than that and made Stacey promise not to say anything to Raven.

"What are you talking about?" Raven asked. "I checked Monique's phone the other day and saw where she had been talking to Tonya." "How do you know it was Tonya?" Raven asked puzzled. "You don't even know Tonya number." "Yeah, I don't but I know what she looks like and her picture was with the number," Stacey recanted. "I don't believe you" Raven screamed as she backed away from Stacey. "You don't believe me?" He asked. "Well believe what you read! Check the fucking phone records Raven! I'm not the one hiding shit!" Raven was confused, she didn't know what to say. "I'm sorry!" She turned and walked to the house. Moments later the kids came running from the house. "We're ready daddy!" Omari said. Stacey and the kids got in the car. He made sure they were buckled up and ready to go, but just as he was about to pull off… "Daddy can we wait a few seconds before we leave?" Kelly asked. "We didn't get a chance to say bye to Tonya." Stacey was so pissed by the statement that he reeved his engine and sped away.

Raven called Tonya's phone it went straight to voicemail. She dialed it again. Raven knew Tonya was on the phone, but she wasn't saying anything. "I know you're there Tonya! Where are you?" Raven asked. "Oh, now you're worried about me!" Tonya yelled. "When you were all hugged up with that nigga I wasn't on your mind!" "It wasn't like that Tonya! Can we please talk about it? Where are you? Come home please!" Raven shouted into the phone. The line went dead, moments later Tonya walked through the door. Raven ran to her and threw her arms around her. "Baby I love you! Stacey will never come between us! Never, I promise!" Tonya grabbed hold of Raven and kissed her like her life depended on it.

Even as she made up with Tonya, Stacey's words burned in her mind. Why would Tonya and Monique have the need to talk to one another? Raven knew she couldn't confront Tonya without proof, so she kept her cool about the situation. As Raven was mentally analyzing Tonya situation Tonya was doing the same. She just wasn't ready to let go of what she had saw. But until she had proof she would keep her cool about the situation.

Raven had decided that since they would be leaving the next morning that she would make this a simple night. She ordered Chinese and pulled up a movie on Netflix. After dinner they cuddled up on the sofa to watch The Time Traveler's Wife. Tonya had drifted off to sleep and before she knew it Raven was waking her up to breakfast. "Morning Sunshine!" Raven beamed as she placed the tray of food on top of Tonya's lap. "Are you ready for your surprise?" Raven asked. "Yes Ma'am!" Tonya smiled as Raven placed a piece of bacon in her mouth. After breakfast Raven escorted Tonya up to the shower. While Tonya showered Raven pulled their already packed luggage down stairs in the foyer to await the Limo. She cleaned up the kitchen and living area as she waited for Tonya to finish.

Tonya stepped out the shower and started to dry off. Just as she slipped her wife beater over her head she heard her phone ringing. When she heard the ringtone, her breath caught in her chest. She raced in the room to grab the phone. Monique's picture was flashing across her phone. This bitch has lost her fucking mind. "You better have a good reason to be calling me Monique when you know I'm at home!" Tonya spoke trying to keep her voice low as so not to be heard by Raven. "Why would she have reason to call you anyway?" The voice caught her off guard. "I guess you want to monopolize all the women in my life, huh Tonya. Or better yet you just wanna be me." "What the fuck! Why the fuck are you calling me Stacey?"

Tonya yelled into the phone forgetting about her voice level. "Are you fucking Monique too?" he asked. "Why don't you ask Monique? Better yet whisper my name in her ear and watch her pussy cream. Don't fucking cross me Stacey! Don't take these breasts as a weakness!" Tonya said sarcastically. "Don't call my phone anymore! You or your ratchet ass whore!" Tonya clicked her phone off without waiting for a response. She finished getting dressed and went down stairs to look for the love of her life.

Stacey shut the phone and smiled, Tonya played right into his hands. All he could hope is that Raven checked the phone records. He put Monique's phone back on the stand and joined her in the shower. He aligned his body right behind her. Stacey leaned in, so his mouth was right by Monique's ear. "Is Tonya a better fuck then me?" He asked her. "What?" Monique turned around to face him. "What made you ask me that?" "I'm curious that's all." "Awww handsome, you have nothing to worry about." Monique dropped to her knees and slid Stacey into her mouth. Her tongue caressed every inch of his penis. She knew exactly how to take his mind off what he was thinking. Stacey watched as Monique did her thing, but this isn't how he wanted her. He pulled Monique up, kissed her lips to thank her for a job well done. Stacey turned Monique around and bent her over. He slid his rock-hard manhood into her soft wet center. She let out a gasp as he pierced her core. Stacey pumped all of his rage into Monique. He wanted to erase any thought of Tonya from her mind. Monique accepted every inch Stacey offered, she grinded her hips to match him stroke for stroke. She felt him speed up and she knew he neared eruption. Just as Monique felt the tip of Stacey's penis begin to contract, she pushed him out of her and shoved him down her throat. Stacey couldn't hold back, Monique literally sucked the cum out of him. Without even missing a stroke as Stacey released she swallowed until it was nothing left. Monique stood back up and continued showering as if nothing had happened.

Stacey stood there looking at her astonished by what she had just done. He finished showering, dressed and went to check on the kids. Monique I'm fixing some snacks for the two of them, would you like anything. Stacey called up the stairs. "Yeah sure!" came the response. Monique took the opportunity to finish the job Stacey couldn't. She never had an orgasm with a man and Stacey wasn't an exception. She locked the bathroom door, pulled out her hidden toy, and finished herself while picturing Tonya's hands on her. After she got the release she wanted she put everything back, cleaned herself back up, and jumped in bed to wait on Stacey's return.

Just as Monique was whispering Tonya's name alone in her bathroom, Raven was screaming it in the back of a Limo with Tonya's face buried deep between her thighs. They managed to get themselves back together just as the chauffer pulled the door open at the resort. They stepped out and thanked him for everything, grabbed their luggage and entered the hotel. Once inside the room their mouths dropped, there was no way Raven could have imagined the pure beauty of the suite they would occupy for the weekend.

9

Shattered Glass

Mercedes

Days went by and nothing from Hakeem, Mercedes had wondered if he had finally giving up. Despite the fact that she was relieved that the calls had stopped, she still hasn't found the courage to call Monea. She deliberately made herself busy at the end of the work day, so she couldn't take the deposit to the office. She didn't know what she was holding back for, she really liked Monea. She laid back on the bed and closed her eyes.

As soon as she started dreaming she could hear Hakeem's voice in her ear. "You know I love you right?" she could feel the weight of him on her torso. She could smell the alcohol on his breath. His hands grew tighter around her neck as he turned her head, to expose her ear to his words. Mercedes could barely pass air through her windpipe but to fight him would be cause for worse to happen. With his free hand, he wrapped her leg with his arm and with one gigantic swoop he was inside her. The tightness against her throat, the pressure of Hakeem pressing down on her midsection, was nothing compared to the savageness of what was happening between her legs. As he grew closer to his climax the tighter Hakeem's hands compressed around Mercedes's neck. The sound of the alarm clock brought her back to reality and she jumped up grabbing her throat, coughing and gaging trying to catch her breath.

The day went by fast, which she didn't mind because suffering from lack of sleep she was tired and kind of moody, she didn't want to snap on some unsuspecting individual. Mercedes gathered her things, said goodbye, and left the building. As soon as she walked out the door Mercedes ran right into Monea. Mercedes had a feeling she was waiting there in hopes to run into her, because she'd never seen her come that way before. Mercedes really wasn't in the mood for her right now, her feet and back hurt, she was tired, and hungry as hell. Mercedes tried to get by with just keeping her head down and throwing up her hand in a hello jester. Monea wasn't having it and broke out into a full conversation.

"So, you were just gonna walk by me and not speak?" she asked blocking her path. "I'm not feeling real well Mercedes said trying to go around her." Monea grabbed Mercedes by the arm. "What did I do to you? You act like you can just fuck me and then just turn it off like a switch." She stood there with Mercedes' arm in a vice grip waiting for her answers. "Look I'm going thru something Monea, it has nothing to do with you ok!" Mercedes pulled her arm from Monea, but she side stepped Mercedes and blocked her way again. Just then a couple of the girls from the kitchen came out the door, Monea put a fake smile on her face until they passed and were out of sight. Mercedes could have taken that opportunity to leave but she still wanted Monea and she deserved better. "What the hell Mercedes, what the fuck is going on?" "I'm trying to figure out what the fuck I'm doing right now, it has nothing to do with you!" The words hit Monea in the face like a slap. She dropped Mercedes' arm and stood back looking at her like Mercedes had just spit fire from her mouth. "What the fuck Mercedes!" Monea just kept yelling at Mercedes. "Monea! Please hear me out! Let me speak!" this time Mercedes was blocking Monea's path. "What Mercedes? What can you possible say to me at the moment that could help the situation?" "I'm sorry Monea! I really care about you, but I really have to figure things out," she pleaded. Mercedes check her phone it was almost time for the bell to ring and they were outside of the school making a scene. Monea turned to walk away; Mercedes grabbed Monea's hand and turned her around to face her. Mercedes saw the tears running down her face and her heart sank. Mercedes pulled Monea over and kissed her plush soft lips and told her she was sorry for ever hurting her. Mercedes agreed to meet with her soon to sit down and talk. She kissed her lips again but this time the bell rang, and they pushed apart and went their separate ways.

As soon as Mercedes got in the car the tears started falling, like the sky opened the flood gates. She let them fall, letting the tears burn her eyes. By the time she got home she was overwhelmed and exhausted. The moment

Mercedes heard the door shut behind her, she let the breath out she had been holding in. She went about her normal afternoon duties, but the sadness took over. Mercedes really didn't want to be around the house alone, so she texted Evon's phone and told her to rally the troops. "What's up mom?" Evon and Desmond said as they walked in the door followed by Marie. "Get y'all stuff we're going to Auntie Dee Dee's house." They burst from the kitchen and was back in a flash with bags of things they wanted to share with their cousins. Mercedes opted to leave through the front door, since the calls from Hakeem started again she would change up her routine a few times a week.

Mercedes pulled up in front of Dee Dee's house and before she could get out the car good Hakeem had started blowing up the phone. She didn't bother to answer; she just put the phone on silent and headed for her sister's house. "Hey sistea girl," Mercedes said giving Dee Dee the biggest hug she could muster without bursting into tears. "What's up sistea girl" Dee Dee said hugging her back. The look on Mercedes' face gave her away because as soon as the kids were out of ear range Dee Dee hit her with the question. "So little sis, what's wrong?" "Nothing why you ask me that?" Mercedes asked. "You're my kid sister, you don't think I know when something's wrong with you?" Dee Dee replied. Mercedes put her head down but didn't let her sister break her just yet. "There's nothing wrong, I just wanted to see you." Mercedes uttered. "Well ok, if you say so. Let's go sit outside, I need to smoke these damn kids are working it for me." Dee Dee said getting up and heading to the side door.

They sat outside Dee Dee smoked and Mercedes listened. For well over thirty minutes Mercedes listened to her sister talk about her and her hubby's problems. In Mercedes' eyes she didn't really feel like they had any problems, but she was on the outside looking in. Just like for the people who didn't see what she was really going through. It looked to the outside world like she had the perfect life, but in reality, she was constantly drunk, and she was afraid to go to sleep. Mercedes didn't mind listening to her sister, because this was the only escape she had to regain her sanity.

They tried lightening the mood a little by talking about all the good times they had growing up. Dee Dee talked about all the trouble they used to get into, before Mercedes knew it was well past eleven o'clock. "I didn't know it had gotten so late" Mercedes said. So, she rounded up the kids, thanked her sister for a wonderful evening, and headed home. Mercedes dreaded going home but she sucked it up and drove slowly to the house.

When she got home it was eerily dark in the house. Mercedes was almost contemplating going back to Dee Dee's house. She slowly walked thru the house. She went room to room opening up the doors slowly, the tension in the air was heavy. Nothing, but the uneasy feeling wouldn't leave her.

Mercedes was so frightened that she went in the room with the kids and locked the door. She couldn't sleep so she stayed awake the whole night. Mercedes didn't know what time but between 3 or 4 am her body gave in to the tiredness and she dozed off. The sound of the phones alarm startled her making her jump up. Mercedes' entire body was stiff and exhausted she had slept sitting in the corner with her back against the wall. Mercedes woke the kids up and went and lay across the sofa.

When the alarm went off for the second time she got up and dragged her sack of bones to the bathroom to get dressed for work. Mercedes came out the bathroom grabbed her stuff went out the back door and jumped in the car. Mercedes made it about 3 blocks before she pulled the car over and broke down. Mercedes was a nervous wreck, she was so stressed out, she lit a cigarette and headed to work.

The next couple of weeks were rough for Mercedes; she was having pains all over her body and couldn't really function at work. Being at home wasn't any better. Hakeem was back to his old tricks again. The stress was becoming overwhelming, Mercedes felt like she was losing her mind. Mercedes did what she always did to help her ease her mind, she popped an 800 ibuprofen, then she down two large shot of vodka. She then laid across the sofa and let sleep take over.

The sound of the TV woke Mercedes up from her slumber. She thought she was awake, but in reality, she still lay sleep on the sofa. Upon focusing her eyes Mercedes saw Hakeem staring out the window. Without saying good morning, he spoke with demands. "You need to get up and get dressed. John and his brothers are on the way here," Hakeem's eyes never left the window. "I'm tired" Mercedes responded weakly. "I think I'll just lay in the room today." "I guess you're in one of your stuck-up moods today" he said sarcastically. Mercedes looked briefly at Hakeem before she turned and walked away. Mercedes knew that his little crew would be over to start their drunken escapade for the weekend. Despite her feelings Mercedes gathered her things and jumped in the shower.

The knock on the door singled it was show time. Mercedes finished her hair and went to greet her awaiting guests. 11 o'clock in the morning and the house was filled with blaring music, Newport smoke, and loud conversation. Mercedes played her role as a good hostess bringing drinks and cleaning up behind grown ass men. By the time the kids came in for lunch, the crew had finished off their first case of beer and were in the process of making a beer run. "Hey Uncle John," Evon, Desmond, and Marie shouted as they burst thru the door. John dispensed his customary five dollars to each child and they happily ran off to get ready for lunch. The guys left to go scavenging for beer while Mercedes feed the kids and taxied them to the weekend destinations.

Mercedes returned home carrying two boxes of Church's chicken. As she walked to the kitchen she overheard the guys making plans to go to the new pool hall down the street. Mercedes felt exhausted and didn't want to go. However, she knew that if she didn't there would be problems later on with Hakeem. Mercedes put the food down on the stove and fixed herself a plate. "What's up Big Balla?" John said coming up to Mercedes at the table. "Hey John," Mercedes replied. "Do you mind if I help myself to some food?" John asked. "That's why it's here," Mercedes retorted trying not to sound agitated. "You hanging with us tonight Big Balla?" John asked as he pulled a chair up to the table. Mercedes mind was thinking like I have a choice, but her lips said "Of course. Who's all going?" She asked thru a mouth full of chicken. "The guys, but Sara said she would fall thru," John said as he devoured his food. Sara was John's leading lady of the moment. Sara was one of those white chicks that try to act black. Not the kind you knew had to have grown up in the hood but the kind that tried way too hard to fit in. Mercedes had to admit she was cool people, but she really had to laugh at her sometimes. Sara coming was a relief to Mercedes, she was glad she wasn't gonna be the only female with the guys all night.

Mercedes finished her food got up and threw her trash away. "I think I'll go rest for a min," Mercedes excused herself. She retreated to the confines of the room for some peace and quiet before she had to get ready. About a half hour later Hakeem peeked his head into the door apparently trying to keep tabs on her whereabouts. Mercedes knew he was there, but she didn't move. Guess he'd gotten the satisfaction he was anticipating because without a sound he shut the door and left.

Three hours later Mercedes emerged from her room a portrait of beauty. She was wearing black stretch pants, an off the shoulder white shirt with black and gold designs on the front, and her favorite black and gold platform heels. To set her outfit off Mercedes adorned her 23in ponytail and extra-large hoop earrings. Hakeem walked up to his woman and looked her over. He gave Mercedes a kiss of approval on the forehead. Everyone gathered into the two awaiting cars and left for the pool hall.

They arrived at the pool hall where Sara was already waiting. "Hey girl"! Sara said putting her arms around Mercedes. Mercedes smiled and returned the show of affection. The ladies found a table and the guys quickly surrounded a pool table in the corner. "So, tell me girl, what you been up to?" Sara asked trying to start up small talk. "Nothing much," Mercedes stated. The conversation with Sara always ended the same. Sara didn't like Hakeem and she wanted Mercedes away from him. Mercedes and Sara talked until the guys came over with wings and two pitchers of beer. Sara gave Mercedes a child please look then she turned her attention to her man. "I bought wings baby," Hakeem said to Mercedes. "No thanks babe, not really hungry," Mercedes replied to her mate. Mercedes was starving but the fact that everyone was putting their hands in the food made her stomach turn. If she would have told Hakeem that, he would've said she was being stuck up again or worst. The drunker he was the worst the outcome would have been.

Everybody was enjoying themselves and about 3am they prepared to call it a night. John's brothers piled into one car, leaving Mercedes, Hakeem, John, and Sara who had gotten dropped off in the other car. Everybody said goodbye and Mercedes drove home. As Mercedes pulled up she told Hakeem she was hungry and that she had wanted to go to the Waffle House. "I bought food for you, you should have eaten that." he yelled. Mercedes parked the car but didn't get out. Hakeem gets out the car and walked around to the driver's side of the car. Before anyone knew what was happening he snatched the keys out of the ignition and tossed them across the street. John and Sara just stood there staring in disbelief. "Come on Hakeem man let's not start this tonight," John said grabbing Hakeem and leading him toward the house. Mercedes and Sara got out and went to search for the keys. "Mercedes, I think we should stay out here until he cools down and goes to sleep," Sara grimly spoke. "He's not gonna go to sleep as long as I'm out here," Mercedes responded.

They found the keys and headed up the stairs toward the house. As soon as Sara and Mercedes reached the top of the landing John and Hakeem were coming out of the house. John was trying to subdue Hakeem, but Mercedes didn't have time to react, she didn't even see it coming. Whack! he smacked her right across the face. The sheer force of the impact knocked her out of her shoes and across the patio. Mercedes landed hard on the concrete and her phone landed down the steps. A few feet to the right and she would have landed down there with it. John grabbed Hakeem and Sara rushed to Mercedes in an effort to help her up, "Are you ok?" She asked. "Come on man! That shit not called for!" John yelled at Hakeem. "Mercedes, you need to leave his ass!" Sara screamed. "Shut the fuck up bitch!" Hakeem screamed at Sara. "Oh yeah! You some kind of man you know! Putting your hands on a female!" Sara responded. "Bitch I'll put my hands on your ass if you keep talking." Hakeem continued to yell. "Fuck you Hakeem!" Sara turns to usher Mercedes into the house. Hakeem shoved John and began attacking Sara. Sara was fighting back but she was no match for Hakeem's massive punches. John steps in between Sara and Hakeem. "What the fuck is wrong with you!" John yelled at Hakeem. "Stay out of this John," Hakeem stared as if he would kill him. "Stop it! Stop!" Mercedes screamed. It had only been moments, but her side and leg had become painfully stiff. "John can you grab my phone please," Mercedes said grabbing Hakeem and lead him into the house.

Mercedes silently removed her clothes and got into bed. Hakeem was lying on top of the covers still fully dressed. Despite having on sunglasses Mercedes knew he was asleep because he was snoring. There in the blackness of her shame Mercedes wept. The tears that fell down her cheeks awaken her, and she opened her eyes. Mercedes didn't know if this was dream or reality. Mercedes gathered herself to head to her bed. As she lay back in bed she took several deep breaths to help clear her mind. She closed her eyes and this time she really did sleep, sleep which was filled with nightmares. Nightmares that seems to carry on in real life. Even as she slept the tears continue to fall down her face.

10

Love is Not Always Enough

Nashunta

athan took Nashunta back to his mother's house where he helped her get cleaned up. "Who did this to you?" Nathan asked angrily. "Lameka," Nashunta confessed. "You're supposed to be girlfriend?" Nathan asked. "Why the hell would she do something like this to you? Nashunta you have got to leave this girl alone." Nathan said as he got up off the sofa. "Girl, how about I fix us both a drink?" Nathan went over to his mother's china cabinet, reaching around the back he pulled out a bottle of Grey Goose. He went to the kitchen and within seconds they were drinking Vodka and pineapple juice.

Nashunta took several quick sips to calm her nerves, and then she proceeded to tell Nathan about her relationship with Lameka. Nathan was outraged he couldn't believe how she had let this person use, abuse, and manipulate her. Nashunta continued her confession, she felt especially stupid when she told him about Montana and the plethora of other females she tolerated along the journey with Lameka. "You need to be careful with that girl Miss Thang," Nathan said. "People like that always tend to have a dark side." "Nathan you have to promise me you won't tell anybody this stuff. I've never shared these things with anybody," Nashunta timidly spoke. "I'm not afraid of Lameka, yes, she gets mad, but she would never lose it with me." Nathan looked at his friend, even though he didn't want to he agreed. "Well I still say be careful, she looks unpredictable." he said to Nashunta.

Nathan and Nashunta talked for hours, Nashunta felt so relieved to have someone to confide in. Nathan made them dinner and they watched movies until they fell asleep on the couch. "Oh my! Now isn't that just adorable!" the sound of Nathan mother startled them both awake. Nashunta had fallen asleep lying on Nathan's chest and they looked like an adorable little coupled all nestled there on the couch. Before they had a chance to say anything Yolanda was on the phone with Mrs. Jones proclaiming victory.

They agreed to let their moms have that little piece of joy. Nashunta excused herself and went inside the bathroom. She sat on the toilet put her head in her hands and wept. The vibration in her pants made her jump, having forgotten that she had put her phone on silent. Checking her phone Nashunta saw she had over thirty missed calls and texts. Majority of them was from Lameka but there was one from her mom and another from Montana. Nashunta knew her mom more than likely wanted to confirm what Yolanda had told her about her and Nathan. Nashunta made a mental note to check her voicemail later and deleted her call log and all texts from Lameka.

"Everything ok?" Nathan asked Nashunta as she can back into the living room. "Yeah sure," replied Nashunta. "I really need to talk to her and officially break things off, but I don't want to see her right now. Lameka has this way of manipulating my emotions. If I go to her now within seconds she'll have me out my clothes and would have snaked her way back into my heart." "Promise me you'll break it off for good. Nathan stated getting up and walking over to Nashunta. "I promise," Nashunta replied, "I'm gonna give her a couple of days to cool off, and then we'll talk." "Well I'm going back to school next week, but I'll still be only a phone call away." Nathan and Nashunta embraced each other. "I think I should be getting home now before it gets too late" Nashunta said. Nathan helped Nashunta cover up her face with makeup and then he drove her home.

Lameka paced from her room to the kitchen and back. She had tried several unsuccessful times to contact Nashunta. She had left countless voicemails to no avail. All she could hear in her mind was Nashunta saying if she hit her again it was over. The more times she dialed her lover's number the more the rage in her grew. What you think your just gonna walk away from me? You think it's that easy to walk away? Lameka threw questions in the air. I can't see you with no one else! Lameka said as the tears started cascading down her face. If there can't be an us then there won't be a you, believe that. Lameka grabbed her keys, jumped into her car, and sped off.

Lameka pulled up in front of Montana's house ready to make good on the statement she had previously made. Unaware that Montana's car was not there Lameka walks up to the door and begins to knock. After waiting several moments, she pulls out her phone and dials her number. Instead of the customary ring she hears the operator. The number that you've called has been temporarily disconnected. What the fuck! Lameka yelled. She ran to the back of Montana's house and kicked her door in. Once in the house she quickly notices that the house looked the same way it did they last time she was there. Montana hadn't been home since that day. Coming to her senses, Lameka remembered the alarm system. Leaving out the way she had entered Lameka bounced before the police showed up.

Now Lameka was really angry. Nashunta was ignoring her and Montana had disappeared from the face of the earth. Lameka stopped her car a few houses up from Nashunta's house. Lameka spotted Nathan's car, everything in her wanted to get out and smash his window's out. She rolled her a blunt and smoked to calm her a little. Just as she finished Nathan and Nashunta walked out her door and stood on the porch. She was too far away to hear what they were saying but their body language said it all. Nathan wrapped his arms around Nashunta's waist and she wrapped her arms around his neck. The embraced had Lameka's blood boiling. "Take care of yourself baby girl," Nathan whispered to Nashunta. "Sure, thing" she answered back. They made promises to call each other every chance they got. Nathan turned and walked to his car, got in and drove off. Lameka ducked down in the seat as so not to be seen by Nathan. A million things were running thru Lameka's head. She tried a few more times to reach Nashunta but still no answer. She savagely hit her steering wheel until her hands hurt. Lameka didn't know what else to do. She started her car and went home.

Nashunta avoided her mom as much as she could. She didn't want her to see her swollen face. Despite her effort Mrs. Jones wanted to get the details of her day with Nathan. Knock knock! "Honey do you mind if I come in?" Mrs. Jones asked as she knocked softly at her daughter's door. "Mom I really don't feel like talking right now." Nashunta said from the safety of her room. "I promise I'll tell you everything another time. Ok sweetie!" Nashunta could hear the disappointment in her mother's voice. "Are you ok?" Mrs. Jones asked. "Yes Mom, A little sad that Nathan is leaving," Nashunta lied. "Oh, is that all!" Mrs. Jones spoke. "I'm pretty sure he'll be back here before you know it. Do you want me to make you some tea?" Mrs. Jones asked trying once more for the opportunity to have girl talk with her child. "No thanks mom, I'm just gonna crash." Nashunta said. "Mom," Nashunta started to tell her mom everything but thinking back to her dinner she decided against it. "Yes honey," Mrs. Jones answered. "I love you," Nashunta said. "I love you too baby girl," her mom said before she turned and walked back down the stairs. Nashunta made sure her window was locked and her curtains were closed, remembering Lameka sneaking in her window. Nashunta down a Motrin 800 with a little bottle of vodka from her stash, turned on her mp3, put her earphones in, and waited for sleep to take her.

A couple of days later Nathan was all packed and ready for his drive back to the safety of his college apartment. Nashunta had come over the day before to say her goodbyes and help him pack. He was glad he had met her, having an ally at home would defiantly come in handy. Nathan brought all his stuff to the front door to start packing up the car. Yolanda walks over to her son and grabs some bags. "Nathan I'm so proud of you," Yolanda said. "You do know that don't you baby?" "Yes mom," Nathan replied. "I know it's lonely around here without me." Nathan said walking over to his mom and giving her a hug. They walked outside still semi embracing one another. Nathan walks over to unlock his door and stopped dead in his tracks. The look on his face made Yolanda drop the bags and run over to her son. "What in the world!" Yolanda screams. Looking at Nathans's car the tires on the driver's side had been cut to shreds. "Who would do this?" Yolanda asked looking from Nathan to the car. "I think I know exactly who did this." Nathan said grabbing his phone he calls the police. Several hours later after the police left and the tires repaired Nathan said his goodbyes to his mom and drove off. Instead of jumping on the highway he decided to go drop by Nashunta's house.

Opening the door Kimmie was shocked to see Nathan standing there. "I thought you were supposed to leave today," Kimmie says as she steps aside to let him in. "My sister's in her room she never leaves it now a days. You can have a seat and I'll go get her." Before Kimmie turned to leave Mr. Jones entered the living room. "I thought I heard a young man's voice in my home." Nathan stood and introduced himself to Mr. Jones. Kimmie took the opportunity to run get her sister. Nashunta sat staring out the window when Kimmie knocked on the door. "Yes!" Nashunta called out. "Nathan's downstairs and I think you better come quick because daddy's down there interrogating him." Kimmie said to her sister's door. At the mention of

Nathan and her father together Nashunta was down the steps in a flash with Kimmie on her tail. Much to her surprise Nathan was handling his own with her father. Mr. Jones came over and hugged Nashunta, "I like this one," he said. "Come Kimmie let's give them some time to talk." Kimmie looked disappointed at the thought that she couldn't be nosey. Mr. Jones sensing her reluctance he put his arm around her and led her away back through the kitchen. He had the biggest smile Nashunta had seen from him in a while.

Nathan told Nashunta about his car and the thought he had about who was behind it. Nashunta was embarrassed and apologized repeatedly to Nathan. "It's not your fault," Nathan said. "I'm really afraid for you because this shows she has violent tendencies. My tires were shredded; the policeman said they were stabbed multiple times with some kind of large knife. What scares me even more is the fact that she knew where I lived," Nathan continued. "That means she had to have been following us," Nashunta said. The thought of Lameka following her around sent shivers down Nashunta's spine. Nathan and Nashunta finished their conversation, until Nathan decided he better get going before it got too late.

Lameka sat in her car watching as Nathan exited his car and walk toward her girl's house. This fool thinks he can mess with my girl, he has another thing coming, Lameka thought as she popped the cap off a double deuce of Icehouse and guzzled it down. I guess he didn't get the message this morning, she thought as she savored the beer coolness going down. After a few more guzzles she had finished it off and was in the process of popping another when she saw Nathan and Nashunta come from the house. The rage grew inside Lameka at an alarming rate. She couldn't think, she couldn't breathe, what the hell was happening to her. Lameka felt like her brain was melting.

Nashunta walked Nathan outside to his car oblivious to the fact that they were being watched. Nathan put his arms around Nashunta and squeezed her tight. Before Nathan had a chance to get inside his car they heard tires screeching. "Watch out!" Nathan yelled as he knocked Nashunta out the way. A bottle shattered on the ground in front of them. The car sped off down the street and out of sight. "Are you ok?" he asked as he brushed off the bottom of his pants. Nashunta nodded her head but her mouth was wide open in shock. "Was that her?" Nathan asked. "Yes!" Nashunta said. This time letting the words escape her lips. Nashunta assured Nathan that she would be fine. Against his better judgment Nathan got in his car. "Be careful ok?" He said as he started his car. "I will" Nashunta shot over her shoulder as she run back up to the house. She waved bye as Nathan drove off.

Weeks went by and Nashunta felt like she was at her wits end. Everywhere she turned Lameka was there staring at her. It would have been different if she would have at least tried to talk but she just stared. Lameka would call her phone at all times of the night and hang up without a word. She sent text messages that were blank. Even though Nashunta never spotted her she knew Lameka watched her as she walked to and from the house every day. Nashunta didn't know what to do, she felt stranded on a deserted island. Nathan hadn't called in weeks, and she had no one else she could talk to. Nashunta became depressed locking herself in her room. She rarely ate or even talked to her family.

Mrs. Jones grew concerned about Nashunta and tried to reach out to her. As Nashunta came home Mrs. Jones was waiting by the door for her to come in. "Hey Honey!" Mrs. Jones spoke as Nashunta shut the front door. "Hey Mom," Nashunta replied. Nashunta wasn't in the mood to deal with her mom. All she wanted was to get behind the safety of her room door. Mrs. Jones stood and blocked Nashunta's path to the stairs. Looking at her child Mrs. Jones couldn't believe what she saw. Nashunta looked as though she had lost weight. Her hair pulled up into a ponytail looked dull as if she hadn't washed it. She looked tired; her eyes were swollen with bags underneath. Mrs. Jones reached for Nashunta's hand, but she pulled away. "I thought we could go have dinner together," Mrs. Jones stated. "Your father and Kimmie had plans and it's just us tonight." "I really don't feel like it mom," responded Nashunta. It wasn't a cordial invitation, Mrs. Jones stood there with her hands on her hips. "I think it's time we had a talk." Nashunta gave up without a fight and they left the house.

They ended up at Chill's in a secluded booth in the back. They took a few moments to look over the menu. Nashunta told her mom to order whatever; she didn't care what she ate. Mrs. Jones ordered their food and Nashunta excused herself to the bathroom. As soon as the bathroom door closed Nashunta pulled a mini vodka out of her bag and swallowed it down. She made a mental note to go refill her stash. The guy at the corner package store liked her and would let her and Lameka buy without carding them. The thought of Lameka made tears burn her eyes. Nashunta washed her face and quickly hurried back to the table before her mom came looking for her.

"Baby, I notice something is going on with you," Mrs. Jones took the spotlight of the conversation. She wasted no time getting to the real purpose of the dinner. Mrs. Jones gave Nashunta a pep talk, trying to open her up as so she would talk to her. She talked until the food came. Nashunta was ready to confide in her mom. She was tired of carrying her burden alone. She wanted so much to release all that she had bottled up inside. "Mom!" Nashunta started but before she could finish Mrs. Jones cut her off. "Let me just say how proud I was of you for stopping all that gay nonsense and giving Nathan a try. I know you're sad because you haven't spoken to him and Yolanda assured me that Nathan was busy with finals and nothing else. Yolanda said she had talked to him and he promised as soon as he had completed his last final he would call you. See honey! Doesn't that cheer you up a little?" Nashunta sat shocked in her seat. She couldn't believe how self-centered her mother sounded right now. She didn't want to get into it with her mom in public, so she just went along with it. Mrs. Jones talked the duration of the meal Nashunta put on a brave face. She faked smiled, nodded and pretended to engage in the conversation. "I'm glad we had this moment to ourselves" Mrs. Jones said as she drove home. Nashunta thanked her mom for dinner. She lingered around in the living room momentarily, so her mom could feel she accomplished something with her. "I'm tired mom, Nashunta commented I think I'll go jump in the shower and head to bed." "Ok sweetheart!" Mrs. Jones said as she picked up the phone. She walked over and kissed her mother goodnight.

Even though her mind was a jumble of confusion Nashunta actually felt a little better. Having dinner with her mom got her mind off Lameka for a while. As she got to the top of the steps something didn't feel right and Nashunta stopped. Nashunta didn't remember coming up stairs when she came home but her light in her room was on. Get a hold of yourself Nashunta, she said under her breath. Just as she was about to turn the doorknob she thought she saw a shadow moved across the room from the bottom of the door. Did I lock the window? Nashunta's heart was beating so loudly in her ear that she didn't hear her mom come up behind her. "What's wrong honey?" Mrs. Jones asked. At the sound of her mother's words Nashunta jumped out of her skin. "I sorry, I went in your room and opened the window," Mrs. Jones said. "It was stuffy in there, so I wanted to let a little air in. I know you say we invade your privacy. I meant to close it back before we left for dinner." "That's ok mom," Nashunta said breathing a sigh of relief. Mrs. Jones kissed her child again and was back on the phone gossiping as she walked to her room.

Nashunta opened the door to her room. She had to cover her mouth from the scream she wanted to let out. First, she made sure no one was in the room, checking under the bed and in her closet. Then she shut her door and closed her window and made sure it was locked. Looking around the room Nashunta surveyed the damage. There were piles of cut up pictures scattered on the bed. Beheaded stuffed animals lay strewed all over the floor with their stuffing hanging out like disemboweled organs. On top of the bed was a letter she had written Lameka. She picked it up and on the reverse side in large letters it said It Isn't Over Until I Say! Nashunta sank to her knees and silently sobbed.

Nashunta cleaned up her room making sure to tuck the trash bag in the back of her closet. She would take it out the morning of trash day. In her mind she was ready to end this. She picked up the phone and texted Lameka's phone. We need to talk, is all it said. Within minutes a message came back. I'll pick you up in the morning before school. Nashunta agreed to meet with Lameka. Feeling a little relieved she decided to jump in the shower. As she came back to her room she heard her phone ringing. Hello, Nashunta said as she combed through her hair. "Hey stranger!" Nathan yelled into the phone. "Hey stranger yourself!" Nashunta answered. "Sorry it's been crazy around here," Nathan said apologizing for not being able to call her. "How is that situation coming along?" Nathan asked. Nashunta lied believing that she was gonna rectify everything tomorrow. "Oh, it's cool, Lameka just needed sometime to cool off is all." "You haven't been sneaking off with her, have you? Because that girl scares me," Nathan said. "No!" Nashunta responded. Nashunta hated lying to people but she had the situation under control.

They talked for several hours about what was going on in each other's life. Nathan promised to drive down in a few weeks to visit. He had found out about this new spot and since Nashunta's 18th birthday was rapidly approaching he wanted to take her. "I miss you being here with me," Nashunta said to Nathan. "I feel so isolated here without you." "I know," Nathan replied. "Only a short time left and you'll be on your own little journey." They said their goodbyes and Nashunta climbed into bed.

The alarm sounded waking Nashunta up from the worst dream she had ever had. She dreamed Lameka was standing over her choking her and she couldn't breathe. The dream felt so real she was gasping for air and choking as she jumped up in the bed. Hitting the dismiss button for the alarm Nashunta noticed that she had a text message. Nashunta opened the message and it read. We can meet at the usual spot, I'll be waiting. She didn't even bother to reply. Nashunta dragged herself out of bed and proceeded to get ready for school. Feeling much better today she decided to pin her hair up and wear some makeup. By the time she was finished Nashunta looked like her old self again. Nashunta leaned forward and kissed the mirror leaving a lipstick image of her lips behind. She grabbed her bag and headed down the stairs.

"Good Morning Sweetheart!" Mrs. Jones says as her daughter bounces into the kitchen. "Aren't we looking nice this morning." "Thanks Mom!" Nashunta replied. Nashunta grabbed a glass and poured OJ from the fridge. After she drank it down she goes over kisses her dad goodbye and hits Kimmie on the head. "Oww you spaz!" Kimmie says as she turns to hit her sister back. Nashunta sidesteps the attempt. She hugs her mother and turns to say she loves them before she leaves to start her day.

Nashunta walks up the street and around the corner. As she turned the corner she spotted Lameka's car. Spotting her Lameka started the car and pulled up to Nashunta. "Get in" Lameka said as she let the window down, so she could be heard. "Where are we going?" Nashunta nervously asked. "Nowhere special" Lameka replied. "Get in Nashunta," Lameka said again. Everything in her body was telling Nashunta not to get in the car. "I don't wanna go anywhere" Nashunta said through the partially let down window. "Nashunta you want to talk or not? I don't have all day," Lameka stated more calmly than Nashunta had seen her in a while. Going against what she felt inside she opened the door and got in. Nashunta shut the door and Lameka put the car in gear and drove away.

11

She Loves Me Not

Raven

Tonya thanked Raven over and over again for her surprise. They never left the room once the entire weekend. Raven had never felt as loved as she did when she was in Tonya's arms. Before they knew it, it was time to get back to reality. Raven packed their things back up and prepared for the arrival of the limo to take them home. Not wanting to ruin the weekend but Stacey's words wouldn't get out of her head. Raven decided she would put a little bait out there and see if Tonya would take it. "Hey babe!" Raven called to Tonya over her shoulder. "If you knew someone even if it was in another lifetime would you tell me?" Raven asked coyly. "Sure babe!" Tonya quickly responded. "Why do you ask?" "Nothing really," Raven replied. Tonya's mind quickly went to Monique.

Tonya knew she should tell Raven about her but what would she say. Tonya walked over to her lover standing behind her she wrapped her arms around her. Raven's scent teased Tonya and the arousal inside her began to wake up. Tonya began to kiss Raven's neck, and her hands went from her waist up to her breast. Raven turned around and let her lips collide with Tonya's. "I Love you so much," Raven said as she unzipped Tonya's pants. Before she could reply with a I love you too Raven's fingers were massaging her clit and the only thing that escaped her lips were moans of pleasure. Raven vigorously rubbed Tonya until she was dripping wet. Without a word Raven slipped two fingers inside Tonya wet cave. Tonya's pussy was so tight, the feel of it squeezing Raven's fingers made Raven nut on herself. As Raven fucked Tonya she leaned down so her words went directly into Tonya's ear. "Whose pussy is this?" Raven asked. The fact that Raven had taken control was driving Tonya insane. "It's yours!" Tonya moaned. Raven lifted Tonya's right leg and pushed deeper inside her lover wetness. "If I ever find out that you're lying or cheating there's gonna be hell to pay you understand," Raven said in her lover's ear. "Yes!" Tonya breathlessly replied. Raven felt the bulge growing inside Tonya's center and really gave it to her. "O baby! Oh! Oh! Yes baby!" Tonya screamed. Tonya's juices squirted out in a spontaneous burst of nectar.

The knock on the door was barely audible over Tonya's screams of pleasure. The doorman hearing Raven and Tonya's love making session through the door grew excited. He placed his ear to the door and rubbed his expanding penis through the front of his pants. Down boy! He said to his engorged manhood. He straightened his uniform and knocked harder. This time Raven heard the door. She removed herself from Tonya's moist center. With her tongue Raven devoured the left-over essence of her lover from her fingers. Tonya fixed her clothes as Raven casually walked over to the door. "Who's there?" Raven asked. "The bellman Ma'am, your car is out front and I'm here to help with the bags," the bellman replied.

Raven opened the door and stepped aside to let the doorman in. Tonya walked up to Raven, "don't think because you had me hollering like a bitch that I don't still wear the pants around here." Raven smirked and smacked Tonya's ass as she walked pass to grab the bags.

Tonya was sleep before the car hit the highway. Raven had really given it to her that morning. Tonya wasn't use to a woman fucking her. Don't get it twisted she wasn't a touch me not, but she wasn't one for penetration. Raven watched her favorite girl sleeping next to her. "Tonya!" Raven whispered. After she didn't receive a response Raven did the unthinkable. She reached inside Tonya's pocket and pulled out her phone. Tonya had her phone off all weekend and that really didn't sit well with Raven. Turning the phone on Raven went directly to the call log. The first name that popped up in the phone made Raven's heart drop to her knees. Monique! What the fuck! Raven wanted to slap the shit outta Tonya. She composed herself, I'll wait to we get home to deal with this. Just as Raven was about to cut the phone back off, the message not downloaded signal began to flash. Curiosity got the best of her and she wanted to see what the message was. Tonya started to move and so Raven hurried, shut the phone off and put back inside Tonya's pocket.

Tonya opened her eyes but the look on Raven's face made concern register in her head. "What's wrong babe?" Tonya asked. "Nothing we'll deal with it when we get home," Raven replied and turned to face the window. Tonya had an uneasy feeling in her stomach, something wasn't right.

Once they were home Raven busied herself putting their things away. She was totally nonchalant to Tonya. Tonya decided to let her alone to cool off she grabbed her stuff for a bath. After her water was finished she removed her clothes and submerged herself in the hot soothing water. She grabbed her phone to turn it on; she purposely turned it off for the weekend. She didn't know what Stacey was up to, but she didn't want him spoiling their weekend getaway. Tonya hits the power button, but the phone was already on and the message tab indicating she had a text was up. Tonya hit the notification tab to open the message. Download complete was what the screen said. Download complete, what the fuck! Tonya said to herself. She pressed the ok button and Monique's naked body appeared on the screen. Tonya quickly deleted it from her phone. Is that why Raven was pissed at her? She thought. She didn't know what the fuck was up, but she was definitely going to get to the bottom of it.

Raven was downstairs sitting at the table thinking while Tonya was in the tub. She didn't know why Tonya would be talking to Monique. Raven's phone began to ring, cutting through the silence of her thoughts. Looking at the caller ID she sees that it's Stacey. "I thought you were gonna bring them home," she said before he had a chance to speak. "Yes, I was," Stacey replied. "I was in the process of taking them to dinner and the kids wanted to know if you could come too." Raven could hear her kids in the background yelling. "Yeah please Mommy!" "Ok sure!" Raven said give me a minute to get ready. "Where do you want me to meet you?" Raven asked. Just come over here, you can leave your car and we can take mines. Stacey said. Raven agreed she scribbled a note for Tonya, grabbed her keys and left.

Stacey hung up the phone and gave his kids a hug. He can't believe he was using his kids. He had prompted them on what to say when he was on the phone with Raven. I don't care he thought to himself. I want my family back and I'm not gonna stop until I get what I want. "Ok guys go get ready," he said to the kids. They dashed off the get ready for their date with mom. Stacey dialed Monique's number. "Hey!" She said "I'll be heading that way in a few." "Don't worry about it," Stacey said. "The kids wanted to spend some alone time with me before they have to go home. I'll call you later." And with that he hung up. Monique was left standing there holding her phone. Damn no bye or anything, she closed her phone and finished her shopping.

Tonya finished her bath and got dressed. She went looking for Raven, but she was nowhere to be found. Walking into the kitchen she spotted a note hanging on the fridge. I'm off to pick up the kids; I'm taking them for dinner. I thought they might like a little one on one time with their mom. We shouldn't be too late, Love you. "Fuck!" Tonya yelled. She knew she was in the doghouse for real.

Tonya picked up her phone and called Monique. "Hey sexy!" Monique said after the second ring. "We need to talk like right now!" Tonya spoke into the phone. "Lucky for you my man is off to have dinner with his kids and I'm free," Monique replied. "What?" Tonya said harshly. "What part of that statement didn't you understand," Monique replied. "Where are you now?" Tonya asked. "I'm in Decatur, why?" Monique replied. "Meet me at Twain's in 45minutes," Tonya said. Monique agreed, and Tonya hung up.

Raven pulls up in front Stacey's house, she texts his phone to let him know she was outside. What the hell are you doing? Raven thought. It's for the kids she tried to reassure herself. She leaned the seat back and let the soulful sounds of Vivian Green wash over her. Right when Ms. Green was about to break it down Stacey and the kids came out the door. Raven replaced her seat to its original setting, turned her car off, and got out. "Mommy!" The children ran up to Raven and she kissed each one on the forehead. "Where's mines?" Stacey asked. "Yeah right" Raven replied. They all plied up into Stacey's 2008 Cadillac Escalade and headed to dinner.

Tonya arrived at Twain's before Monique, so she grabbed a Corona and a table in the back by the pool tables to await her arrival. Thirty minutes later Monique sashayed in wearing some black low riding jeggings that looked like they were painted on and a black halter vest that showed off her belly ring with no bra. Monique was stopped by several guys with drink offers that were declined before she reached Tonya. Every guy in the place had faces of envy when Monique walked up to Tonya. Tonya had to stunt on them, making sure to let her hand brush across Monique's voluptuous apple bottom ass. Monique giggled like a girl as she felt Tonya's hand on her backside. She grazed her lips lightly across Tonya's cheek.

"So, what do I owe the pleasure of your invitation?" Monique asked as she waved her hand for the waiter. The waiter came over to the table. "Can I get you anything ma'am?" "I'll have a Corona and a Texas Margarita please. Can you start us a tab?" Monique asked. "Yes, Ma'am I'll need your driver's license please." The waiter responded. The waiter gathered what he needed and left. Tonya walked over to Monique and sits down at the table. "What the fuck you and Stacey got going on?" Tonya asked. "What you mean?" Monique quickly shot back. "Why is Stacey calling me from your phone and then this morning nude pics of you appear on my screen." "What?" Monique asked puzzled by what she just heard. Come to think about it Stacey had been acting weird lately Monique thought to herself. "I assure you whatever Stacey has been doing has nothing to do with me." Monique said with a naughty smirk on her face. "Is that the only reason you asked to see me?" Monique asked Tonya. Not wanting to hurt Monique's feeling, Tonya just looked at her and disregarded the question.

Stacey pulled up in front of Red Lobster and escorted his family inside. He enjoyed playing the family man. This was much different from when he went out with the kids and Monique. Monique was a sexy individual, but she looked out of place when they did they family thing. Raven was gorgeous and very elegant. She carried herself like a wife and mother. They followed the hostess to the table. Stacey pulled out the chair for Raven; she seated herself and thanked him. Raven felt butterflies inside, the kids really seemed to enjoy having this time with both of them. Raven knew in her heart she didn't love Stacey, but she wanted to come up with a way they could have more days like this for the kids' sake. They ordered their food, and everyone engaged in conversation until the food came.

The waiter walked over, handed Monique back her license, and placed their drinks on the table. "Can I help you with anything else ma'am?" "Bring us another round in about 15 minutes," Monique stated. The waiter nodded and walked away. Monique let the savory tequila glide it way down her tongue. Seeing the satisfaction, she got from her drink made Tonya chug her Corona. Tonya and Monique played pool while they drank several more rounds. Watching Monique bending over the table was making Tonya want her in the worst way. Tonya had to get a grip, so she decided to start up a conversation. "So, what did you think about Stacey taking Raven and the kids for dinner?" Tonya asked tryna play Monique for information. "What are you talking about?" Monique asked turning to look at Tonya. "Stacey is out with the kids, right?" Tonya asked. "Yes," Monique looked puzzled at Tonya. "Well Raven left me a note saying she was going to pick up the kids and have dinner with them. I didn't put two and two together until you said Stacey was having dinner with the kids." "Why that sneaky bastard!" Monique yelled. "He told me he wanted to spend some quality time with the kids before they went home." Monique spoke loudly but in the back of her mind she was really thanking Stacey and Raven. Monique excused herself and went to the restroom.

Raven and Stacey laughed and talked like old times, and Raven really enjoyed it. She thought Stacey was becoming the father she knew he could be. "Stacey I've been thinking," Raven said as she took a sip of her rose Moscato. "Since the kids really enjoy being with us both that maybe we can try to plan other outings like this once a month." Stacey tried to hide the disappointment on his face before he spoke. He was hoping she would say something about them becoming a family again. "Yes, I think that might be great. Do you think Tonya would go for it?" He asked trying not to ruin the moment with that bitches name in the air. "Let me deal with that part of it," Raven quickly stated. What Tonya doesn't know won't hurt her Raven thought as she down her wine and singled for the waitress to bring another. There was an awkward silence between them until the waitress came with the drinks. "Mommy I have to go to the restroom," Kelly said. "Me too!" Omari chimed in, and with that Raven escorted her children to the restroom.

Like clockwork, time Raven disappeared around the corner Stacey's phone rang. Seeing Monique's face appear on the screen, at first, he started to ignore the call but thought twice and answered it. "Hey babe!" Stacey said casually into the phone. "Hey handsome!" Monique didn't want to let on that she knew about him being with Raven. "How's dinner with the angels going?" She asked. "Everything's good they are really enjoying this time with daddy," Stacey responded. "What you up to?" Stacey asked. "Nothing much hanging with the ladies, but I would much rather be with you guys," Monique said lining him up for the kill. "Aww! Sweetheart, I would have liked that, but I know you're busy," Stacey said sounding sincere. "Oh, but I'm not, I could ditch the ladies and be there for dessert," Monique joked knowing Stacey should be about to shit bricks by the statement. Stacey was taken aback by Monique's response, but before he could come up with a lie Raven and the kids had turned the corner and were headed back to the table. "Oh, babe that won't be necessary, but look I gotta jet the kids want to go to the potty." Before Monique could respond Stacey had ended the call.

Even though Monique relished the thought of spending the evening with Tonya she hated the thought of that bastard tryna play her. She wanted to make sure she ended up on top in the end and that fucker with no one. She wanted to make sure Raven knew Stacey was playing her. Monique knew she had to play her cards right or this shit would blow up in her face. She washed her hands and went back to join Tonya. Once back at the table Monique decided to sit beside Tonya instead of across from her. Tonya quickly assessed the situation and knew it was time to make her departure. "So, you want to split the bill?" Tonya asked. "No, I'll take care of it!" Monique seductively replied. "Are you sure because I gotta jet," Tonya stated standing preparing herself to leave. "Where you headed?" Monique asked. "Can I come with?" Monique added not wanting this evening to end without getting what she wanted, which was Tonya's tongue inside her steamy hot center. "Naw I'm sorry, I'm about to call it a night and take it in." Tonya stated as she waved for the waiter to bring the check.

Tonya waited on Monique to pay the check and she walked her to her car. Monique put an extra bounce in her walk making her ass jiggle with every step. Watching Monique's ass jump was giving Tonya fever, which mixed with a little over half a 12 pack of Corona was pushing her close to the edge. Tonya quickly gave Monique a hug which was accompanied by a hasty peck on the cheek. Tonya backed away to her car before Monique even responded, she knew she couldn't give her a chance to speak or she would be face first between those chocolate legs of hers. The thought of Monique's legs around her neck made Tonya clit pulsate. Tonya jumped in her car and shut the door. Fuck! Tonya said striking the steering wheel. She tried clearing her mind, but the thought of Raven with Stacey entered her head. Fuck it! She breathes a loud. She reached into her dashboard and pulled out her purple passion vibrator. She grabs her phone and dials Monique's number. "Damn baby you miss me already," Monique whisper into the phone. "Tell me you wanna fuck me!" Tonya yells into the phone. Tonya unzips her pants and lays the vibrator against her already tingling mound. "I want you to fuck me!" Monique readily obliged Tonya. "Close your eyes and rub your pussy," Tonya responded. Monique slid down in her seat parted her already anxious thighs and began vigorously stroking her clit. "Do you feel my tongue as I wrap it around that precious pearl," Tonya whispered into the phone. "Ugh!" Monique sighed.

"I miss the way your mouth feels on me!" The words sent fire down to Tonya's clit and it radiated like waves of pleasure with every syllable. "Oh my! You're about to make me cum!" Monique hissed. "Cum for me! Please cum for me!" Tonya begged. Hearing Monique climaxing threw Tonya over the edge of ecstasy causing her to achieve the release she was seeking. "I wish I could taste you" Tonya said to the breathless Monique. "Whenever you would like," Monique stated hoping she could get a little more than just phone play from Tonya. "Maybe another time," Tonya stated as she zipped her pants and started her car. "Thanks for the pleasure," Tonya said and clicked the phone before she heard a response. Tonya pulled out of the parking lot leaving Monique dazed and confused about what had just happened.

Stacey pulled up to his house and stopped the car. He knew he didn't want this moment to end. The kids were sound asleep in the back. "I guess we're gonna have to carry them to my car," Raven said staring at her babies. Stacey put his hand on top of Raven's, "I think we need to talk. He said to her. I miss my family so much and I'll give anything to have you and the kids back with me," Stacey said to Raven. "Stacey, I care about you but I'm with Tonya," Raven replied. "Do me a favor." Stacey said. "Consider it please. If anything happens between you to I'll be here to catch you." "Why would you say that?" Raven asked. "Nothing Raven! I just don't think she's the person she claims to be." Stacey said jumping out the car. Instead of him opening the back door to get Kelly he walked around to where Raven was standing in the door to pick up Omari. Stacey grabbed Raven and turned her to face him. He lowered his lips to her and wrapped his arms around her making their bodies collide. Raven never felt as safe as she did at that moment and she let Stacey's tongue conquer her lips and invade her mouth. Stacey's tongue danced around inside her mouth feasting on the tantalizing sweetness of it.

Tonya arrived at home and headed straight for the shower. Taking a quick shower relaxed her and she tried to take her mind of Raven lying to her. Despite her angry disposition Tonya couldn't keep her mind off the way Monique's ass bounced as she walked. After her shower Tonya went to the kitchen to fix her a bite to eat. Tonya finished off her sandwich and settled on to sofa to watch a movie. Before she knew what hit her Tonya was asleep and the movie was watching her.

Just as Stacey was kissing Raven, Monique pulled up to the stop sign directly in front of Stacey's house. When she saw them kissing she had to take a double take because she could believe what she was seeing. Monique quickly grabbed her phone and snapped a picture of them. Not wanting them to see her she rapidly turned left and parked down the street. Raven snapping back to her senses pushed Stacey from her. "What's wrong Raven?" Stacey asked looking down into Raven's eyes. "This is wrong Stacey! I can't let the overwhelming feeling from us having a family outing get to me. I don't love you," Raven spoke. "That's not what your body is saying," Stacey replied. "Of course, my body reacted to you we have history, not to mention two kids. You're the only man I've ever truly loved but that's over now. I'm in love with Tonya!" Raven yelled more for herself then for Stacey. She picked up Omari and headed for her car. She opens the door and put the sleeping child in and buckled the seatbelt. Without waiting on word from Stacey she returned back to his car and grabbed Kelly and did the same with her. "Raven please be reasonable just think about us, for the sake of our children. They deserve to live in a two-parent home," Stacey tried to convince Raven. Raven was not interested in hearing his pleads. She had been down this road with him before.

Raven started her engine and put the car in gear but before she drove off she let the window down. Stacey walked over to the lowered window awaiting her words. Raven placed her hands on the sides of Stacey's face. "You're selfish about this whole situation" Raven started off. "You're ready to be a family right," she asked him. "What about Monique? Where does she fit in all this? Furthermore, what about Tonya, what's to happen to her?" "I love you Raven! I love our kids! Nothing else matters to me!" Stacey yelled. "I care about you Stacey but I'm not in love with you. I don't think I'm ready to sacrifice my life, so my kids can have their parent live unhappily ever after." Raven kissed Stacey's forehead then rolled up the window and drove away.

Monique waited several minutes after Raven's departure before she called Stacey's phone. Even though she was sitting in her car down the street from his house she wanted to gauge the situation. Stacey picked up the phone, but his voice was barely audible, it sounded as though he was crying or had been. "You ok baby?" Monique said into the phone. "Yes, I'm fine! Why wouldn't I be!" Stacey yelled. "Are you still entertaining the little ones, or can daddy get his grown man on finally?" Monique asked seductively. The sound of the word daddy sliced through him. "If you don't mind I think I need to be alone tonight." Stacey said. "I'll give you a call in the morning" and before Monique had time to respond Stacey clicked the phone shut. "What the fuck is with everybody hanging the phone up on me!" Monique yelled. Monique started her car and drove to her two-bedroom apartment she shared with a roommate in College Park. Even though she stays at Stacey's house majority of the time Monique knew better then to let her place go. The flash of Stacey and Raven kissing infuriated Monique. Sitting outside in the parking lot Monique thought to send the picture to Tonya but thought against it. I need this for leverage she thought to herself. Monique gathered her things and went inside.

Raven drove down the street but before she got to the house she reached in her purse grabbed her phone and called Tonya. Tonya's sleepy voice can through the phone after the second ring. "Babe I'm about to pull up, do you think you can come out and help me with the kids." "Yeah sure," Tonya said. Tonya stood in front of the chair and stretched her arm in the air. She wiped the sleep from her eyes and walked to the front door to await Raven's arrival. Tonya anxiously wanted to confront Raven about having dinner with Stacey, but she didn't want to reveal how she knew the information. Raven pulled into the driveway and she saw her sexy stud standing in the doorway. Raven didn't care about the shit Stacey was tryna put in her head she loved Tonya and that was it.

No sooner than Raven put the car in park she was out of the door. She ran straight into Tonya's arms. The sheer force of Raven's unforeseen strike almost knocked Tonya threw the glass door. "What's all this for?" Tonya asked sarcastically. "I've missed you!" Raven spoke as she gently kissed her lover's neck. "Yeah, I'm sure," Tonya replied removing herself from Raven's grasp. Tonya sidesteps Raven and opened the back door of the car. She picks up Kelly and heads toward the house. Raven grabs Omari hits the alarm on the car and falls in step behind Tonya. "What's wrong with you?" Raven asked as she shut the door to the kids' room. "Did you see Stacey tonight Raven?" "What kind of question is that?" Raven catechized. "Of course, I saw Stacey! Where do you think the kids were?" Raven barked. "How close did you get to him?" Tonya asked as she turned to face her mate. "What?" Raven barked. "The fuck you mean by that?" Raven stood with her hands on her hips. Tonya was so pissed off that she was pacing back and forward. "Did you fuck Stacey tonight?" Tonya stopped and banged her head on the wall. "Hell no! Why would you ask such a question?" "Raven your such a fucking liar! Your clothes smell just like his cologne!" Raven never thought about that she was struck speechless.

Raven walked over and tried to rest her hand on Tonya's arm. Tonya snatched her arm away from her. "Answer me!" Tonya demanded. There was nothing Raven could say. She had lied about her whereabouts in the first place. How was she gonna explain the kiss she shared with her ex-husband. Tonya took Ravens silence as an omission of guilt. "You fucked him!" Tonya screamed enraged at the thought. "No baby, I didn't" Raven tried to plead her case. "What then Raven!" Tonya yelled grabbing Raven by her arms. She was squeezing so tight that Raven could feel Tonya's nails digging into her skin. "Baby please your hurting me!" Raven whimpered. "I gave you my all and this is how you repay me." Tonya slapped Raven across the face with the backside of her left hand. Raven fell to her knees and hid her face in her hands. Tonya wanted to kick the shit out of her, but she forced herself to contain her anger. "I didn't do anything!" Raven yelled. She stood up and tried a desperate attempt to get her point across. "Get the fuck outta my face Raven!" Tonya yelled. "Please listen to me! I didn't do anything!" Ugh! Tonya picked up the glass vase on the desk and tossed it against the wall. Tonya walked out the room slamming the door behind her. Raven fell to her knees balling like a baby. She had to come up with something quick. Why the fuck did she let Stacey put her in this situation in the beginning.

Monique was awakened by the smell of cannabis smoke pouring from up under her door. "Wake and bake bitch! Get your ass up," yelled Eric Monique's roommate as he beat on the door. Monique rolled out of bed and unlocked the door. "I ain't seen you in a mouth of Sundays," Eric said handing Monique the blunt. Once Eric saw the look on Monique's face he knew they needed a sistea to sistea talk. Eric was a sexy mocha chocolate specimen of a man. He was too much man to be a girl and too much queen to be anything other than gay. Eric walked over and sat on Monique's bed. "Now chile I've known you for way to long. What's up?" He asked taking the blunt for his turn in the two-man rotation. "It's Stacey," Monique said. "I know he wants to get back with his ex, but yesterday he lied about going to dinner with her and the kids. Then when I arrived at his house I saw him kissing her." Monique was never the one to fall in love. She never misled Stacey on that part, but she wasn't ready to give up the lifestyle she had with him. Stacey pretty much gave her what she wanted and always left her to her own devices. Eric chuckled at his roommate looking like a wounded sparrow. "Are you falling for Stacey?" he asked getting up off the bed to light his Newport. "Hell no!" Monique replied. "I just don't wanna have to worry about keeping up my appearance by myself until I find someone else. I'll be damn if I go back to nickel and diming it." "Well Miss Thang, looks like you better worry more about getting Stacey to put a ring on it and less about him kissing Miss Raven." Eric finished smoking and left the room. Moments later she heard him partaking in his favorite pass time, gossiping. Monique so desperately wanted to tell Eric of her plan that she had been working on for months now, but she didn't want to hear his judgment. Monique pushed her door closed and decided to go claim her man.

Tonya opened her eyes but didn't recognize where she was. She rubbed her hand across her face and realized that she was in the den. She was mad as hell at Raven, how could she betray her like that. Tonya wasn't sure if Raven had actually slept with Stacey, but he had gotten close enough to her for him to leave his scent. Tonya thinking about Stacey's hands all over Raven made the anger inside her grow to enormous heights. Tonya could feel her blood boiling inside her so much so that the tears that ran down her cheek seemed to burn her skin. She sat up on the sofa, said a small prayer and got up to get ready for work.

Raven didn't sleep at all that night; she desperately wanted to talk to Tonya. What would she say? Raven thought to herself as she let the water cascade down her in an effort to wash away her sins. Raven got out the shower and walked over to the mirror. She touched her face where the purplish bruise had started to transversely form on her cheek. The tears dropped heavily down her face. Everything was all her fault. How could she prove that she didn't sleep with Stacey if she was hiding the fact that he kissed her? On the other hand, if she says he kissed her how could she prove she didn't sleep with him if she lied about the kiss. Raven didn't know what to do. She pined up her hair and went to go wake the kids for school.

Stacey lay awake in his bed starring at the ceiling. He wished he could roll over to the beautiful face of his wife again. He longed to touch her, caress her, and make love to her body again. The thought of making love to Raven made Stacey's body become aroused. The phone rang breaking Stacey's thoughts. The ringtone indicated that it was Monique. Stacey shrugged repositioned himself and reluctantly picked up the phone. "Morning sexy!" Monique chimed in before Stacey had a chance to speak. "Morning Monique!" Stacey spoke trying not to sound dry. "I'm at the door and I have breakfast!" Monique said disregarding Stacey gloomy disposition. Stacey looked up at the ceiling again then down at his throbbing shaft. Fuck it! He thought that's what she's here for anyway. Stacey got up off the bed and went to let Monique in.

Once Stacey opened the door and saw Monique, you could have driven a semi threw the gaping hole that was in his mouth. Monique had on sweat pant three sizes to small and a GSU sweatshirt that was sliced to wear it stopped barely below the breast area. Stacey could tell she had on no bra and by the way her ass jiggled when she moved, no underwear either. Stacey took the bag of food from Monique's hand, and headed to the kitchen table. "I'm gonna run to the restroom while you set everything up." Monique said while Stacey rummaged through the bag. Monique hurried up the stairs, she went into Stacey's room and over to the nightstand. She slides open the drawer and picked up the box of condoms her and Stacey uses. She switched them for the box of condoms that she punched holes in earlier. Monique had been switching the condoms for about a month and a half now. She also had stopped taking her birth control. She was gonna make sure she got Raven's ass out the picture for good as well as insure her own comfortability at the same time. Monique returned back downstairs as Stacey was sitting down ready to dig in. She walked over to him and stood directly in front of him. With her hands on her hips Monique was standing there looking like Lynda Carter minus the wonder woman costume. Her luscious camel toe was mere inches from Stacey's face begging for the attention of his tongue. All of a sudden Stacey's mouth wasn't craving food anymore. When he looked up into Monique's eyes she knew exactly what he wanted.

Stepping back from Stacey Monique leaned against the wall and removed her shoes. She slipped out of her pants revealing the belly chain that was attached to her navel ring. Stacey leaped up from the table and pinned Monique against the wall. He lifted her up and kissed her ferociously as the need to have her overwhelmed him. Monique wrapped her legs around him pressing her smoldering hot sex against his hardened shaft. Stacey carried Monique to the bedroom and laid her face down on the bed. Pulling her to him he lowered himself and buried his face inside her wetness. As Stacey ate Monique's pussy from the back the scent of her drove him wild. Stacey licked and sucked her clit until she was about to burst. Monique started to shudder, and Stacey removed his tongue from her mound and licked the rim of her anus. As Monique screamed his name, Stacey drove his tongue inside her tight anus over and over until she released herself and saturated the sheets below with her nectar.

He gave pleasure to Monique's pussy with his tongue until she purred, and it was sticky and glistened with cum. Stacey made sure to please her pussy because he was about to beat it up in the worst way. He paused briefly, long enough to slip on a condom from the nightstand. Stacey rubbed his hand up and down between Monique's cave making sure she was nice and saturated. Monique wiggled with anticipation as Stacey gently inserted his 9 and a half inch shaft into her already marinated center. Stacey dove into Monique with all he had, and she accepted it like the pro she was. Monique switched it up pushing Stacey back against the bed. She jumped on top of him mounting Stacey like a jockey at the horse race. Feeling Stacey's powerful muscular body up under her had Monique climaxing continuously. Monique felt Stacey's body grow taut beneath her and she took off like she was at the camp town races.

As Stacey climaxed he yelled out Raven's name and simultaneously gave Monique what she been plotting and planning for months. "What!" Monique yelled. "Did you just scream that bitch's name while you were cumming inside me?" "Oh, Baby I'm sorry!" Stacey pleaded as Monique jumped up and ran into the bathroom. "Fuck you Stacey!" she yelled through the door. "I go out my way to please you and you treat me like I'm shit," Monique continued to rant and rave as she dressed. "Monique please just let me talk to you! I didn't mean it!" Stacey continued to plead for Monique's forgiveness as he beat his head against the door. Monique sat on the toilet smoking a Newport as Stacey voice echoed through the door. Fucking bitch! Monique thought to herself. She can't just have one perfect mate she has to have them all. Ima see to it that she gets exactly what's coming to her. Monique threw her cigarette in the commode and walked out the bathroom. She walked up to Stacey and took his hand. "Look I know we agreed but I love you, this really hurt me, and I need some time." Hearing those words from Monique made Stacey gasp. Monique kissed her lover's lips and walked out the house. Stacey slumped down against the wall. I'm chasing a woman who wants nothing to do with me and disregarding a gorgeous woman who has my back. Stacey dropped is head into his hands and wept like a baby.

While Raven put the kids on the bus Tonya hurried and got ready for work. Raven came back in the house and stood in front of their bedroom door to wait on Tonya to come out. She wanted so bad to go inside the room, but her nerves prevented that. Just as she was about to abort and walk away the door opened. Tonya looked up and found herself face to face with Raven.

"I think we should talk," Raven spoke first. "Get the hell outta my way Raven!" Tonya irritably replied. "No, I think we should discuss this!" Raven yelled as she moved to block Tonya's path. "Look, I'm really pissed off and I think it wise if you would move." Tonya spoke the words as if she was speaking to one of the inmates inside the jail. "No!" Raven defiantly screamed. Before Raven knew what had happened Tonya had her pinned against the wall by her throat. Raven tried to yell but her airway was blocked. She clawed at Tonya's hand, but they were like tree trucks and were unmovable. Tonya leaned down to Raven's ear and said, "don't fuck with me Raven, because it won't end pretty." Tonya released Raven, grabbed her things, and walked out the house. Raven collapsed to the floor holding her neck and gasping for air. She was so visibly shaken that her legs were wobbly as she tried to stand.

Raven sat on the floor and gathered her thoughts for a moment. Then she went to the phone called her job saying that she had an unexpected meeting at the kids' school and she would be a few hours late. No sooner did she hang up the phone did she come undone. Raven had to smoke two Newport's and drink a glass of wine to be able to get herself prepared for work. She made up her face making sure to cover the bruise on her cheek. Raven quickly dressed finishing it off with a satin scarf around her neck. Raven smoked one more cigarette, downed two Tylenols, grabbed her things, and left for work.

12

Side Chick or Main Squeeze

Montana

Montana arrived at her best friend Katrina's house. Katrina helped Montana with her bags; she noticed that her friend was trembling terribly. As they walked to in the house Katrina bombarded Montana with an array of questions. "Girl what's wrong?" she asked. "Was it Lameka again?" Katrina absolutely hated Lameka. She felt like Montana had always been stupid for that girl. No matter how much Montana would brag about the love they shared in the end she would always be crying at the hands of Lameka. "Look, please don't judge me ok!" Montana yelled reading the look on her friend's face. "How about you make us a drink and I'll tell you everything." Katrina agreed and dashed into the kitchen to whip up some drinks.

Katrina brought two Ketel One martinis and handed one to Montana. Montana downed half of her glass in one sip in a desperate attempt to calm her nerves. "Did Lameka do that to your face?" Katrina asked standing over Montana. Montana had forgotten all about her appearance, she hadn't even looked in the mirror at herself yet. She sat the glass down and rushed into the bathroom. Montana gasped at the sight of the reflection staring back. The right side of her face had a large hand print from where Lameka had slapped her. Her right eye was puffy and swollen. The other side of her head had dried blood matted in her hair line where she hit her head on the wall when Lameka hit her. There was a purplish bruise already forming just below her eyebrow. Montana definitely looked like she had been at the losing end of an ass whipping. Katrina's face appeared in the mirror. "I know you're gonna report this to the police, right?" Katrina asked. "No!" Montana snapped. "No, she'll kill me if she found out." Montana broke down as the memory swam back into her mind. Katrina held her friend letting her sob uncontrollably on the bathroom floor.

Montana got herself together and she followed Katrina back to the living room. They both sipped their martinis and Montana relived her accounts of what happened. Katrina knew Lameka had been physical before but never anything of this caliber. She was utterly terrified for her friend. "Montana you gotta go to the police with this," Katrina said trying to persuade her friend. "No!" Montana screamed. "Please Katrina don't push me on this. You didn't see the look in her eyes." Montana sound desperate as she spoke. "She'll kill me, I know it!"

"Well you're welcomed to stay here along as you promise that it's over between the two of you." Katrina demanded. "I can promise you this" Montana spoke; "I don't ever what to come face to face with Lameka again. To tell you the truth I'm terrified for Nashunta." "Fuck her!" Katrina blurted out. "Do you think she gives a damn about what happens to you?" Katrina asked as she finished off her drink and got up to make some more. Montana dropped her head, "maybe you're right Katrina." "I know I'm right!" Katrina said from the kitchen. Montana and Katrina talked until right before midnight. Katrina waited until Montana was settled in and asleep before she went off to bed.

The next morning Katrina made Montana change her phone number. For her own safety Katrina also suggested that they switch cars seeing that Lameka had no idea where Katrina worked. Montana got herself together and headed off to work. Arriving at work super early Montana drove around the parking lot before she parked and hurried inside through the back door. Montana informed Patricia the front desk receptionist that she had a lot of work to complete and if anybody called or came in to see her she was out of the office until further notice. Patricia agreed, and Montana went off to the back to get her work started. The day was going quite smoothly until Montana was standing by the sliding glass window talking to Patricia when she saw Lameka enter the office. The window was barely open but if Lameka had looked up she would have saw her. "Are you ok honey?" Patricia asked as she looked up at Montana. "You looked like you've seen a ghost." Montana was standing next to Patricia's desk with her body pressed hard against the wall. Seeing her coworker's reaction Patricia knew something was wrong.

When Lameka rang the bell for assistance Montana was practically hyperventilating. Patricia put on her customer service smile and slide the window open. "Good afternoon! How can I assist you today?" she asked still smiling. "Yes," Lameka started off. "I was wondering if Ms. Montana Santiago was working today." "I'm sorry but Ms. Santiago will be out of the office for a couple of days." Patricia replied. "Why? Is something wrong with her?" Lameka asked trying to sound more concerned than she was. She was really only interested in doing damage control. "I do apologize for not being able to assist you, but I can direct you to our supervisor and maybe she can assist you further." Lameka became visually frustrated but she kept her cool. She stood there for a minute as if she was contemplating her next move. "No thanks," Lameka replied then she turned around and walked out the door. Montana released the breath she had been holding. She tried to move but her legs buckled, and she collapsed to the floor on her knees. Patricia rushed to her coworker's side. Montana was shaking like a leaf in the wind. "Did something happen to you honey?" Patricia asked helping Montana to her feet. "No Patricia I'm fine." Dr. David and some of the other staff came rushing over. "I'm just not feeling to well; I think I need to leave," Montana grabbed Patricia's hands, "please don't say anything about this," Montana whispered to Patricia. Against what Patricia felt inside she agreed. Montana got up grabbed her things and was out the back door. Everybody was left staring at Patricia for answers.

Once her car door was shut Montana broke down crying uncontrollably. Reaching into her purse to grab a Newport, Montana noticed Lameka sitting in her car near the front entrance of the office. Montana was frozen like a deer stuck in headlights. She sat there still for several moments until she realized she was in Katrina's car. Lameka had no clue that Montana was there. Thank heavens for window tint Montana prayed as she started the car and drove away.

Days went by without incident from Lameka. Montana had even spoken to Katrina about going back home. Out of the blue Montana's phone rang. The caller ID indicated that Montana's alarm company was calling. Montana felt her stomach turn over. "Hello"! Montana said into the phone. "This is Alert One calling for Montana Santiago" The male voice said through the phone. "Yes, this is Montana Santiago speaking." "Ma'am your alarm has indicated a possible break-in. We've dispatched police to the location. Are inside the house at this time?" The caller asked. "No! Montana said I'm not home." "Ok ma'am I've just been informed that the police are at the location at this time. We suggest that you head home and meet with police to survey the damages." Montana agreed, and she thanked the caller before hanging up. Montana and Katrina jumped into the car and headed toward Montana's house.

Arriving at her place Montana was shocked. The back door had been kicked in and she just knew all her things would be gone. An officer walked over and introduced himself. "How are you doing ladies I'm Officer Jay Johnson. Which one of you is Ms. Santiago?" Officer Johnson asked. "I am!" Montana said raising her hand as if she was back in elementary school again. "Well I just want to inform you that we arrived at the residence and noticed that the back door had been kicked in. My partner, Officer Patrick and I proceeded to enter the house. We did an extensive search of your residence, but it looks as though nothing was taken. We were thinking maybe it was some kids and the alarm scared them away." Officer Johnson stood there waiting for a response before he went on. Katrina looked at Montana and her eyes were screaming tell him. Montana just stood there with her mouth hanging open. "Is something wrong ma'am?" Officer Johnson asked. "Oh no! I was just thinking that maybe you were right." Montana blurted out. "About the kids I mean." Montana gave Katrina a shut your mouth glance. Katrina put her hands on her hips, rolled her eyes and went to go sit inside the car. "Are you sure that everything is ok ma'am?" Officer Johnson asked. "Yes, I'm sure." Montana replied. "Would you like to walk through to make sure nothing was taken?" "Yes of course!" Montana said following behind Officer Johnson.

A few hours later the door was repaired, and the ladies jumped back in the car to head back to Katrina's house. As soon as they pulled off Katrina started in on her. "Why didn't you tell the police about Lameka?" "Because, I not certain that it was her." Montana said. "You heard the Officer it looked like it could have been kids." "Are you serious right now?" Katrina shouted. Katrina wanted to smack her friend upside the head. She couldn't believe what she was hearing. "I mean, I don't want to get Lameka in any trouble if it was only kids." Montana dropped her head sounding unsure of herself. "Lameka deserves to get into trouble for what she's done to you!" Katrina yelled. "Why are you letting her get away with this?" "It's not that simple Katrina!" Montana retorted. "Well make me understand!" Katrina shot back. Katrina snapped her head around facing Montana. "Oh, please don't tell me that you're still in love with her!" Shaking her head Katrina took Montana's silence as a divulgence of guilt. "Come on Montana!" Katrina shouted. "This girl has been treating you like shit for a long time. This time she went way too far. You have to stop her before she kills you or somebody else." "What was I supposed to say Katrina?" Montana asked. "That my girlfriend got a little too rough with me during sex." "Yes!" Katrina replied. "Don't forget that she came back beat the crap out of you, and you suspect that she kicked in your back door looking to come kill you." "But we don't know for sure that was even her!" Montana yelled. "Oh please!" Katrina screamed. "Stop taking up for her Montana you're starting to sound like a real victim right now." Montana and Katrina rode the rest of the way home in silence. Deep down inside Montana knew Katrina was right.

13

Once The Closet Door Opens

Mercedes

Mercedes woke up, but it felt as though she was a hollow shell of what she use to be. She had become depressed and withdrawn from her family. Mercedes didn't even want to get out of bed anymore. It was like with every call or text Hakeem sent, the more the doorway open to her tormented past. Mercedes felt as though she was being sucked inside the closet of secrets she had created. She was tired of allowing herself to suffer in silence. Mercedes grabbed a pillow dropped it over her face and began screaming. Screw this Mercedes said as she jumped up off the bed. She grabbed her phone and dove back across the bed. Placing the phone to her ear she could hear ringing and then there it was, her soft voice. "So, you finally decided to call?" The sweet sound of Monea's voice was so soothing and comforting. "I'm ready to talk." Mercedes replied to Monea's statement. "I'm ready to come clean, can we meet somewhere?" There was a short pause on the other end of the phone. Mercedes started to recant her offer but before she could get the words out Monea started to speak. "I can't today, but I'm free tomorrow if that's ok." Mercedes was so elated that she wasn't shot down she quickly agreed before Monea thought to change her mind. They both decided to meet the following day around noon. Mercedes thanked Monea and ended the call.

Without even giving her mind a chance to act against her she jumped up, opened her door and yelled "who wants ice cream?" The kids yelled in unison, "me!" "Ok, you guys have ten minutes to be dressed and loaded in the car." Within minutes everyone was dressed and loaded in the car and heading for Bruster's. Once there the kids were out of the car like lighting and running to get in line before the other one. Mercedes took her place in line behind her children.

After the children had devoured their cones they chased after each other in the grass. Mercedes watched her children, she loved them more than life itself. Despite the person who was their sperm donor was she never regretted what he helped her to make. The Lord always knows when to show up and right before Mercedes started feeling sorry for herself the phone she had nestled inside her bra began to vibrate. She pulled it out in order to look at the caller Id before she answered it. The phone lit up and the name flashed Monea. Mercedes was so excited to see her name that she fumbled the phone, and in the process of trying to catch it she dropped her half eaten double scooped chocolate chip cookie dough ice cream cone on the ground. "Shit!" she screamed more to herself than anything. Mercedes straightened the phone hurriedly trying to catch it before she hung up.

Letting out a long breath, she switched the talk button to on. "Hello!" "Hey!" Monea said in return. "are you busy?" Mercedes was so mesmerized by Monea's voice that she almost forgot to respond on cue. "Umm! Not really, I brought the kids to get some ice cream. Everything's ok with you?" Mercedes asked. "Everything's ok," Monea responded. "I was thinking about you and wanted to hear your voice. I've really missed you. I know things have been real crazy for you, but you don't know how many times I wanted to call," Monea paused. She was becoming overwhelmed and she didn't want her emotions to run Mercedes away.

As she listened to Monea, butterflies swam and fluttered although her stomach. There was a pause and Mercedes took that time to attempt to plead her case. "I'm so sorry for the way I just abruptly stopped talking to you. You deserved way more than that. "Let's not talk about that yet." Mercedes said in an attempt to change the subject. "So, you missed me huh?" She continued. "Kinda!" Monea replied through small cute laughs. The conversation between the two carried on even after Mercedes corralled her crew and drove home. It was as if they picked right up and no time between them had passed. She was so intertwined with her conversation with Monea that she didn't even notice the texts that had come thru. The phone beeped singling she had an incoming, but she never skipped a beat as if oblivious to the fact. As Mercedes pulled into her usual spot she was so involved in her conversation as if the world's troubles no longer matter. She was finally able to breathe, her mind felt so free. While still holding the phone Mercedes quickly secured her car and ushered everyone inside.

Hakeem sat in the car he had borrowed and parked next to the dumpster staring up at his ex's apartment she shared with their kids. If he had been minutes earlier, he would have saw them driving away. He had been parking there for weeks watching her comings and goings. He knew to come after the morning work rush and he would leave just before five avoiding the people coming home from work. Hakeem would also sit sometimes late at night. He didn't even know why he was doing it, he didn't care. She belonged to him, his kids, his wife, and his family. Hakeem picked up his phone and called Mercedes. Once the call started ringing call waiting popped up on the screen, indicating that she was on the phone, deliberately ignoring him. She would usually send his calls to voicemail, but this time was different. As Hakeem sat in the car he became more and more enraged. He sent a few texts, but that only added fuel to the fire.

He got out to stretch walking back and forward from the back of the car and the dumpster. He was making sure to stay out of sight from the on-coming traffic as he smoked a cigarette. Hakeem got back in the car and leaned the seat back and turned the radio on. No sooner as he clicked the radio on Mercedes pulled into her normal parking spot. Usually she would look around twice before hurrying inside, she feared him, and this excited him. The very thought of Mercedes' terror cause an erection to form in his pants. Hakeem waiting on them to get out the car, his anticipation caused his breath to become loud and heavy. As Mercedes got out the car he could see her on the phone. The sight of her laughing and enjoying someone's voice cracked the veil of arousal. This time she didn't even look around once before she grabbed her thangs and casually walked inside with the kids.

Hakeem was so pissed off that he grabbed the large switch blade from under the seat and got out the car. All he saw was red, he looked around as he slowly walked over to Mercedes' car. Just as he was about to bend down to slash the back tire, a police car bent the corner and started heading his way. Hakeem bent down to pretend to tie his shoes and stuck the huge blade in his socks. He stood up just as the police car was driving up slowly, Hakeem lit a cigarette gave a smiling node in the officer's direction. Once the car had passed he crossed the street, got back in the car, and sped off in the other direction.

Unbeknownst to what was going on outside, Mercedes sat at the kitchen table talking to Monea while the kids made themselves busy in their rooms. She heard her phone beep several times while she talked but she didn't want to ruin her mood by looking at it if it was from the wrong person. After another hour or two on the phone they finally ended their phone conversation. Without even looking at the phone she laid the phone face down on the table and Mercedes moved to the living room to relax and watch tv before bed. With nothing on tv she settled for the movie Tombstone, Mercedes placed a sofa pillow behind her head to enjoy one of her favorite movies.

Mercedes stood in the sunlight holding hands with Monea. The smile on her face always seemed to make everything fade away. Pulling Monea to her, Mercedes' pressed her lips against Monea's. Her lips tasted of menthol from the Newport's she smoked and spearmint gum. The scent of Monea's Waikiki coconut beach body spray, the softness of their commingling bodies, and the aroma of the Spring season caused arousal to rise inside of Mercedes. Mercedes wanted to have Monea in every way possible, her body, her ambience, as well as her love. The two lovers locked hands and continued walking down the sidewalk.

The two rounded the corner to go up the backsteps towards Mercedes's apartment. She rarely used the front entry because it was an enclosed stairwell and she had a fear of being cornered in there by Hakeem. The couple had just made to the landing of the concrete steps when the was a deep familiar sounding voice calling Mercedes' name from behind them. The breath was caught in Mercedes' chest and she could hear her heart beating up between her ears. She pushed Monea behind her as she swirled around to face the voice. "Is this what you doing?" "You embarrassing me like this?" "So, what you dyking now?" the bombardment of questions from Hakeem was continuous. "How did you find us?" was the only thing that was able to come out her mouth. At that moment the world was a black box and only the three of them existed in it. Suddenly Mercedes felt Monea's hand squeeze her hand and began to pull her toward the steps.

Things were moving so fast yet so slow. Just as Monea began to pull her arm Hakeem grabbed her by the collar of her shirt. Pure instinct made Mercedes snatch away from his grasp. Doing so only added fuel to the fire and Hakeem pulled from behind his back a large silver hand gun. There was no sound, no movement of any kind at that moment. All she saw was the barrel of the gun pointed directly at her. "Monea run!" Mercedes yelled out and the two took off in an effort to save themselves. The cannon like sound that came from the gun as it erupted, sent pain through Mercedes' ear drums. Within an instant Mercedes loses her grip on Monea's hand. She stops running and turns in enough time to see Monea as she hits the ground. At this point nothing else matters, not the gun, not Hakeem, Nothing.

Kneeling down beside Monea she noticed blood coming from a hole in the midsection of her shirt and under the bottom of her. The force of the shot knocked her to the ground and she was unconscious. Mercedes quickly grabbed her phone to dial 911, but before she could speak into the phone a blinding force caused the world to fade to black. The force from the impact caused Mercedes to suck air in just as a person coming up out the water. She jumped clean off the sofa onto her feet. Gathering her bearings Mercedes found herself within the safety of the walls of her apartment. Mercedes grabbed her pack of cigarettes and lit one as quickly as she could get the flame to the tip. She said thank you God over and over to herself and out loud. It had only been a dream.

14

When I Love You Never Come

Nashunta

Mrs. Jones arrived home after work; she went upstairs to get comfortable. Twenty minutes later she was back down in the kitchen preparing to cook dinner for her family. The smell of food brings Kimmie wondering into the kitchen. "Hey Mommy!" Kimmie said kissing her mother on the cheek. "How was your day sweetie?" Mrs. Jones inquired as her continued to cook. "It was ok!" Kimmie replied. "Nothing special happened." She said as she opened the fridge. "Where's Nashunta?" Mrs. Jones asked. "I don't know she hasn't got home yet." "Really? Did she say anything about staying after school today?" Mrs. Jones asked. "Not to me!" Kimmie said as she grabbed an apple and exited the kitchen.

Mrs. Jones wiped her hands on the kitchen towel and grabbed her phone. She dialed her daughter's number and put the phone to her ear. The phone rung several times before Nashunta's voice chimed in telling her to leave a message. "Hey honey! Call me when you get this message. Love you!" Mrs. Jones said. She hung up the phone and finished cooking.

Mrs. Jones was setting the table when she heard her phone ringing. Thinking it was Nashunta she rushed to grab it. "Hello!" she spoke into the phone. There was a brief pause and then a computerized voice began to speak. "This is an automated message from Chamblee High school. Your student Nashunta Jones missed one or more periods today from school. Thanks, you!" There was another short pause and the line clicked and the call ended. Confused Mrs. Jones quickly dialed the school. "It's a great day at Chamblee High School! I'm Mrs. Duncan, how can I direct your call?" "Good evening Mrs. Duncan, I just received a call stating that my daughter missed some classes today." "Yes, Ma'am I can check that out for you. What's your daughter's name?" Mrs. Duncan asked. "Her name is Nashunta Jones." Mrs. Jones replied. "Oh, I know Nashunta." Mrs. Duncan stated. "I'm pretty sure I didn't see Nashunta at all today, but I'll check to make sure." Mrs. Duncan placed the call on hold for several minutes. "Mrs. Jones?" Mrs. Duncan said coming back to the phone. "Yes, I'm here." Mrs. Jones replied. "No ma'am she wasn't here today." Mrs. Duncan stated. "Are you sure?" Mrs. Jones questioned. "Yes, I've checked, and she was marked absent from all her classes. I'm sorry I can't be more of an assistance." "Oh no, you're fine! I thank you for your help." Mrs. Jones said. She thanked Mrs. Duncan again before she hung up the phone.

Mrs. Jones called Nashunta's phone several more times receiving the same outcome. There was a nervous uneasy feeling starting to grow inside her stomach. Mrs. Jones was so wrapped up in her thoughts that she didn't hear her husband and child enter the kitchen. Mrs. Jones walked over to the table. "Nashunta wasn't at school today and she's not answering her phone." Mr. Jones and Kimmie both started at her unblinkingly like she was speaking a foreign language. "What do you mean?" he asked his wife. "I received an automated call from the school saying Nashunta had been absent from school." "Oh mom! They send those even if one of your teachers mark you absent." Kimmie said trying reassure her mother. "I thought it might've been an error, so I called the school. I spoke to a Mrs. Duncan, she checked the records for me and she said that Nashunta had been marked absent from all her classes. You don't think she'd run, away do you?" Mrs. Jones asked to whomever was listening. "I think something's wrong Mike!" Mrs. Jones yelled to her husband. "Don't over react honey." Mr. Jones said as he came over and put his arm around his panicking wife.

Kimmie followed her mom up to her sister's room. As they looked around everything seemed to be in place. The only thing missing was the bag she took to school every day. Sitting on the bed Mrs. Jones placed her head in her hands. "Something's not right!" she yelled through small sobs. Kimmie sat down next to her mom on her sister's bed. "Mom I'm sure she's fine."

Kimmie said hugging her mom in an effort to console her. "I think we should call the police!" Mrs. Jones shouted as she got up and headed back down stairs with Kimmie on her heels. "Baby I think you're overreacting! Please let's just eat dinner and we'll try calling her again." "I can't eat Mike! I feel like something's wrong!" Mrs. Jones yelled as she left the kitchen. Mr. Jones and Kimmie ate dinner in silence. Kimmie cleaned the kitchen while her father tried several times himself to reach Nashunta. After leaving messages of his own he silently prayed that everything was fine.

By ten o'clock Mr. Jones went inside Nashunta's room where his wife was sitting. "Honey I think it's time to call the police." he said grabbing his wife's hand. The police arrived at the house within 20 minutes. The officers were not treating this as a missing person's case. They acted as if Nashunta had simply run off. "Was she upset about anything?" One of the officers asked. "No" Mrs. Jones replied. "Has she run away before?" The officer asked. "No! Nashunta would never do that!" Mrs. Jones yelled. "Why are you acting so nonchalant? My damn child is missing!" she screamed at the officers in her living room. "Ma'am your daughter is probably somewhere blowing off steam. However, if you want us to help you we have to ask questions." The officer that was doing the writing said. "How old is she?" The officer asked. "Nashunta is seventeen; her eighteenth birthday is in a couple weeks. She was extremely excited about her upcoming birthday. She had already made plans with her friends." Mrs. Jones stated to the officers. "Does that sound like a girl that wanted to run away?" "I understand your frustration ma'am but officially she has to be gone for 24 hours before we can say she's missing. Do have a recent photo of her?" The officer asked. Kimmie went and grabbed Nashunta's 11th grade picture of the mantel. The officer took the picture and placed it on top of the paper he was writing on. The officer that was asking all the questions stood up and handed Mr. Jones a card. "This is the officer that will be handling your case. If you hear from Nashunta or have any more information call the number on the card." He followed behind them as they walked to the door. Mr. Jones shook their hands and thanked them for coming.

Just after midnight a semi-hysterical Mrs. Jones dials her best friend Yolanda's phone. Yolanda was a night owl and she was up watching reruns of Amen when her phone rang out the blue. She was shocked to see her friend's name on her caller ID. "Hey girl! You and Mike burning the midnight oil?" Yolanda said teasing her friend. "Nashunta didn't come home tonight!" Mrs. Jones blurted out. Hearing the sobs that escaped her friend Yolanda knew she was serious. "What do you mean?" Yolanda asked. "Nashunta didn't come home tonight and she never made it to school this morning." Mrs. Jones continued to sob. "Are you saying she's missing? What happened? Did you guys have a fight or something?" Yolanda was so confused that the questioned were never ending. "No! Nothing!" Mrs. Jones screamed. "I feel like there something wrong Yolanda!" Hearing the desperation in her friend's voice caused tears to form and roll down Yolanda's cheeks. "I'll call Nathan and check to see if he's spoken to her. I'm sure she's just mad somewhere, everything's gonna be fine. Stay by the phone and I'll call you right back." Mrs. Jones agreed, and they hung up. Yolanda jumped up from the sofa rushed to her room and threw on the first thing she saw. She silently prayed that everything was ok, but she still wanted to be there for her friend. When Nashunta came home Yolanda wanted to be there to hold her down while her parents beat her ass for pulling a stunt like this.

2:45am Thursday morning Nathan was awakened by his phone ringing. Glancing at the caller ID he saw that it was his mom and his heart starts pounding in his chest. Before he could even get the phone to his ear he was yelling out to her. "Mom is everything alright?" "Nathan have you talked to Nashunta at all yesterday?" Yolanda asked disregarding his question all together. "Yeah, I spoke to her the other night. Why do you ask? Is she ok?" Nathan asked. The line stayed silent a little too long and the fear inside him jumped into his throat. "Mom please! Tell me what's wrong!" Nathan yelled. "Nathan, Nashunta didn't come home last night." "What!" He blurted out. "When was the last time she was seen?" "Yesterday morning when she left for school, but she never made it to school." "So, what, she's missing? Has anybody called the police?" "Yes!" Yolanda responded. "They said she have to be missing for twenty-four hours before they can classify her as a missing person. Mrs. Jones said they were acting like she was a run away or something." Nathan was speechless for a second. "Mom I'm coming home! Honey are you sure?" Yolanda asked her son. "I think, no mom I know something's wrong!" Nathan hung up the phone, he packed as much as he could as fast as he could and jumped in his car. If anything has happened to Nashunta, Lameka Ima find and kill your ass. Nathan thought to as he sped away.

The sky outside turned from dark to light as Mrs. Jones sat staring out the front window with Yolanda by her side. "Would you like some coffee?" Yolanda asked as Mr. Jones came down the stairs as stood next to his wife.

The overwhelming feeling of guilt hit him, and he wanted to breakdown. Mike knew he had to be strong for his family. He whispers morning to his wife, but she didn't move or respond to his presence. He looked at Yolanda for some kind of validation, but she couldn't offer him any. "I can't sit around here Yolanda, I'll go insane." "That's understandable." Yolanda replied. "Call me if anything!" Mr. Jones said. Yolanda nodded her head. He bends down kissed his unresponsive wife on the forehead said he loved her and was out the door. Mr. Jones got in his car and drove away. He only made it as far as the stop sign before he broke down. The tears came down in huge drops like massive raindrops during a summer thunder storm. Heavenly father I'm sorry! My daughter tried to speak to me and I wouldn't listen If you bring my child home safe to me I promise I'll accept her just the way you made her.

Mr. Jones prayed out loud through the sobs. Lord please give me a chance to fix it with my daughter. In Jesus name I pray amen. Realizing he was still sitting at the stop sign Mr. Jones wiped his face and drove off.

Arriving at work Mr. Jones went directly into his office. Before he even put his things down good he was on the phone calling home. Yolanda picked up the phone on the second ring. "Hey Yolanda, anything yet?" Mr. Jones inquired. "No! I tried calling her phone again, but now it's saying her voicemail is full. How's Monica doing?" "She hasn't shown any change Mike. She hasn't moved from in front of the window at all this morning." "Yolanda I'm at a loss, I don't know what to do." "I think you should call the police again." Yolanda said. "I have the card, I'll call the detective right now." Mr. Jones was about to end the call but thought twice. "Yolanda!" "Yes Mike?" "Thanks for being here!" he said. "There's no other place I would have been." Yolanda replied. There was pause as they both silently appreciated each other.

Mr. Jones sat in his chair staring at the card the officers had given him the night before. He wiped his tears and cleared his throat before he picked up the phone to call the number on the card. The phone rung several times before the pleasant feminine voice answered. "Good morning missing persons, this is Detective N. Moss speaking. How can I help you?" "Um, morning! I'm Mike Jones, I was given your card by a couple of officers that were at my house last night." "Hey Mr. Jones, yes, I have your file right in front of me. I was about to give you guys a call this morning. So, Mr. Jones please tell me your calling with good news." "I wish that I can say that I was."

Mr. Jones stated. "Nashunta still hasn't come home. We continue to try to reach her by phone but now her voicemail is saying that it's full. This is so unlike my daughter; her phone is her lifeline. Even more so she would never willingly make us worry like this. If she was upset with us she would have at least called her sister to say she was alright." Detective Moss had a bad feeling in the pit of her stomach. Hearing the emotions of a father for his daughter touched her heart. This is exactly why she chose this field to dedicate her life.

"Alright Mr. Jones you have my undivided attention. Now all I want you to do is focus on your family let me take over and handle the rest. I'll put an APB out for Nashunta." Detective Moss stated. "If you want better results I think you should involve the media. I don't know if my wife is well enough to face the media." Mr. Jones replied. "I completely understand but if you get your daughter's face out there we'll have more than just the police looking for her." Mr. Jones let out a sigh. "Ok," he agreed. "Thank you so much!" Mr. Jones said. "No thanks needed this is what I do! I'll do everything in my power to help your family. I'll be contacting you soon," Officer Moss stated and ended the call. Detective Moss put the APB out for Nashunta. Afterward she called a connect she had at the news station. An hour later her connect called back with news of a press conference at the Jones' house around noon that day. Detective Moss thanked her friend and promised she'd spring for lunch the next time they had mutual free time. She grabbed her things and rushed out the door.

Detective Moss arrived at the Jones' house to get some more information and inform them about the press conference. "Who is it?" Yolanda called from the other side of the door. "Detective Moss ma'am!" "Do you have any information about Nashunta?" Yolanda asked before she could get the door opened completely. "Unfortunately, I don't, but I spoke to your husband this morning and I was wondering if I could speak with you a moment." "Oh no, I'm not Mrs. Jones! I'm a close friend of the family." "Well is Mrs. Jones available?" Detective Moss asked "I'm sorry" Yolanda said stepping to the side to allow the Detective room to gain entrance in the door. "She's not doing too good." Yolanda said over her shoulder. "She's been sitting in the window since last night, I'm worried about her." "Do you think she'll be able to speak to me?" Detective Moss said as they entered the room where Mrs. Jones sat staring into oblivion. "There is nothing wrong with my mouth!" Mrs. Jones spoke out of the blue. "I do apologize ma'am would you mind if I spoke with you a moment? I know this is a difficult time right now. I just want to make sure we're all on the same page."

Mrs. Jones agreed and offered the Detective a seat. "I spoke with your husband this morning we discussed the option of a press conference. I wanted to get Nashunta's face out there so the police wouldn't be the only people out looking for her. If you're up to it there's a press conference scheduled for noon today in front of your house." The tears built up inside Mrs. Jones eyes. Again she couldn't believe the conversation she was having in her living room. Was she really about to have a press conference because her child was missing? The room was completely quiet and still except for the ticking of the clock on the wall. The front door opened, and everyone held their breath. After a tensed couple of seconds Mr. Jones walked into the area where everyone was sitting.

I need to ask some more questions because I need a little more information. Detective Moss said. "Is there anyone who might want to hurt you or any member of your family?" she asked looking mainly at Mr. Jones. "No!" They both said in unison. "No, I don't know of anyone who would what to hurt us," Mr. Jones replied putting his arm around his wife the thought of someone wanting to deliberately harm his family sent chills down his spine. "Is Nashunta dating anyone right now?" The detective continued. Yolanda and Monica Looked at each other. "Well she's been talking to Yolanda's son but no one else that we know of," Mrs. Jones said. "Where's your son?" Detective Moss said focusing her attention on Yolanda. "He's away at college, but... Before Yolanda could finish her sentence, the detective cut her off. "Have you spoken to him since Nashunta disappearance?' "Yes, I called him right after Monica called me." "What was his initial reaction?" "He was shocked and said he was coming home." "Do you think Nashunta could have run away to be with him?" "No! Nathan wouldn't let Nashunta worry her family like this! If he knew her where abouts he would have said so!" Yolanda shouted coming to defense for her son. "I'm not tryna hit a nerve but I'm just tryna catch a lead."

Detective Moss turned back to the couple sitting across from her. "Do you mind if I look around Nashunta's room?" "No, of course not." Mr. Jones said get up to lead the way to Nashunta's room. Mr. Jones walked up the stairs with Detective Moss in tow. He walked up to the door to Nashunta's room and stopped. "Are you ok sir?" she asked. "Detective its funny how you never pay attention to certain things until it's too late. My daughter loved body sprays, she would always run to the mall when they had a new fragrance she wanted to try." "I understand, but what brought that memory to you?" The detective asked. "I say that because just as we walked up I could smell her just as if she was standing next to me." The hair on the back of detective Moss' neck stood on end. She was a firm believer in the spirit world, but she didn't want to believe that Nashunta was a part of that world. As Mr. Jones opened the door there was a gush of cold air that rushed past them. Detective Moss shook her head for an instant she could have sworn she smelled the enchanted aroma of cucumber melon. She dismissed the thought and followed Mr. Jones into the room.

At first glance everything seemed to be in order, maybe cleaner than the average teen age girl's room would be. Detective Moss looked around the room, she used her experience to identify things that might seem out of place. She walked past the mirror and saw the lip imprint left on it. Walking further into the room she was walking past the closet and the smell of cucumber melon fully engulfed her. "Mr. Jones what was Nashunta's favorite fragrance? Mr. Jones looked at the Detective. "Um something fruity, cucumber something I can't remember." he said. Detective Moss felt as though Nashunta was standing in front of her. She stepped forth and opened the closet. She found the string and pulled the light on. Detective Moss moved the clothes from side to side, she didn't know what Nashunta wanted her to find. She was about to turn to leave but something caught her attention. Detective Moss bent down and grabbed a trash bag from the back of the closet. "What's that?" Mr. Jones asked as the Detective came out the closet holding the bag. "It may be nothing, but do I have your permission to open it." "Yes of course!" Mr. Jones replied. "If we find something I'm gonna have to ask you not to touch anything." Detective Moss tore open the bag and poured the contents out on the bed. The room was eerily silent as they stared down at the things on the bed. The bag was filled with cut up and beheaded teddy bears, cut up photographs, and torn up letters. There was one letter that was still intact, the detective pulled a glove from her pocket and picked it up. The letter was written by Nashunta to someone named Lameka. The Detective flipped the letter over and in large letters written on the back said "It ain't over until I say!"

"Mr. Jones did Nashunta have any female friends she hung out very closely with?" "No! I don't know!" "What's that have to do with anything?" "I think your daughter was being stalked! Don't touch anything!" Detective

Moss said as she pulled out her phone. "Hey this is Moss can I get a CSI team at 4088 Magnolia Lane? It's a possible abduction! ASAP, I mean I need this like yesterday!" She ended the call and turned back to Mr. Jones. "We need to leave this room; I'm making it a crime scene." "Detective my daughter wasn't kidnapped from the house we all watched her leave". "Yes, I understand that but the person that did this was in this room. My guess is they came through the window." "I'm not understanding what's going on here! Mr. Jones said looking from the bed to Detective Moss. "I'll explain once we get back down stairs."

Detective Moss and Mr. Jones entered the room where Yolanda and Mrs. Jones were sitting. "What's wrong?" Yolanda asked seeing the looks on their faces. "I've dispatched a CSI unit to come to the house." Detective Moss stated. "What is that and why are they coming here?" Mrs. Jones asked. "It's a crime scene investigation unit and I called them because I have reason to believe your daughter was being stalked. While we were up in Nashunta's room we found a bag full of cut up teddy bears, pictures, and letters that was hidden inside of her closet." "Why would she hide something like that?" Mrs. Jones asked more to her husband than anyone else. "This may be hard to hear especially from a stranger, but I think your daughter may have been gay. I think she may have been dating or was involved with a girl named Lameka. Does this name ring any bells? Maybe a friend she hung out with a lot?" Detective Moss asked looking around the room for some answers.

"Wait! Come to think about it she was acting different lately." Mrs. Jones said walking over and sitting down next to Detective Moss. "I thought she was just missing Nathan since he had gone back to school." "We're talking about your son Nathan, right?" Detective Moss said pointing at Yolanda. "Yes!" Yolanda replied. "So, Nathan and Nashunta were dating?" "Yes, we hooked them up!" Mrs. Jones and Yolanda said sounding so sure of themselves. These people haven't a clue about their kid. Detective Moss thought to herself. "Look from where I'm sitting my guess is that your daughter was gay. My intuition also tells me that her girlfriend was a girl named Lameka. I'm also guessing that this thing between her and Nathan was just a cover relationship to keep you guys off her back."

"You have no clue of who my daughter is!" Mrs. Jones snapped as she stood and walked to the window. "Pardon my bluntness, but I feel that it is you who don't have a clue of who your daughter is. I'm not here making these thinks up, the facts are right here in your face." The knock on the door cut through the room catching everyone off guard. "I'll go see who that is." Yolanda said heading for the foyer. "Hopefully it's the CSI unit I called for." Detective Moss said getting up and following Yolanda out the room.

Mr. Jones walked over to where his wife was standing at the window. "Mike how dare her come into our home and say these things about my baby." "Monica you know as well as I do that the detective is right about Nashunta. We need to accept what we've heard and move on. We have to work together to bring our baby home." Mike Jones grabbed his wife pulling her to him. Mrs. Jones let her husband envelope her in his powerful arms. For the first time since Nashunta's disappearance she felt how weary her body was. "Sweetheart you really need to get some rest." Mr. Jones whispered into her ear. "I know but my mind won't let me." He kissed her forehead and held his wife tight.

15

Ticking Time Bomb

Raven

Weeks went by and the tension between both couples was still visible. Tonya lay in bed staring at the ceiling. The anger inside her was like a slow burning fire. The moment you think you've extinguished it you turn your back and it blazes back up. She just couldn't get past the thought of Stacey touching her woman. I don't know if they had sex but whatever happened I'm gonna figure it out. Tonya closed her eyes but all she saw was Stacey's arms wrapped around Raven. She yelled but there was no sound escaping from her lips. She ran towards them, but her body never left the spot she stood in. Stacey's head turned into a wolf's face and he stared at Tonya as he licked Raven with his gigantic carnivorous tongue. The alarm clocked blared shanking Tonya back into the real world.

Stacy tried everything in his power to get back into Monique's good graces. He sent flowers to her house, bought expensive gifts, and went out his way to make her feel special. Stacey sat on the edge of his bed holding his phone. He was debating on calling her or not. They had said they wouldn't do the love thing, but still she had said she loved him. "Fuck it!" He swore out loud and dialed Monique's number. When Monique answered the phone, she didn't sound like her normal self. "What's wrong babe?" Stacey asked hearing the weak coarseness of her tone. "I think I'm gonna have to take a rain check on our date today. I think I'm catching the flu or something." "You sure?" Stacey replied sounding more disappointed than he wanted to. "Yeah, I've been so sick these past few days." "Well ok I hope you feel better, call me a little later when you feel up to talking." "Thanks Stacey." Monique said ending the call.

Before she could lay her head back on the pillow she had to jump up and make a mad dash for the bathroom. Monique bowled Eric over as she was running by to make it to the toilet. "Are you ok Miss Thang?" Eric asked as he was picking his things up off the floor. He looked in the door after he received no response. Monique was on her knees face down praying to the porcelain god. "Oh, chile did you eat something bad?" "I haven't been able to eat anything!" Monique replied. "Oh, Bitch please don't tell me you have a stomach virus!" Eric said moving away and grabbing the Lysol can. "It's not funny Eric I'm really sick!" Monique said pulling herself up off the floor. "You don't think you might be pregnant, do you?" His words hit her knocking her breath away. Monique ran back to her room. Grabbing her phone, she pulled up her calendar. What! Unsure of what she was seeing. "Eric what's todays date?" The reply she heard sent shockwaves through her. She turned back to Eric, "I missed my period."

No matter what Raven was going through at work she always put her best face forward. "Good Morning! How can I assist you?" She always performed well for the public. Despite how she felt on the inside the world always saw a happy Raven. Her smile was big and bright but inside she was terrified. Tonya had choked her, and Raven didn't know how to deal with that. She knew she loved Tonya if she could just move past this Stacey thing she was stuck on. Raven had let her mind drift away. "Miss! Excuse me Miss!" The lady yelled from the other side of the safety glass. "I'm sorry ma'am, how can I help you today?" "I would like to make a deposit." The lady said irritably. "Yes, ma'am I apologize I can assist you with that." Raven swiftly assisted the customer, but as soon as the lady walked away Joyce, Raven's supervisor walked over. "Is there something the matter with you dear?" "No not at all. Why would you ask?" "It just seems like your head has been up in the clouds lately. That's not usually like you." Joyce said. "I'm fine just a little tired, but I assure you it won't happen again."

Eric and Monique stood anxiously in line at the CVS. Monique knew she had been trying to get pregnant on purpose, but she didn't think it would really work. What the fuck had she done! She screamed to herself. She paid for her test and they headed back to the car. "Can I confess something to you?" Monique asked as she started the car. "You know you can tell me anything." "I know but I don't want you judging me." "I can't make you any promises especially if you've done something stupid." Eric replied holding up the pregnancy test. "I felt like I was losing it all!" Monique yelled. "Losing what? Stacey?" Eric asked confused. "Yes! He was always talking about his family, Raven, and his kids." "Monique what did you do?" Eric asked. "I stopped taking my birth control pills." Monique replied. "When did you make that decision? You told me that you weren't in love with Stacey!" "I love him yes, but I love my security more. I thought that if we had a baby he would stop thinking about that bitch Raven and focus back on me." "How the hell did you get Stacey to sleep with you without a condom?" Monique looked up at Eric. "I've been poking holes in his condoms for months." "What! How the hell are you gonna convince Stacey you're having his baby if y'all been using condoms the whole fucking time." "I don't know! I didn't think that part through." "Oh my God! Monique your stupid as hell!" Eric grabbed his friend and hugged her tight. "First things first let's go take this test."

Tonya had to go to the gun range today, so she could qualify for her annual accreditation. She had to get her head off this, so she could focus. She pulled up at the range and parked her car. Several of her coworker had already arrived before her. She walked inside found her designated area and signed in. Instead of sitting with the crowd Tonya chose to sit by herself, she wasn't in the mood for pleasantries. Almost half an hour later they were ready to begin. The instructor called off everybody's name and the order of which they would shoot. Tonya had number fifteen which was fine with her just as long as she wasn't first. She hated to be the first in line to shoot. Tonya stood back and watched her coworkers take their turn at the targets. Standing there watching, Tonya's mind drifted off to her and Raven. Deep down inside she knew she loved Raven. I think it's time for me to move past this stupid shit. I can't let this nigga know how he can affect me. Tonya was so deep in thought that she didn't hear the instructor call her. "Head out of the clouds officer they're calling you." Tonya got set up and aimed at the target, before she could fire the target turned into Stacey. She lowered her gun and wiped her eyes. "What's wrong Officer? We can't wait all day on you!" The instructor yelled from the side. Tonya decided to use that to her advantage she aimed right between Stacey's eyes and pulled the trigger. She hit the target from every distance. Tonya left the range feeling 100% better. I'm not giving Stacey my family she jumped in her car and headed home to wait on Raven.

Monique sat on the toilet peeing on the little plastic stick that held her future. Eric sat on the tub reading the box and smoking a blunt. It says you have to lay it flat once you've peed on it and wait for several minutes. After a few minutes you will either see a line in one window for a negative result or a line in both windows indicating a positive result. Monique walked over to the sink laid the test on a napkin and washed her hands. She grabbed the blunt from Eric. Well we can't just sit in here it's gonna drive us crazy.

Stacey was in the store picking up some soup and things to take over to Monique. He was standing undecided about a bouquet of flowers when his phone started ringing. The ringtone indicated it was Raven. "Hello!" Stacey said into the phone. "Hey, I'm on the way to drop the kids off." "Oh shit! Damn I'm sorry Raven!" "Don't tell me you forgot about your kids." Raven yelled into the phone. "No!" Stacey lied. "I just lost track of time. I'm just in the store grabbing dinner. Let me pay for this stuff and I'll be heading that way." "That's fine." Raven said and ended the call. Stacey added frozen pizzas and some juice to his basket. On his way out the door he grabbed a couple of movies from the red box. He left the store and headed home, he would get the kids, and then take the stuff over to Monique.

Tonya arrived at home and thought she would cook dinner for Raven to surprise her. She went upstairs and jumped in the shower. Tonya let the water cascade down her body. Lost in thought she closed her eyes to succumb to her day dream. The sound of a gunshot rang through Tonya's head. Jerking open her eyes Tonya had to hold on to the curtain rod and the wall to steady herself. She gasped for breath and her hands were shaking uncontrollably. She regained herself finished showering and got out. She looked at her reflection in the mirror. Lord please don't let that dream come true. Tonya quickly dressed, cleaned up her mess, and headed to the kitchen to whip something up for her queen.

"I can't look Eric please go look for me." Monique and Eric sat on the sofa neither one of them wanted to venture in the bathroom for the results. "Ugh bitch this is sad!" Eric said getting up and stomping into the bathroom. Seconds felt like an eternity to Monique as she waited for Eric to check the results. "Monique get your ass in here now!" Eric shouted. Monique jumped from the sofa and dashed into the bathroom. Eric was bent looking over the test on the sink. "Where's the box bitch?" "I don't know!" Monique shouted as she ran back to the living to grab the box. "How many lines do you see?" She asked reading the paper from the box. "Two!" Eric said. "Please tell me you're lying?" "What does the paper say?" Eric said coming over and taking the paper from the speechless Monique. They stood silent in the middle of the bathroom. Neither one wanted to verbally admit the obvious. Monique sank down to the floor. Eric came over to offer as much support as he could. "What are you gonna do?" Monique looked up at her friend "I'm not sure of anything at the moment. Fuck it!" Monique yelled. "It's now or never." She got to her feet, packed up the test, she grabbed her things, and headed for the door. "Where you going?" Eric yelled behind her. "I guess I'm going to see what Stacey has to say about all this." She turned and walked out the door.

Raven sat outside waiting on Stacey to get home. She stopped and got the kids McDonalds', so they were preoccupied at the moment. Raven took the opportunity to close her eyes and rest since she hadn't been sleeping well. "Daddy!" The kids yelled simultaneously as they jumped up and down. The car shaking woke Raven from her slumber. "Ah now! Sit down or y'all gonna get it!" she shouted. "It's Daddy!" Omari pointed at Stacey as he walked up to the car. Before Raven had a chance to protest they were out the car bags in hand running to their father. Raven rolled down her window as Stacey approached. "Do you have a moment?" Stacey said into the open window. "Sure!" Raven replied. She rolled up the window and got out of the car. "Daddy can we go inside?" the kids yelled. "Love you mommy!" Kelly said giving her a hug. Seeing the show of affection stopped Omari in his tracks. He turned and ran back to his mother. "Love you too mommy!" But before she had a chance to reply they had dashed off toward the house. "How are you doing?" Stacey asked. "I'm good." She replied. Stacey looked Raven over. "Are you sure because you look tired?" "Yeah, I'm sure just had a few restless nights." "I've known you for a long time and I still know when you're lying." Raven dropped her head and before she knew it she was crying. Stacey came over and embraced her, despite what they went through they were still friends.

Monique drove as fast as she could her nerves were on end. She searched every aspect of her brain for the right word to say. In spite of her best efforts to calm herself the nervousness got the better of her. She had to pull over quickly, so she wouldn't throw up inside the car. Monique rinsed her mouth out with a bottle of water she had in the car. She tossed in some gun and lit a Newport. Once her stomach settled enough she started her car and was back rolling on her way to Stacey's house. Monique reached Stacey's house and the moment she turned the corner her heart felt like it exploded in her chest. Stacey had his arms wrapped around Raven with her head on his chest. Stacey you lying son of a bitch! Oh, I love you Monique! It's over between me and Raven! The anger inside Monique erupted. After all she had went through this nigga was still stuck on this bitch. The devil works so rapidly, and he uses even the slightest spark of anger to do his work. Monique quickly remembered the picture she had taken of Stacey and Raven kissing. Before she had a chance to think about the consequences of her actions she forwarded the picture to Tonya. Monique parked her car on the street on the opposite side of Stacey's house. She reached inside her purse and found a napkin and a pen. On the napkin she wrote her name in big letters wrapped it around the pregnancy test with a rubber band from her hair. Monique jumped out the car and snuck around the back of the house to where Stacey's car was in the drive way. Searching the ground, she found the biggest rock she could safely carry. Taking the rock and chunking it as hard as she could Monique sent the rock careening through the window of Stacey's vehicle. She tossed the test in through the window and dashed back behind the house to her car. Monique managed to make it back to her car before anyone came around the house. She cranked her car and sped off.

Stacey was enjoying the feeling of Raven in his arms when he heard the sound of glass breaking. At first, he thought the kids in the house had broken something. Him and Raven both broke into a full run to see what had happened. By the time they reached the porch the kids were running out the house. "What happened are you guys alright?" Raven asked before Stacey could speak. "We heard glass breaking and we thought you were fighting." Everybody was standing around looking dumbfounded. The sound of tires screeching on the other side of the house broke everyone from their spell. "Stay here with the kids I'll go check it out." he said over his shoulder. Raven took the kids back inside while Stacy went to check things out. Stacey went behind the house, but nothing seemed out of place. It wasn't until he came back around did he notice the glass on the ground by his truck. "What the fuck!" Raven heard the words penetrate the walls. "Stay here" she told her kids and she ran outside to see what had happened. Once outside she saw Stacey standing by his car with his hands on his head. "What happened?" She asked him. "Somebody broke my fucking window!" He yelled. "Did Tonya know you were coming over here? Did she follow you?" "Of course, Tonya knew I was coming over here, but she had to go to the gun range today. She was still there when I brought the kids here." "Shouldn't you call the police or something?" Raven asked. "I swear if I find out that that bitch of a girlfriend of yours had anything to do with this Ima fuck her up!" "I assure you Tonya had nothing to do with this." Stacey opened the door and let the glass fall onto the ground. "What's that?" Raven asked. "What?" Stacey replied harshly. "On the floor. Was that always there?" He looked down and grabbed the napkin. "I don't know where that came from. It looks like a pregnancy test!" Raven said looking at Stacey. Taking off the rubber band he opened the napkin. Monique's name was written in big letters on the napkin. Stacey looked at the test then the napkin and finally up at Raven. "What the fuck?" "Well I guess you have your culprit! Looks like you might need to go and call her. If you need to talk just call me later." Raven turned and walked back to her car.

Tonya was in the kitchen music blaring dancing around like a teenager in love. Stephanie Mills sang about how good she felt as Tonya browned the chicken breast on the stove top. The crescent rolls fluffed up in the oven and a magnificent salad chilled in the fridge. Everything was coming together, and she was so engulfed in what she was doing that she didn't hear the phone announce that a text message had arrived. After everything was perfectly set up she grabbed her drink made of lemon aid spiked with chilled Grey Goose from the fridge and proceeded into the living room. She popped in a slow jam CD and settled back against the sofa to await her love. Music swirled around the room creating the perfect ambiance. Song after song blared from the speakers as the time ticked away. Tonya began to worry what was taking Raven so long and the notion to call jumped into her thoughts. Damn my phone! Tonya thought as she patted herself down. Retracing her steps, she found her phone on the counter where she had laid it before washing her hands to cook. With the phone back in her possession she returned back to her comfort zone on the sofa. Pressing the home button, the icon on the top of the phone indicated that there was a message that needed to be downloaded. Pressing the download button, the message popped up indicating that it was from Monique. What the fuck did she want!

Raven drove home in silence she couldn't help but wonder if Monique saw Stacey consoling her. Enormous butterflies spread their wings and took flight inside her abdomen. Dare she call to inquire about what had happened? The kids were there, she could use them as a means to call. Grabbing her phone Raven dialed Stacey's number as she tried to keep focus on the road. "I can't talk right now!" Stacey yelled before the phone seemingly had a chance to ring. The call ended, and Raven was left speechless.

"What the fuck Monique!" Stacey yelled threw the phone. "Why did you break my window? That shit is gonna cost more than two hundred bucks for the glass and the right tint job!" He continued to rant like a mad man. "To top it all off you telling me you're pregnant. I thought you said that you weren't sleeping with no one else?" The question flew from his mouth one after the other. Monique didn't have a chance to rebut anything he slung her way. "I'm sorry about the window!" She said catching Stacey off guard. He hadn't expected her to own up to what she had done. "I'll pay to have it fixed. I'm just so fucking tired of this little game you keep playing between Raven and me. Seeing your arms wrapped around her was the last straw. Yes, I'm pregnant Stacey and it's yours!" The words penetrated every fiber of Stacey's conscious being. "What!" He screamed like venom from a black mamba. "You can't possibly believe that you're carrying my child? I've used condoms from the first time we've ever laid together. I know what type of female you are, I would never create an offspring with the likes of your mentality." Tears stung Monique's eyes, but she wouldn't give him the satisfaction of hearing her cry. "You can deny it all you want Stacey, but DNA don't lie. If you chose not to accept it now you will pay when it is born." With that Monique slammed the phone shut with everything in her. Tears ran down her face in rapid procession. This is not how it was supposed to be. He should have confessed his love and they were supposed to be a family. Eric heard the sobs and came into the room to check on his friend. "I'm sorry Hun!" He said from the door. "I really fucked it up this time," Monique said "but I bet the bitch Raven gets hers too."

The message had completely downloaded when Tonya heard Raven come in the front door. She laid the phone down to go greet her lover. Raven came around the corner and was stunned to see the dining room set up in its romantic setting. "Does this mean I'm back in your good graces?" "Let's just say I'm open to have that talk." Tonya replied. "How about you go shower and I'll get everything ready." Raven kissed Tonya's lips seductively before she turned and headed for the shower. Tonya quickly went to work putting out the food and pouring the drinks. The buzzing sound completely caught her off guard. Damn I forgot about that text from Monique. Tonya's intentions were to delete the text before Raven returned. She accidently hit the view instead of deleting. The image of Raven immersed in an embrace as Stacey tasted her mouth appeared on the screen. Tonya's heart dropped into her midsection. The breath inside her lungs clung thick in place. The world as she knew it faded to black.

16

The Quiet Before the Storm

Mercedes

Morning came with the sun shining down on the world. Monea lay in her bed staring up at the ceiling. Something inside her couldn't stop thinking about Mercedes. Everything about her drove Monea into a frenzy. The way she stood back in the cafeteria and watched as she walked through always made her heart flutter a bit. Even though she pretended not to notice she always saw her. The smell of her cucumber melon Suave shampoo and conditioner, the way her neck always smelled of whatever body spray she wore that day mixed with coco butter are all things the swirled around her head when she thought about her lady love. Monea touched the bottom of her full plush lips with her index finger as she longed for the taste of Mercedes' strawberries and cream EOS lip balm she always wore. She prayed that whatever it was that was bothering Merccdes would have no effect on where she wanted to take things between them. "Take things between us!" Monea said the words out loud. She let out a breath of air and pushed herself off the bed to go get ready for her rendezvous with Mercedes.

An hour later Monea was dressed in a casual but sexy sundress that hugged in all the right places. The color was an orange that looked like it was kissed by the sun. she complimented the dress with a strappy wedge sandal that was flashy enough for a night on the town and comfortable enough for a long walk in the park. She checked herself in the mirror grabbed her things and headed out the door. She made it right around the corner from Mercedes' house, but she couldn't find the address to the place they were supposed to meet. Grabbing her phone Monea dialed Mercedes' number. After the fourth ring the answering service picked up. She tried several times with the same outcome. Seeing that it was still early Monea took a chance hoping she haven't left home yet.

Five minutes later she pulled next to Mercedes's car, checked her face in the mirror, and got out the car. Monea opened the door to the front stairwell of Mercedes' apartment building and walked in. After the door closed Monea started to see why Mercedes said she never used this way. Even with the small window at the end of the hall on each landing it was still dark. After her eyes adjusted to the darkness Monea started her way up the two landings of stairs to get to Mercedes' door. Halfway up the second set of steps on the first landing the hallway lit up indicating the door to the outside had opened. Monea paid no mind and continued moving toward the second landing.

Whoever came in the door was moving at a very fast pace, running almost. They sounded as though they were right behind her and something inside her began to feel uneasy. She reached for her phone but realized in her rush she left her phone as well as her purse that contained her pepper spray on the seat in her car. She placed her keys between her fingers in a last effort to defend herself if she had to. Monea stepped to the side just as a tall slender gentleman came in to view. "excuse me miss lady" he said as he went past. Monea leaned against the wall and let out the breath she had been holding in and she relaxed her guard. She smiled to herself and turned to continue on her way when she was forcefully snatched up.

Mercedes woke up and the sun was shining, not only outside but also in her heart. The kids had gone over friend's houses for the weekend because she wanted no distractions later. She planned on making up to Monea all night and all morning too. The thought of making up to Monea made moisture form in her lower region. She slides her hands inside her underwear and was horrified. She desperately needed to manicure her grass. Mercedes checked the time and made a mad dash for the shower. Once in the bathroom Mercedes turned on her little bathroom radio and proceeded to dance and sing her way to cleanliness.

It took way too long to finish shaving, seeming that she had grossly underestimated the amount of hair that she had accumulated. Mercedes toweled off and headed back to the room to dress. After moisturizing her body Mercedes stood in her birthday suit staring in her closet, she did know what she wanted to wear. Mercedes was inside her closet matching outfits together. She didn't notice her phone which she had put on silent last night when Hakeem started calling, flashing indicating a call coming through. By the time she was finished in the closet, clothes covered the entire bed including the phone which continued to ring.

When everything was all said and done Mercedes went with light denim leggings coupled with a white and blue halter top. She brushed her hair into a side ponytail with long curls the lay perfectly at her breast. Mercedes brushed her teeth, did her makeup and double checked herself in the mirror. "What time is it?" She said a tad bit to loud inside her own head. It was at this moment Mercedes realized she had not seen her phone in hours. After searching under mounds of clothes, tops, bras, and countless pairs of lace thongs Mercedes finally found her missing device. "Fuck!" Mercedes screamed when she realized that she had three missed calls from Monea from over thirty minutes ago.

As quickly as her fingers could move, Mercedes dialed Monea's number. The answering service chimed in after a few rings. The pit of Mercedes' stomach began to twist in knots. She redialed the number only to get the same result, but this time she left a message. After the beep she spoke with a shaky tongue. "Hey beautiful, I was in the shower when you called." "I really hope you weren't calling to cancel on me." She said with a small chuckle. There was a small awkward moment of silence. "Well I'm just gonna head to the place, hope to either hear from or see you soon." Mercedes ended the call and let out a stressful breath of air. Grabbing her smokes off the table, she lit it and took a drag so deep she could feel the nicotine racing through her tugging at the knots in her stomach.

Mercedes tried Monea one more time as she finished smoking. The same result, Mercedes put out her cigarette in the ashtray, and grabbed her things. On second thought she went back to check her appearance in the mirror. Just as she was about turn and leave out her room she heard the doorbell ringing. The doorbell ringing meant someone was at her front door, which was odd since anyone who knew her knew how much she hated that entrance. With that she had only two opinions of who it could be, personnel from the leasing office or Jehovah Witnesses. She didn't have time for either at the moment. Her plan was to see who it was and then silently creep out the back door. So, without making a peep Mercedes tiptoed to the door and peered through the peephole. Everything in Mercedes radiated with joy, because even though the person on the other side of the door had their head down she knew at first glance it was Monea. Forgetting about the pleasantries of who is its, Mercedes hurried with the deadbolt locks to free the door from its bondages.

Mercedes adorned the biggest smile she could muster and swung open the door. Monea lifted her head and it stopped Mercedes in her tracks. Monea once perfect makeup now ran down her checks as black tears that streaked their way all the way down to the top of her dress. Mercedes reached out her hand to grab for her but before she had the chance to move Monea was forcefully pushed towards her and the both fell back inside the door.

Hakeem pulled up at in front of Mercedes's apartment, turned off the engine, and adjusted the seat. He had no clue as to where his current actions were taking him. He wanted to teach his ex a lesson, he just didn't know how. As Hakeem took his time running ideas through his head he took out a fresh pack of Newport's. He flipped the pack over smacked them across his hand a few times to settle the tobacco in the cigarettes, then torn off the plastic wrapper. After placing the cigarette between his lips, he realized he couldn't find his lighter. He patted all his pockets, felt between the seats, even checked the center console, with no luck. I don't know what it is about jonesing for nicotine, but no one wants to smoke worse than a person that can't find their lighter. The more he searched for the lighter the worst the need became for him to have it. Hakeem was about to crank the car and drive to the closet store when a young man came around the dumpster to dump his trash with a lit Newport blowing in the wind. "Ah yo!" Hakeem said as he got out the car. "Can I get a light from you?"

The young man handed Hakeem a lighter and they both stood there talking and enjoying their cigarettes as if they've known each other for years. Once he finished his smoke the guys excused himself and headed back the way he came. The young man stopped suddenly turned around and ran back towards Hakeem. Not knowing what to expect Hakeem slide his hand inside of his pocket and let his hand rest on the small handgun he kept there. "I thought you might could use these." The young man said as he produced a book of matches and handed them over to Hakeem. "Good looking out" Hakeem said showing his gratitude.

Hakeem stood there alone behind the dumpster finishing his cigarette. Just as he was about to turn back to the car, Monea flew passed in her car, jumped out and headed toward Mercedes' apartment. The sight of his ex's lesbian lover enraged him. He took one more drag from his cigarette and flicked it to the ground. He looked around making sure no one was insight and he headed in the direction right behind her. Once inside the dark stairwell he had to let his eyes get adjusted to the darkness.

Hakeem took the steps two at a time and he quickly caught up to Monea. However, he slowed his pace as he came up behind her. He could have easily taken her then, but he passed her instead and waited as she relaxed and lowered her guard. He snatched her up quickly and the force knocked her into a corner. Hakeem had the handgun that was once inside his pocket pressed to the side of Monea's temple. "Ok Bitch, if you want to make it out of this do exactly as I say!" Monea didn't know what to do, in her mind she was about to be raped in the dark stairwell that her future girlfriend warned her about using.

With the gun still pressed against her temple, Hakeem took his free hand and pressed it firmly around Monea's neck. "You are going to Mercedes's door and ring the bell." He spoke slow but harsh with his lips inches from her ear. "If you say anything or if I even think your lips are moving, the next thing you'll see will be your GOD." He ushered his captive to her spot and positioned himself just outside the line of sight of the peephole. Monea stood frozen in place, she was so afraid that she never reached up to ring the bell. Hakeem took one hand off the gun to ring the bell.

The tension swam around them thick and heavy. Hakeem aimed the gun directly at the side of Monea's face. A strong wind and he could've ended Monea with a simple pull of a trigger. Monea stood there repeating the Lord's prayer as she desperately tried not to wet herself. The seconds it took for Mercedes to come to the door seemed like it was never ending. Without warning the door swung open. Mercedes must have saw her through the peephole. At that moment the world around them moved in slow motion. They were like three synchronized swimmers preforming a well-choreographed routine. As Mercedes reached for Monea, she lurched forward and they both tumbled to the ground. Hakeem stepped from around the door and stood towering over the both of them.

It was like an image from one of her nightmares, Mercedes couldn't decipher dream from reality. Her breath was caught in her chest. Her brain had ceased to function, she had lost all ability to convert oxygen into carbon dioxide. Everything around her faded from existence, her apartment, the outside stairwell, as well as Monea. There was only the two of them, her and

Hakeem. Mercedes was so focused on Hakeem's face that she didn't see the gun he had pointed down at them.

Hakeem stepped inside the doorway like a television character coming to life. Without taking his eyes off the frighten ladies cowering on the floor he shut the door. He walked up to Mercedes, took her face in his fingers, and brought it so close to his that she could smell the essence of alcohol and tobacco on his breath. "I bet you thought when you left it was gonna be the last time you saw me, huh?" Hakeem asked. Before Mercedes could muster up the voice to speak Hakeem raised his hand and came down hard with the butt of the gun. The force of the impact of the gun hitting the side of Mercedes' face flung her backwards onto the floor causing instant blackness.

17

Desperately Seeking Answers

Nashunta

Yolanda opened the front door to find her son standing in front of her. "Oh, Nathan I'm so glad to see you." "Have they heard anything about Nashunta?" He asked even before he embraced his mom with a greeting. "No but there's a detective here and they are supposed to have a news conference today. "I must speak to the detective" Nathan demanded as he rushed past his mother and into the Jones' house. Nathan stormed into the living room and startled everyone upon his entrance. "Nathan!" Mrs. Jones yelled breathlessly as she raced to welcome him. "Has Nashunta called you? Do you know where she is?" The questions continued to slide off her tongue like melted ice cream.

"Mrs. Jones, I know you're desperate to find your daughter, but you must let me do my job." Detective Moss said standing to greet Nathan. "How are you doing, Nathan I presume?" Without giving Nathan time to respond to the question she continued. "I'm Detective Moss and I would like to ask you a couple of questions. Would you like to go somewhere private or is it ok to stay here?" "We can stay here" Nathan said "I have nothing to hide." "It has been brought to my attention that you and Nashunta were romantically involved." "We were friends, I wouldn't say that we were involved romantically." So, you guys were only friends? Did she tell you things about her private life she couldn't tell her parents? "Yes, she often told me that I was her only outlet and that she had no one else to talk to." "If I can be so open Nathan but are you gay?" "What?" Yolanda screamed out. "My son is not on trial here!" "Mother it's quite alright, it's time for some truth in this house. Hidden secrets have already caused enough pain."

"Yes, Detective Moss I am gay and so was Nashunta. Our families were so hell bent on making us straight that we had come up with a plan to start a fake relationship, so our parents would be happy, and we can live in peace." The rest of the room sat in silence as Nathan spoke. All three adults in the room knew that the words being spoken were the truth. Detective Moss didn't want to look around the room in hopes of not letting Nathan lose his nerve. "Nathan do you know wither or not Nashunta was seeing someone?" "When I first met Nashunta she was involved with a girl named Lameka." Hearing the name was like a slap in the face for Mrs. Jones. She couldn't bring herself to make eye contact with the detective. She already knew the things that the detective said was true, but she didn't want to believe them. "Do you know Lameka's last name?" "Unfortunately, detective I don't." Nathan replied. "I do know this if something has happened to Nashunta Lameka is the first one you need to look for." "What makes you say that?" Detective Moss asked as she sat down directly in front of Nathan as to not miss a word coming from his mouth. "On the night of our first date, Nashunta said she swore she saw Lameka following us. Then a few days after that Nashunta called me frantic saying she needed me to pick her up. I agreed and when I arrived I found a hysterical Nashunta. She looked like she had been beaten up. When I got her to the safety of my mom's house, she confessed that that wasn't the first time Lameka had beaten her up." "At any of these events did you see Lameka?" Detective Moss asked. "I never saw any bruises on Nashunta!" Mrs. Jones stated. "If my daughter was being abused I would have known, it. How could I not have known!" "There is no need for blame, sometimes parents see only what they want." Nathan commented looking up at his mother. "Nashunta told me how good she had become at concealing the black eyes and bruises from you. No offense but she said that the two of you were so wrapped up in your perfect life that you guys never notice anything. She said that she could give birth in her room where she and the baby could live undetected." Detective Moss took this time to interject. "Did you witness any events that you personally saw Lameka?" "Well on the day I was supposed to leave going back to college I came outside, and my tires were slashed." "I remember that!" Yolanda yelled. "Are you saying that psycho knows where we live?" "At first, I didn't cast blame on anyone because I didn't want to believe it. However, when I went to Nashunta and told her what happened that was the first name that came out her mouth. We both came to the conclusion that she had been following us around and I told Nashunta to be careful and she walked me outside to my car. While we were talking a car sped by barely missed us with a bottle. I had to throw both Nashunta and myself to the ground. I didn't recognize the car, but she immediately said that it was Lameka."

"Did Nashunta say that Lameka was stalking her?" "No but the last time I spoke with her she said she had the situation under control." Nathan replied. "Can you give me any other useful information like Lameka's last name or what kind of car she drives?" "I don't know her last name, but I think she drives a tan Toyota or maybe an Acura. I'm not sure the car was moving pretty fast." "That's fine, any information is better than none at all." Yolanda came over and grabbing her son she began tearfully apologizing about everything she'd felt she's been doing to him. Seeing her best friend embracing her child Mrs. Jones felt sparks of envy rise inside her. She wanted desperately to hold her own child. Mrs. Jones wanted to be able to express understanding, to shower her with love and end the endless turmoil she felt the need to hide. She rose to her feet and walked out the room towards the kitchen.

Detective Moss saw her leave and followed behind. "Is everything ok Mrs. Jones?" "No Detective everything is not ok! The mere fact that you're standing in my home would tell you everything's not fine!" "I'm here to do whatever humanly possible I can do to get your daughter back to you." Detective Moss said. Before Mrs. Jones had a chance to respond the door was struck by a forceful knock. "Are you expecting anybody else?" Detective Moss asked at the forcefulness of the knock. "No!" Mrs. Jones replied. Detective Moss quickly unsnapped the button on her gun strap and walked cautiously toward the door pushing Mrs. Jones behind her in the process. Whispering over her shoulder she instructed Mrs. Jones to answer the door. "Who is there?" Mrs. Jones said trying not to let the nervousness of her voice be audible. "Ma'am I'm Officer Davis from the Crime Scene Unit, I'm here upon the request of Detective Moss." Detective Moss snatched opened the door. "Dude you should watch how you knock I almost shot you!" she said playfully dapping and hugging the other officer. "Well I've been here knocking ten minutes, I was finna call you, but I heard voices, so I decided to knock again." "Oh, is that how you greet your right-hand man?" Officer Davis asked still staying at the opened front door.

Mrs. Jones greeted Officer Davis and invited him in. she showed him into the living room where everyone was sitting preparing for the press conference. "So, what you got for me?" Officer Davis asked putting his trolley of equipment to rest behind him. "Ms. Nashunta Jones didn't come home from school yesterday. I went up with her father to look around her room did a routine check of her things. Upon investigating her closet, we found a bag in which Mr. Jones gave me permission to open. I opened the bag and found evidence which to me it looks as though the young lady was being stalked. I would like fingerprints and DNA analysis done on all the things in the bag as well as the window by the bed. Do you think you can handle that?" Detective Moss asked Officer Davis. The knock on the door startled everyone. "Oh My! This is turning into a mad house!" Yolanda said from her seat on the couch. "That should be the people from the news." Detective Moss stated. "Mr. Jones can you please instruct them to set up outside away from any identifying marks of your house while I get Officer Davis squared away upstairs. Don't anybody say anything to the press until I return to prep you guys on what are key things to speak on." Detective Moss said. Everybody agreed Mr. Jones headed to the door as Detective Moss and Officer Davis headed up the stairs to Nashunta's bedroom.

Mr. Jones stood as the patriarch of his family along with his wife, Detective Moss, Yolanda, and Nathan in front of the news media. His heart and his mind raced out of control as he tried to make words come from his lips. "Yesterday morning my seventeen-year-old daughter Nashunta Jones left home to go to school, but she never made it." a tearful Mrs. Jones held up a picture of her oldest daughter. "It was brought to our attention that her good friend Lameka may have been the last person to speak with her. Lameka you're not in any trouble the police would like to talk to you to see if maybe Nashunta spoke with you or if you saw anything. If anybody has any information on the where about of my daughter Nashunta Jones or her friend Lameka please contact the police." The media tried to ask questions, but Detective Moss escorted the family and friends of Nashunta Jones back inside the house.

With everyone back in the house Detective Moss raced back upstairs to check on the progress of Officer Davis. Officer Davis was packing up his equipment as she walked into the room. "Hey man thanks for coming out so quickly." Moss said to Davis. "How fast can you have those results ready for me?" she asked the officer. "Turn away from them girls and let me take you out you can have them first thing in the morning," Officer Davis said candidly looking over his shoulder. "Nigga please! Don't play me you know I don't roll like that!" she remarked with her award-winning GQ smile. "Alright then Bro! I guess you can still have them first thing in the morning." "You can freeze me with that Bro shit too!" Detective Moss sarcastically replied as she punched her long-timed friend and coworker playfully in the arm. She helped him with the equipment down the stairs.

Walking back in to the living room Detective Moss announced that she was heading back to the office. "If you need me, doesn't matter how minor you think the question maybe, call me." she stated giving Mr. Jones her card with her personal number on it. Mr. Jones grabbed her hand but instead of shaking it he pulled her in for a full embrace. "Thank you for opening my eyes. I hope I get the chance to tell my daughter how proud I am of her." Detective Moss was caught off guard by the hug. "I appreciate the gratitude sir." she said not allowing herself to think back on her own father. She pushed back the tears turned and walked out the door.

Detective Moss waited for Officer Davis to pack up his equipment and get inside the state issued crime scene van. "Don't forget to call me first thing in the morning! She yelled thru the window of her black jeep." "I got you man! Don't worry about nothing." Officer Davis replied before driving off down the street. Detective Moss checked her messages from her phone while she sat in her car. Slightly irritated by the lack of messages she threw her car in drive and sped down the street toward the office.

Detective Moss sat behind her mahogany stained desk eating her extra-large burrito from Taco bell when the phone on the desk rang out. "Detective Moss Missing Persons! How can I assist you?" She spoke tryna balance the phone with her neck and lunch with her free hand. "Yes, is this Detective Moss?" The sultry Latin accent asked in return. "Umm Yes! Detective Moss Missing Persons, how can I help you ma'am?" Moss stated trying not to sound to irritated. "My name is Montana Santiago I saw the news today and I have some information about Nashunta Jones and Lameka Rogers." Hearing the two names from the sexy Latino caller made Moss drop her burrito down on the desk. "Umm yes Mrs. Santiago would you mind coming in to talk to me?" "Come in? Why can't I just say over the phone?" "Don't be alarmed, it's mainly protocol. If you're afraid I can come to you and we can speak in private. Where you would like to meet?" Detective Moss asked trying to calm the caller. "If I come can I bring someone?" She asked with uncertainty in her voice. "You can do whatever makes you more comfortable, but I would like it to be today! Preferably as soon as you could get here!" Detective Moss held on while Ms. Santiago spoke to someone that was with her. After a brief moment she came back to the phone and agreed to meet with the detective at her office.

Detective Moss was so overwhelmed by the new lead she tossed the remaining bits of her lunch in the trash. She jumped to her feet to go share the news with the rest of her team. She gathered everyone to brief them on the case. "As you guys know I'm handling the Nashunta Jones disappearance. Well I just got off the phone with Montana Santiago. She's on the way to give us info on our missing person as well as the person of interest." Moss's contemporaries stood stock still at the information. They were just amazed she finally got a tip that was viable. Everyone came around giving her pats on the shoulders. She enjoyed her short-lived moment because the reality was that Nashunta was still missing. Back to her office she went to gather her files and wait on Ms. Santiago. She was so excited about the lead that she forgot to call out to the front to inform them about her guests. After she hung up the phone she started to get an uneasy feeling in the pit of her stomach. She sat back in her chair turned on her Pandora flow and tried to relax her mind before her witness arrived.

18

Running Scared

Montana

Montana was in her underwear dancing and lip singing to Whitney Huston's I wanna dance with somebody. Letting herself get lost in the music she began grinding her hips to her own reflection in the mirror. This was her first morning alone at her own house. She hadn't heard anything from Lameka, no calls or texts. Nothing! Montana secretly felt liberated. She found herself wondering why she had wasted so much of her time on Lameka anyway. She had taken some time off work after the day Lameka came to the office looking for her. She was so shaken up by the incidence that she wondered if she needed to relocate to their other office. Laughing at herself for her mixed emotions she went back to clean her room.

Montana had to literally rearrange her entire room. She entered her room and the night Lameka choked her instantly popped in her head. After a few vigorous hours of moving her bedroom furniture around she finally came up with something she could live with. Montana decided to complete her bed first so if anything, her bed would be complete, and she could finish the rest later. Sliding down to the floor after the last pillow was safely placed on the bed she felt her stomach growling. Damn! She thought to herself. This was supposed to be a quick pick up and off to breakfast. She checked the time on her phone. Ugh! It was just pass 12. Oh well, lunch time! She jumped up and headed to the kitchen. Montana made a quick salad and warmed up the salmon she had left over from Chili's last night.

Montana turned on the TV in her dining room to the news then returned to the kitchen to get her food. She grabbed her food off the counter top and headed to the table. Food in hand Montana was standing in front of the table but instead of sitting down she was frozen in place. In big letters at the bottom of the scene read seventeen-year-old Nashunta Jones missing. Her heart started beating a hundred beats a second. The words pouring from the man talking on TV felt like the most important thing on earth. Once she heard him say that Lameka was a person of interest her plate fell from her hands landing in a heap on the floor and she dashed up the steps for her phone.

"Pick up the phone!" Montana yelled as she dialed Katrina's number for the third time. Montana was prepared to hit the call button again, but the phone flashed that Katrina was calling her. "This better be important! I'm in the middle of our afternoon huddle." Katrina barked into the phone. Montana tried to explain the reason for her call, but she was going so fast the Katrina didn't catch any of what she was saying. "Montana you have got to slow down! I can't understand a word you're saying." "On the news just now, I heard them say it!" She yelled in return. "You heard them say what? What are you talking about chile!" "Katrina, are you listening or not?" Montana yelled. "I'm trying to, but ok go ahead." Katrina shot back. "On the news just now, they just said Nashunta was missing." Montana said taking her time to articulate every syllable. "Nashunta? Wait that's the girl your friend was seeing? You don't think? Oh My God Montana you have to call the police!" "I'm afraid!" Montana yelled back through the phone. "Stay put I'm on my way!" Katrina screamed and ended the call before Montana could say otherwise.

Montana paced back and forth while she chained smoked a pack of Newport's. Panic traveled through her every time she tried to sit down. She just kept repeating how she tried to warn Nashunta. She grabbed the bottle of vodka out the fridge to calm her nerves. Katrina swerved in and out of traffic narrowly missing a soccer mom and her kids. The soccer mom blew her horn scaring the kids inside. "Fuck you bitch! Learn how to fucking drive!" Katrina yelled. Apparently, she could read Katrina's lips because as Katrina passed the car she saw her quickly giving the finger. No, this silly white bitch didn't just give me the finger. She lucky I'm in a hurry cause I was finna go gangsta gospel on her ass. WWJD Cora! WWJD! She said in her Medea voice. How the fuck Montana keep getting into shit with this young ass thug! Katrina was having a full blow conversation all by herself. Either

Lameka got a golden strap or she found two of the world's dumbest bitches on the face of this earth.

By the time Katrina reached Montana she was frantically bawling on the bottom of the front hall steps. Next to her was a small ashtray over flowing with discarded cigarette butts. She felt sorry for her friend but only briefly. "Look at yourself!" Katrina yelled loudly to her best friend since high school. She wanted to shock some sense into her. "How you keep letting her scare you like this? What has happened to the diva I use to know?" "It's not me I'm terrified for!" Montana returned. "I felt like I should have done more to warn Nashunta about Lameka." She looked down at her hands and the tears began to fall. "You did what you could! It wasn't your fault she didn't want to listen to you." "She dead! I just know it!" Montana shrieked loudly before crying uncontrollably. "Montana you have to call the police." Katrina grabbed the phone off the steps and dialed 911.

"911 what is your emergency!" "Yes, my name is Montana Santiago I have information about the missing person we saw on the news today." "Can you hold please?" With the remark the line went silent. "Here!" Katrina tried to hand the phone to Montana. "Ma'am the operator was back on the line. Detective Moss is handling all calls of this nature. I'll transfer you I can also give you her direct number for future reference." After receiving the number Montana was transferred and the line began to ring again. The line clicked, and someone began to speak. The person on the other end of the phone said something but Montana and Katrina were passing the phone back and forth and they couldn't make out what she had said. "Detective Moss?" Montana asked tryna make sure she had the right person. The detective gave an answer and Montana shot a crazy look at Katrina. "What's wrong?" she asked. Montana told the detective her name and the reason why she called. "Come in? Why can't I just say over the phone?" Katrina watched as Montana grew more desperate with in the conversation. "If I come can I bring someone?" she heard Montana asking. Montana's head swiveled like an owl. "Come with me please?" Montana asked pleading with praying hands and all. Katrina's mind was saying she had to get back to work but her big mouth said ok. Montana agreed to meet the detective then she hung up the phone. She stood in front of Katrina but didn't understand the look on her face. "What?" she finally asked. "We going or not?" she asked Katrina. "Yes, we are but, do you really wanna go in your underwear?" Montana looked down at herself. The realization of her being in her skivvies set in and she dashed up the steps to dress. Montana emerged seconds later jeans, cut off sweatshirt, and ball cap on. Even though she tried to dress down Montana looked like a model with everything she adored on her rich vanilla cream skin. Katrina tried not to notice her friend's satin skin that peeked from various places of her outfit. She had secretly been in love with Montana since they first met. It was hard not to fall in love with the temptress after she graced you with her presence. Montana had hordes of people both male and female pining after her. This is why she couldn't understand why she willfully subjected herself to Lameka's bullshit. "Ready!" she yelled breaking Katrina from her thoughts. They turned to walk out the door. "Hold on a sec!" Montana yelled as they walked out the door. She dashed back inside only to come out with her fabulous pair of Louie Viton glasses that Katrina gave her for Christmas. "Now I'm ready! I can't face my public with these bags under my eyes." She laughed as she buckled her seat belt.

They arrived at the police department, but Montana became nervous again. Katrina had to practically drag her ass out the car. She changed her mind twice before they made it to the entrance. They walked inside the building and up to the metal detector. "There are no tobacco products allowed and all cell phones must be off or on vibrate." the security officer continuously said as the people walked in the door. "Can I help you?" the guard said once they reach the front of the line. "We are here to speak to Detective Moss from missing persons." Katrina spoke up. "She's expecting you. Please place your things on the belt and walk through the detector one at a time." They did as they were instructed once on the other side the guard directed them to have a seat and Detective Moss would be with them soon.

Montana watched everyone that came out of the doors behind the desk. She was trying place the voice she heard over the phone to a face. After a few minutes of definitely not her, out walks this ebony goddess with dreads that were pulled back. The glasses she chose to wear gave her a strictly business appearance. The clothes that adorned the ebony caramel frame let Montana know without guessing that she was family. Katrina was talking when she realized she wasn't getting a response from Montana. "Earth to Montana!" she said but still got nothing. Katrina turned to look, she had to see what was holding her friend's attention. Katrina wasn't a devout lesbian, but she had dabbled in the art a time or two. However, after seeing the cause of Montana's lapse of being she was seriously reconsidering her sexual preference. "Saw her first" Katrina said to her best friend. "Girl please you ain't even gay." "Yeah, I know but for her I'll shave off my hair and burn my bra!" Katrina's words broke the hold the Detective had on them. "Burn your bra?" Montana said half laughing. "What da hell you gonna burn your bra for?" "Shit I don't know it just sounded right." Katrina replied and they both burst into laughter. They were so wrapped up with laughing that they hadn't saw Detective Moss walk up beside them. "Ms. Santiago?" Moss asked. "Yes, I'm sorry." Montana said standing to her feet. "Hey, I'm Detective Moss; we spoke on the phone earlier." "Yes, I recognize your voice." Montana said extending her hand. "Umm yea I leave that Mrs. Santiago crap for my mother!" Montana spoke sarcastically. "You can just call me Montana, and this is my best friend Katrina." Katrina jumped in front of Montana nearly knocking her over with her hand extended. "Pleased to make your acquaintance." Katrina spoke taking the hand the Detective had offered. Montana playfully elbowed Katrina, "please don't mind her." Montana said looking the very attractive detective in her eyes. "She was dropped on her head a couple of times growing up." Detective Moss smiled at the pair as they joked as if they had been friends forever. "Ladies if you would please follow me." Detective Moss ushered the ladies to the back. Once in the back she led them to the interrogation room. "Ok ladies have a seat, I'm gonna go get some paper work and I'll be right back." The women agreed and found their seats. Detective Moss waited until the ladies took their seat. She turned and left the room.

19

Blood on Your Hands

Raven

Monique sat up in her bed and stared at her friend. "If I can't have my happily ever after, then nobody will." The look on her face was sinister and it frightened Eric to see her in that state. "What you mean by that?" he asked moving from the door to her side. "Don't do something stupid" he said to Monique. "Something stupid!" She laughed. "Like getting pregnant by a guy you agreed not to fall in love with but did. I can't do anything stupider then I already have." She turned her face away, so her friend wouldn't see her cry. "You know what I mean Miss. Thang don't get smart with me. I hope you don't plan on getting even with Stacey." "I'm not worried about Stacey right now. Once my baby is born I'll deal with him. That bitch Raven is who I'm talking about."

"Raven! What the hell you out to get even with her for?" "It's that bitch's fault my life is crumbling all to shit. "Oh right! It's Raven's fault you lied to your man about taking birth control. Let's not forget to blame her for punching holes in your condoms too." "Are you siding with her Eric? Cause its room on my list for you too!" "No, but you are sounding a little neurotic right about now." Eric replied to the comment. Monique turned over her phone and handed it to Eric. He looked down at the picture he had to take a double take. He snatched the phone right out of her hand. "What you gonna do with this picture?" Monique smirked and walked over the nightstand. With a Newport tuck between her lips she flicks the lighter and pulls the flame across the tip of the cigarette. "It's not what I'm gonna do it's what I've done." "What the fuck have you done now? You know I'm old and I can't take all this drama!" Eric said walking over to Monique and taking the Newport right outta her mouth. "AHH!" She yelled in protest. Once he takes a drag he blows the smoke in her face. "Please you're not supposed to be smoking anyway." "Haven't you ever heard of my body my choice?" she replied. "They were not talking about smoking cigarettes dumbass." Eric said. "Maybe you should consider having an abortion!" he commented playfully hitting Monique with a pillow.

Monique turned around suddenly. "Not a chance!" She yelled. "Stacey and Raven are gonna pay for all the pain and suffering they have put me through. You wanna know what I did? I forwarded this nice picture to Raven's so-called girlfriend. Once Tonya sees how much of a liar Raven is she'll leave Mrs. High and Mighty alone. Just as soon as she snatches the wool from under poor little Raven I'll be there to help Tonya pick up the pieces. If I can't have my first choice, then I guess my second runner up will have to do." Monique stood staring out the window like the answer to all her prayers dance just beyond the window pane. "So now you and Tonya are gonna have the big happy family?" The sound of a voice other than hers brought her back to reality. "What the fuck Eric! Whose side are you on?" "I'm for you all day every day but I want you to take some time and think things through." "Yeah you right!" Monique yelled. "Let me start that right now. Can you excuse me I need some time to think!" she angrily said standing at the door waiting for her roommate to leave her room. As soon as Eric was far enough out the door way Monique slammed the door with all her might. Before Eric had a chance to protest or even knock music came blaring from behind the door. Eric shrugged his shoulders and walked away. No use talking to that stupid bitch! I'll be here with vodka when all this shit blows up in her face.

Raven undressed and slid inside the soothing hot water. The water felt wonderful as it cascaded down her worn body. While letting the day's events race round in her head she washed her hair. She was actually glad Stacey and Monique had issues they had to deal with amongst themselves. That would leave her alone to be able to deal with her own family. Raven turned the water off and stepped out the shower. After she dried off she escaped the confines of the bathroom to the openness of her bedroom. She had laid her favorite sundress across the bed. Grabbing the carrot tree oil off the stand she hurriedly oiled her body. She couldn't wait to see what her wifey had in store for her.

"Daddy you not gonna eating with us?" Stacey turned to face his kids. Seeing his children sparked something inside his heart and he started crying. How dumb could he be! He thought to himself. He was never raised to walk away from one of his own. Deep down inside he did love Monique and he knew he needed to be by her side. She didn't deserve to be treated like that. Stacey wiped the tears that were falling down his cheeks. His mind was made up. He would walk beside Monique thru this. When the child is born he will still get a DNA just to be on the safe side. The son he shares with his childhood love places his little hand over Stacey's bigger one. "Daddy you ok?" Omari asked his father. "Yes baby, daddy is just fine." "Then why you have tears running down your cheeks?" his little queen asked. "Parents sometimes cry." he said to his children trying to reassure them that things were fine.

"You mean like the way mommy cries to herself when she and papa Tonya fight?" That statement caught Stacey of guard. "Tonya's not your daddy!" "I know that silly! She can't be a daddy because she's a girl. Not like me and mommy but a papa girl." "A what?" Stacey just had to hear what his daughter would say. "She's a papa girl daddy, girls that are boys on the outside and girls on the inside." Stacey laughed at Raven's attempt to explain being gay to their daughter.

"Sweetheart what did you mean about when they fight? Do your mother and Tonya fight a lot in front of you guys?" Omari looked at his sister. "What's wrong son?" He asked his eldest child. "Nothing, but mom said were not to talk about the things in our house with you or Monique." "Oh really!" Stacey said playfully tickling his son. He knew that if he wanted the answer to his question he would have to get Kelly away from Omari. "Ok kids finish up and I might let you have some ice cream." Stacey kissed both the kids on the forehead and walked in the other room to call Monique. The words of his son swam around in his head. Why would Raven want to keep the kids from talking? Unless she was hiding some hideous secret about Tonya. Sitting in the chair at his desk Stacey dialed Monique's number. The phone rang several times and then the voicemail picked up. Not wanting to leave a message Stacey hung up and pressed redial. Getting the same results as before he hung up the phone. She might be mad, the thought to himself. Of course, she's mad dummy look what you said to her. I'll try again later and if she still doesn't answer then I'll head to her house. Stacey put the phone down and headed back to check on the kids.

They had finished their meal and retreated back into whatever they were doing before. Stacey saw that Omari was deep into a game on his DS, so he took the opportunity to talk to his baby girl. Stopping at the door to his daughter's room he tapped on the door as to gain her attention. Kelly let out a tiny giggle as she looked up at her daddy standing in the doorway. "Hey baby girl. Can daddy come in?" Signaling yes with a head shake Kelly scooted over allowing her daddy a space on the bed. Stacey watched as his baby girl sat mesmerized while The Little Mermaid sang about being a part of their world. Kelly sat with the two middle fingers on her right hand in her mouth and the left hand twiddling her dolls hair. "You know you can tell daddy anything sweetheart." "I know daddy." She said without taking her eyes off the screen. Stacey knew that this was the moment he needed. "Your mommy cry a lot at home baby?" "One time I saw her crying in the bathroom. She was putting makeup on the black mark on her face." "A black mark! Like a bruise?" Stacey asked his daughter. Kelly shook her head yes to the question her father asked. "Omari said it was a black eye. He said that every time mommy wears her big glasses she has one." "What? Have you ever seen Tonya hit your mother?" "No but they yell at each other a lot."

Just as he was about to ask another question he heard Omari calling him from somewhere close by. "Come on baby girl." Stacey said lifting his daughter up in his arms. Let's go get that ice cream daddy promised you. They met Omari halfway between the living room and the kitchen. "You don't have to tell me son I'm heading there now." Stacey fixed huge banana splits for him and his kids. They all sat there enjoying their time and desserts.

Monique was awakened from her nap by another urge to relieve herself. She hurried to the bathroom She felt as though she hasn't peed in years and her bladder was about to explode. After finishing her deed, she washed her hands and left the bathroom. In her mind she wanted to go back to sleep but the fridge called to her. Her body flowed to the kitchen like she was in a trance. When Monique was finished raiding the refrigerator she had a left-over fruit bowl, half a slice cheese cake from the night before, a peanut butter and jelly sandwich equipped with Sweet Heat BBQ chips, and 2 small kosher dill pickles wrapped in cheese slices. She happily grabbed together her goodies like a squirrel stocking up for the winter.

"Honey I'm home" Eric yelled as he walked in the front door. "I brought you some of your favorite!" Eric started out, but his statement was cut short when he entered Monique's room. Monique sat in the middle of her bed surrounded by a smorgasbord of food. "Oh, girl your gonna be one of those Eric can you run down to the corner store for popcorn and a large red slushy at 2am kind of pregnant wife." Monique laughed at her friend and through a mouth full of food she asked. "What did you bring me?" "I brought you your favorite honey BBQ wings from KFC," Eric replied as he sat the bag down in front of her. "Keep eating like this and you're gonna ruin that nice video hoe figure you worked so hard to get." Monique licked her tongue out and grabbed a wing from the box.

20

What Nightmares Are Made Of

Mercedes

A few months earlier

Hakeem had been standing out on the block all morning. He hated having to do these petty nickel and dime deals, but he needed the money to pay probation fees. He knew he was capable to move larger amounts of weight but while he was serving time the streets had changed. Young cats that were petty street hustlers were now running whole operations. Big time dealers and money makers were either dead or doing time for murders and other crimes. The whole process just fucking pissed him off.

As he stood outside the neighborhood corner store, he would catch sight of all the nice-looking women that came and went. He had a few he could call to take care of business with no questions asked but it was only one woman who knew exactly how he liked it. He had molded her for years and she thought she could disappear once he was inside serving time. She had left him time and time again, but he always found her. In Hakeem's mind he always would, she belonged to him. Once he got out he tried looking for her but had no luck. Everybody he knew that knew her had moved or vanished completely.

The afternoon sun had made its way high in the sky. His stomach began to growl, Hakeem pulled out his phone to check the time and saw his battery needed charging. He collected his stash that he had hid inside an old paper bag that he placed on top of the garbage inside the trashcan he leaned on all day. "I'm about to go get some food." Hakeem said as he slapped five to the rest of the fellas hang on the block. Hakeem then turned and walked the two and a half blocks back to his cousin Yolanda's house. Luckily, she was nice enough to let him catch the sofa until he got back on his feet.

He walked in the house and went straight for the refrigerator. "Cuz, ain't no food in here!" Hakeem yelled still standing in the door of the fridge. "Order us something!" Yolanda yelled back in return. "Where from?" He asked. "From Hans, the number is in my phone." "Bet!" Hakeem said more to himself than anything else. Hakeem grabbed his cousin's phone off the counter and started going down her contact list. Half way down the list he runs across the name Cedes and paused. Cedes as in Mercedes, Hakeem thought. "Did you find it?" Yolanda said as she made her way down the stairs. Hearing his cousin coming Hakeem quickly snapped a picture of the contact and pushed his phone down in his back pocket. Got it!" Hakeem yelled just as his cousin entered the kitchen. "Cool, order me the number 17 but I want shrimp fried rice." Yolanda said. "What's that?" he asked. "Sweet and sour shrimp but it comes with plain fried rice." Yolanda answered "Hell yeah, that shit sounds good as fuck" Hakeem replied. He dialed the number, order the food, and went outside to smoke before he went to go grab their lunch. While Hakeem sat on the porch enjoying his momentary nicotine high he pulled up the picture he took and dialed the number. After the fourth ring the computerized female voice indicated that the person called could not be reached. He hung up the phone before the beep, stubbed out his cigarette on the bottom of his shoes, jumped in his cousin's car and sped off to go get their food.

After lunch the day seemed to drag by Hakeem had a few regular customers come by but nothing that would help him reach his daily quota. The slowness of the foot traffic allowed time for his mind to wonder away. He thought about all the good times he had with Mercedes and he had to have her back. As he stood there thinking a lightbulb went off. If it was her number she wouldn't answer for an unpublished number, so he downloaded a computer number from the internet. he opened the app after it was completely installed, and he dialed the number again. There were several rings and just as he was about to hang up someone picked up. "Hello" the voice was so calm and soft. Hearing her voice sent a floodgate of emotions flowing threw him. Mercedes gave a few more hello and received nothing but silence so she ended the call. Hakeem stood there with the biggest smile on his face. Without saying a word, he grabbed his stash and started to walk off. "You out?" one of his boys called out behind him. "Yeah man, I'm tryna go home." And with that he turned and walked off without saying another word.

Hakeem sat at his cousin kitchen table with a beer in one hand and a Newport in the other. He had to find her, and he knew exactly who knew where she was. He sat at that table waiting for his cousin to come home. As soon as he heard her keys turning in the lock he went into his act. He sat there fake tears and all in the darkness of the dimly lit kitchen with all the shades closed. She walked in with her arms filled with bags of groceries. "Why is it so dark in here?" Yolanda said as she crossed the room making it to the table to relieve herself of the bags. Yolanda walked over and flicked on the light and was startled by her cousin sitting in the corner at her table. "What are you doing sitting here in the dark?" she said as she walked over to where he sat, she could tell something was wrong. "What happened?" Yolanda asked as she pulled up a chair and sat next to him. "I can't do this no more Yolanda" he said forcefully as he lit another cigarette. "This hustle life is getting old man. I can't find a job making real money, and I can't do no fast food gig. I don't want to be a burden on you no more, and I wanna see my kids too." To put more dramatics with it at the mention of his kids he let out a little more water works.

Yolanda sat there for a moment and let her cousin vent before offering any words. Placing her hand on his shoulder, she leaned in to rest her head on him. "You're never a burden to me, and as far as the hustling goes, you can always go through a temp agency and get on at one of those warehouse jobs. They are always hiring, and they'll take you with a background. Plus, if you're a good worker with good attendance they will hire you permanent and you'll get benefits and stuff. If you want I can call a friend to see if a can get you an interview." "Shit! Hell yeah!" Hakeem said sitting up straight in the chair. "Man cuz, I know I've done some fucked up shit in my past, but I really just want to see my kids man. I really wanna hold 'em in my arms. Seeing them would be the motivation I need to get on the right track and get my shit together." The moment his cousin sat back in the chair he knew she had bit the bait hook, line and sinker.

Yolanda set there at her table listening to one of her favorite cousins as he poured his heart out. This one has been in and out of trouble his whole life and never once had he ever talked about getting himself on the right track. It was always go inside, get out, hit the block. She prayed that since he was inside for a longer stint this time he would come home ready to do right. So, as he sits here saying the words she prayed he always would she couldn't help but thank God for whatever it was that was the reason behind the turn. "I love you so much Hakeem, nothing you could ever do would change that." "Don't bullshit me though, let me know right now if you really thinking about getting yo shit together." "I'm dead ass for real, I'm getting to old for this shit. I just want to get a job, get my own place, be with my kids, be a damn father this time."

Getting up from her seat, Yolanda walked over to the other side of the table grabbed a Newport, lit it, took a long drag and blew the smoke out through her nose. "Then I'll help you as much as I can. First things first, I'll call my folks in the morning to get you set up with an interview. Just make sure you answer ya phone when she calls you back." Yolanda sat back down in her chair, took another pull from her smoke, and playfully blew smoke out into the air. Yolanda knew Mercedes had told her to never tell her cousin that she saw her, so she lied about exactly where she had saw her. "I don't know exactly where ya kids are at, but I saw Mercedes at the liquor store over there off Covington highway." She just knew that the chances of her little tip leading him anywhere were slim or, at least that's what she made herself believe. There were no words that came from Hakeem, he didn't want to seem overly excited. They sat there finishing their smokes with no words coming between the two. "Thanks a lot cuz, you know just as well as I do that tip is a long shot." He got up kissed her on the forehead and went into the living room to watch tv.

Days passed and Yolanda heard nothing more from Hakeem about seeing his kids, he had even started working the night shift at a warehouse not far from the house. She just prayed that this time he would stay out of trouble. Hakeem's plan went without a hitch, he had gathered as much information as he could from his cousin. He also went on some interviews and actually scored a night shift gig. He also played it cool about tryna see his kids, he wanted Yolanda to think he was over that idea. At first, he started riding around the area in the morning and going to the warehouse job at night but that was getting him nowhere. That's when Hakeem had the thought to literally look for his kids. They had to go to school and chances are they would be catching the school bus. Hakeem would ride around the neighborhood during the times the kids would be getting on and off school buses. He became so obsessed that he missed too many days and soon was fired from his temp position.

Hakeem pulled into an apartment complexed early one morning. He pulled out a cigarette but couldn't find his lighter. He took his eyes off the road momentarily to get the lighter but looked up just in time to avoid hitting a boy darting across the street. He slammed on breaks, threw the car in park, and was about to jump out to yell at the kid when he noticed his daughter Evon walking up the sidewalk. He pulled his hat down close to his face, pulled the car into drive, and rode right by the group of kids meeting up on the grass. No sooner had he passed the kids he saw his son Desmond run from a set of apartments a little way off from the group of kids. Hakeem turned the car around and pulled behind the dumpster to watch his kids playfully walk to get on the school bus.

Hakeem came back later that afternoon in an attempt to spot his ex coming or going. This time when the school bus passed it was the smaller kids coming home. There were two or three ladies walking with the herd of small schoolers. The herd would carefully wait and watch each little person walk into their house. The herd stopped at the building where Hakeem saw his son exit this morning, but instead of someone going in, one lady ushered a little girl towards the back. When the girl turned around to give her friend a goodbye hug, Hakeem noticed the face of his baby girl Marie. He got out the car crossed around back and walked on the opposite sidewalk on the other side of the street. As he walked he was able to see them clearly, the lady walked Marie to the bottom of some steps and the child climbed the steps alone. Once she reached the top of the landing she pulled out a key that was around her neck on a string. She crossed the landing to the door on the right side, opened the door with the keys, closed the door, and waved to the lady from the window. After the lady received the signal the lady walked back to the group and they proceeded on their way down the walk.

At first Hakeem wanted to go up to the door and knock to see if his daughter would let him in. After some consideration, he thought against it and decided to head back to the car. Hakeem made his way back, but his mind was racing. He couldn't think straight. He was so close but yet so far. This was his family, and by all rights his home, he should be in there. Hakeem grabbed a Newport and lit it, he wanted to regain his grip because he knew if he let his anger control him, he was gonna make a mistake. Mercedes had to be taught a lesson and once he's done this time she's never gonna leave. He smoked in silence, just him and his thoughts. While he sat there a vehicle rode up and parked in front of the building he had been watching. It was a green four door Jeep Cherokee, with tinted windows. Once the driver exited the car, Hakeem jumped straight up in his seat, it was like he had seen a ghost.

There she was, Mercedes walking like she didn't have a care in the world. Ducking down as far as he could and still look out the window Hakeem pulled out his phone and called the number he had for Mercedes. After the second ring he sees Mercedes stop, pull out her phone, and answer. He could hear her voice through his phone as she said hello repeatedly. When there was no response from the other end he watches as she looks around in all directions before she hangs up and proceeds around the back of the building. Hakeem sat up quickly, slammed his hand against the steering wheel. "I got ya ass now!" Hakeem starts the car and pulled off.

21

The Enemy of My Enemy is My Friend

Nashunta

Walking as fast as she could back to the monitor room Detective Moss joined the monitor tech in watching the screen. They tried to get some rapport about the new informant and her companion. Montana and Katrina sat oblivious to the fact that they were in a surveillance room and were being watched. Twice Montana lost her nerve and wanted to bail but Katrina held her hand and helped her to breathe through the minute panic attacks.

"Alright!" Detective Moss said standing up letting her hand rest on the tech's back. "Let me get in her before she bolts out the room" Moss spoke before she opened the door and left the room. "I'm sorry ladies the copy machine was acting retarded, so I had to use another machine." Moss pulled up a chair and organized the papers in front of her. "Ok Miss. Montana what you got for me?" Montana looked Katrina in the eyes. Grabbing Montana's hands, she shook her head up and down, go ahead Katrina said. "Go ahead honey tell her." "To start off Lameka and I were involved with it other way before she started going out with Nashunta." "So, it's safe to say Nashunta and Lameka are in or were in a romantic relationship?" Moss asked to get clarification. "Yes, but she was still sexually involved with me." "If you don't mind me asking how old are you and what was the length of the relationship between Lameka and yourself?" "I'm 26 were seeing each other for about 3 years." Montana replied. "That would be 3 years on and off!" Katrina threw in barging into the conversation. "So, you Know Lameka as well?" the detective asked Katrina. "No, I wouldn't say I know her" Katrina started "we've met a few times but she has never been on my list of most liked people."

"Hold that thought" Moss said to Katrina as she turned her focus back toward Montana. "Ok Miss. Montana if you're saying you're 26 then how old does that make Lameka?" "I don't want to incriminate myself by anything I say to you." "Please I assure you that we won't use anything you say to prosecute you in anyway." "Lameka is 19 she was 16 when we met." "Did Lameka's parents know about her sexual orientation and the relationship with you?" "In the beginning no, they didn't but Lameka came out to them. She spoke to them about her sexual orientation and our relationship." "Ok, after she spoke with her parents about the relationship with you what happened then?" Moss continued to question Montana. "Lameka's parents went berserk she replied. They threatened to have me arrested and sue my employer if I didn't leave their daughter alone. That's when I tried to back off from seeing Lameka. But that girl is hardly the type to take no for an answer. She has the art of get her way down to a science." "Only with retarded women like that of yourself." Katrina added. Montana shot her a look. "Montana has Lameka ever been violent with you?" Detective Moss asked trying to keep the ladies on track. This time Katrina spoke first. "Yes, she has and that's why we're here."

Everyone stared at Montana as if she were an actress on stage who forgot her lines. The moment of awkward silence was broken when Montana let out a sigh before she spoke. "You know Lameka wasn't always mean to me Katrina. She had a way of making you feel like you were the only person in the world. It wasn't until you pissed her off that you would see the Mr. Hyde to her Dr. Jekyll. I knew exactly when Lameka and Nashunta started talking. She came over to my house made love to my entire body then afterward told me she had found somebody else." "How did that make you feel about Nashunta?" Detective Moss asked making Katrina sit up and pay attention. "Hey!" Katrina quickly remarked. "I don't think I like the way this line of questioning is going." "Katrina it's cool!" Montana replied waving her hand at her now visually agitated best friend. "I'm pretty sure Detective Moss has my best interest in mind. Shall we continue?" Montana fixed her gaze at the young eager detective. "Of course, madam!" Detective Moss replied playfully tipping her imaginary hat.

"To be perfectly honest Detective, Nashunta and I absolutely hated one another. Yes, it made me furious knowing that I was no longer Lameka's number one love. I tried to back off and leave her alone but Lameka made it painfully clear that I was always gonna be in her life." "So, what you're saying is that Nashunta knew about the relationship between you and Lameka?" "Of course, she did!" Montana replied. "One day Nashunta was snooping threw Lameka's phone or so it seemed to me and found my number. I had to give it to her the girl had huge balls. She called me right from Lameka's phone. I thought it was cute, so I burst her bubble by mentioning her name before she gave it to me. It pissed Lameka off majorly, but she never stopped coming by and Nashunta never called again. I guess she got the picture." Montana finished her statement as she sat up straight in the chair. "Both of y'all looking like two stupid dogs in my book." Katrina blurted out of nowhere.

"Do you know if Lameka ever got physical with Nashunta or not?" Detective Moss asked. "I really can't say for sure because I have never actually witnessed anything. However, Lameka did say that she had to watch her temper around Nashunta." "Do you know what made her say that?" Moss inquired. "Lameka told me she had gotten a little physical with her. She said Nashunta tried to break it off with her, but she promised she wouldn't put her hands on her again if Nashunta would reconsider." "Montana has Lameka ever been violent with you?" The question brought the night at her house back into her mind and she could feel the tears burning in her eyes. "Detective Moss I know with everything I've told you I might sound stupid, but I honestly thought I was in love. Lameka was always very dominating when it came to words. She was very verbally abusive and at first that was all it was to her. However, as she became older she would get more and more aggressive. Yes, she eventually started hitting me, but it was a shove here or a slap there. I really thought I could deal and had everything under control." "What happened that made you change your mind?" The detective questioned. Despite her best efforts the tears became more powerful than Montana and ran from her eyes like an overflowing river after the storm.

Right on cue Katrina came to her friend's aid grabbing her hand willing strength from herself to her friend. "It's ok Montana! Tell her what happened." Montana shook her head giving Katrina the ok signal. Grabbing the tissue off the table she dotted her eyes before she cleared her throat to start. "About a week and a half maybe even two weeks I'm not sure before this stuff with Nashunta I was at home one night and Lameka called me. She was cold very to the point when she spoke to me. I just thought that she and Nashunta had gotten into an altercation or something and she was mad, so I didn't really say anything about it besides I was in need of some sexual healing." Montana tried to joke. "From the time the door open Lameka wasted no time she was super aggressive throwing me against the wall, hitting me, even tearing my lingerie from my body. She was very forceful in how she penetrated me and the look in her eyes was terrifying. I told her to stop she was hurting me and that's when Mr. Hyde came outta nowhere. Lameka grabbed me by the throat and started choking me as she rammed her strap inside of me over and over again. I tried to fight her off of me but the more I struggled against her, the tighter she would squeeze my throat. I felt like my insides was on fired and I couldn't breathe I was terrified. I just knew she was gonna kill me. I felt like my life was slipping away but right when I felt myself about to blackout Lameka climaxed. Without warning she released me, threw on her clothes and was gone. I thought she was going to get something to finish me off, so I laid very still hoping she would think I was dead if she came back. But she never did she had disappeared into the night."

"Terrified I tried to call Nashunta and warn her to be careful about how Lameka was acting but she wouldn't answer the phone for me or ever return any of my texts." "Would you blame her?" Detective Moss said. "No not really!" Montana said letting her head hang a little. "What happened after that?" The detective continued. "Between me and Nashunta nothing but I guess she told Lameka I had been trying to contact her. Because the next day Lameka called my phone but I didn't answer. I wasn't about to hang around to find out what she wanted. So, I threw some things together to head to Katrina's house but Lameka caught me leaving and attacked me. She told me if I messed things up between her and Nashunta she would kill me. I told her it was over, and she told me it ain't over until she says it's over. She slapped me and said she would be back to fuck me again like she had the night before. She told me how much she enjoyed it even told me I was a filthy whore." This time Montana broke down and started crying inconsolably. Katrina wrapped her arms around her friend. Even though her outside was falling apart Montana felt like a weight had been lifted from her heart.

"I'll give you ladies a few moments of privacy." Detective Moss said as she stood up. "I'll be right back. Would you ladies care for anything to drink?" "Sure!" they replied. Detective Moss extended her hand towards Montana. "Don't worry we're gonna catch her and when we do I'm gonna charge her for the attack on you." Montana shook her head but didn't look up. Detective Moss walked out the door. The emotions had gotten to her and she had to get her head back in the game.

After the small break Detective Moss returned to the room where the two ladies sat still clinging to one another. "Ok ladies we're just about finished. All I need now is for you to do a picture line up, so we can positively identify Lameka." Moss had inserted a picture from Lameka's driver's license into a page of random pictures of female mug shots. Before she could even lay the paper down on the table Montana was pointing her finger at the paper. "There! Right there! That's her right there!" Montana shouted. Detective Moss handed her a pen. "Circle the picture, sign your name, and date it." Lifting her trembling hand Montana grabbed the pen and did as she was instructed. Gathering the things on the table Detective Moss stood up and prepared to end the meeting. "I really want to thank you for gathering the courage to come in today. I know this was a very traumatic experience for you. I really want to suggest for you to get victim counseling to help you get thru this." Montana stood up from the chair and without warning wrapped her around the unsuspecting detective. "Thank you so much Detective Moss! Please Find Nashunta and when you do tell her I'm sorry. I really sorry about everything!" Montana broke down crying again and Katrina had to help her walk out of the room. Detective Moss escorted Montana and Katrina back to the opening where they first met. The Detective thanked them again for coming down and silently watched as they crossed the room for the exit to the outside world. At that moment Detective Moss realized that Katrina was head over heels in love with Montana. She also recognized that Montana was clueless to that fact. Shaking the vision out of her head she turned and headed back to her desk.

Information was running through Moss' head like a freight train on the move. As soon as she put her bottom in the chair her phone started ringing. "Missing Person this is Detective Moss speaking." "Hey Moss! The voice on the line said. Yes, what's up? Hey this is Waddell! I have a caller on the phone that wants to report a missing person." "You're gonna have to handle on your own Waddell I'm still swamped with this case of my own." "Yeah, I know The Nashunta Jones case, right?" "Yes! And it's a major one." "I know that's why I think you should take this call," Officer Waddell spoke. Moss thought for a second and then she caved. "Alright transfer the call, it better be worth it or Ima see about you Waddell." "What if it is? Am I down for some lunch or something?" "Umm hmm sure I guess!"

The line clicked momentarily, and a female voice was heard. "Hello?" The unknown female caller spoke. "Yes Ma'am, my name is Detective Moss. I was told you wanted to report someone missing?" "Yes, my daughter! We haven't heard from her in almost a week." "Ok Ma'am is your daughter one for running away?" "My daughter is one that really does her own thing. However, she always keeps in touch and lets us know she's ok. My husband and I are away on business a lot. I didn't really think anything of it until I saw your news conference this morning." "Why would the news conference make you realize your daughter was missing?" Detective Moss asked inquisitively. "Detective my daughter is Lameka Rogers." the female caller replied. The statement knocked the breath out of Detective Moss. "Ma'am is it alright if I come meet you at your home to get more information from you?" "Yes of course." The caller gave her address and phone number where she could be reached. "Do me a favor; please don't move a muscle I'm headed to you right now." Moss said before she clicked the phone. Yes! Moss shouted as she did a little jig in her chair. She stopped quick as she thought about how indebted she was. Picking up the phone she dialed Waddell extension. "Waddell!" The older officer said into the phone. "I got lunch tomorrow" Detective Moss said into the phone. Not giving him a chance to boast she clicked the phone on him without a second thought.

Arriving at the home Lameka shared with her family Detective Moss put her car in park but didn't exit her vehicle. She didn't know where this new lead would take her. On the bright side she hoped that Nashunta and Lameka had just run off with each other. Taking a few deep breaths Moss gathered her things and opened the door.

Reaching up to knock Detective Moss was caught off guard by the door in front of her swinging open. A medium built slender woman appeared in the doorway. To Moss she looked like an older more feminine carbon copy of Lameka. "Detective Moss?" she asked. "Yes, ma'am and you must be Mrs. Rogers." She nodded in concurrence. "Please come in Detective." Mrs. Rogers said as she escorted the young detective inside and to the living room. "Would you like anything to drink?" Mrs. Rogers asked as she watched Detective Moss make herself comfortable in her seat. "No ma'am I'm fine." Detective Moss replied. "So how did you come to the conclusion that your daughter was missing?" "Well detective my daughter has been pretty much coming and going as she pleased since she been 17. To be honest she was found sleeping with a dental assistant at our family dentist office." "You're speaking of Montana Santiago, right?" Mrs. Roger's just looked at her and continued. "I guess she called herself in love, but the lady was 7 years her senior. When we found out it had already been going on for a year. That's when she told us she was gay and that she was in love with the lady. I took it upon myself to confront her. I told her if she didn't leave our child alone that we would report her to the police and sue the dentist's office." "Do you think your tactics worked?" Moss asked. "As far as I know yes, Lameka pouted around for a while and then that's when she met Nashunta."

Detective Moss looked up from the paper she was writing. "So, you knew Nashunta?" "Yes!" Mrs. Rogers replied. "Nashunta was always over here for dinner, she was a wonderful girl. She seemed to keep Lameka from getting into trouble. Don't get me wrong detective I love my daughter, but she had hell's fire trapped in her for a while. She had started to become uncontrollable for a moment. Then she brought home Nashunta and that started to change. My husband and I are away a lot for business. When I got back home I noticed Lameka hadn't been home I tried calling her but got no answer. I didn't think too much of it until I saw on the news that Nashunta was missing? I tried several more times until her voice mail said it was full." "Do you think Lameka and Nashunta would have run away together or something?" Moss asked trying to get a grip on the situation. "Anything could be possible but Lameka took nothing if she did. As far as I can see all her things are still here."

"Lameka has a car registered to her name, right?" "Yes!" Mrs. Rogers agreed. "Could you please give me permission to put an APB out for her car? That way if her car is spotted we can know where they are and find them." Mrs. Rogers agreed and gave Detective Moss all the information she needed. As Moss walked back to her car she started feeling the definite signs of fatigue. After she put an ABP out on Lameka's car she would grab a bite to eat and take it in for the night.

22

When the Smoke Clears

Raven

Tonya's breath caught in her chest and burned the inside of her lungs. Everything she knew and felt about her relationship with Raven was a lie. The anger and rage inside of her took over she ran on pure adrenaline and motor functions. With two swift movements Tonya cleared the table of its effects. The plush teal green carpet was decorated with the remnants of a perfect dinner for two. Tonya stormed through the kitchen destroying everything her hands came in contact with. The pupils that should have saw the staircase of her home only saw Stacey with his hands all over Raven. Tonya had no clue where her feet were taking her. It seemed like every part of her body was doing something opposite of what she wanted. As she emerged at the top of the stairs Tonya heard Raven singing from behind their bedroom door. The blood that ran thru her veins heated to a boil. Just as her unsteady hand reached for the door knob the door swung open and an unsuspecting Raven appeared in the doorway. The sight of Raven standing there made Tonya snap.

Raven shocked to see the demeanor of her lover had changed dramatically. She opened her mouth to speak but before she could enunciate a single word Tonya's hand was across her face. The sheer force of the slap made Raven stumble back into the door. "What the fuck Tonya!" Raven yelled. "What are you doing?" "You wanna know what the fuck? Huh do really wanna know? I trusted you with everything and you gave me your ass to kiss." "What the fuck are you talking about Tonya?" Raven continued to yell. "This is what I'm talking about!" Tonya yelled as she tossed her phone into Raven's hand. The picture of her and Stacey kissing completely caught Raven off guard. "Where did you get this?" Raven asked dumbfounded.

Tonya's conscious was in turmoil as her good and bad sides fought for superiority. She wanted to talk it out as her calm side suggested. However, the more she watched and listened to Raven the more primitive side took control of the helm. Slapping the phone out of Raven's hand was the image Tonya was seeing in her head. It wasn't until she heard the crack of the phone when it broke as it crashed into the wall that she became aware of what was happening. With each step anger replaced the pain and at this point any feeling was better than the pain in her heart. Without warning Tonya attacked Raven again. She tried desperately to defend herself, but Raven was no match for Tonya's brute force.

Raven struggled to stay on her feet as Tonya continued to pommel her from every way possible. "Please stop!" Raven yelled. "Please you promised you wouldn't hit me again." Raven continued to plead. The words from Raven meant nothing to Tonya. Raven's mouth was moving but the sound didn't reach Tonya's ears. Blood trickled from the side of Raven's mouth as she tried retreated from the attack. The wall smacked her in the back as she found herself trapped in a corner.

Monique picked up her phone to check the time but saw that Stacey had called. Despite what her mouth said she was totally in love with him. The fact that he tried reaching out to her made her heart do flips. Well I guess it's now or never, she uttered as she dialed his number. Stacey lay across the bed with his arms folded behind his head. Monique ran through his head every chance she could. He just couldn't shake how horrible he felt for treating her like shit. They had had sex plenty of times without a condom. He would suck it up until he proved the baby wasn't his and then he could move on with a clear conscious. The phone rang but Stacey didn't move at first. He was in deep thought and his mind didn't pick up on the singing until the chorus. Jumping up he grabbed the phone and put it to his ear. "Hello!" He yelled in to the phone. "Are you alright?" Monique asked. "I'm cool. Why you ask me that?" Stacey replied. "Well hell you're yelling in the phone and you sound out of breath. Oh no it's nothing like that. I didn't hear the phone ringing and had to run for it." Stacey said into the phone.

There was an awkward silence as neither one of them knew what to say next. "So, I see that you called me." Monique said tryna break the silence.

"Yea I did. I really wanted to say I'm sorry about all that dumb shit I said to you." Hearing the apologetic words from the man she loved brought tears to her eyes. "I was stupid to doubt you" Stacey continued. "I know you love me and to be honest I really love you too." "You what?" Monique replied. "I said I love you girl!" Stacey could hear over the line that Monique had begun to cry. "Are you alright?" he asked. "Yea! Just hearing those words from your lips mean so much to me." So, am I forgiven?" Stacey asked. "Of course, but you do know you have a lot of making up to do right?" "On the subject of making up let's discuss this window issue." "All is forgiven! Monique quickly shot back. "I thought that's what you would say." They both burst out laughing. "How about you come over and watch a movie with me and the kids. I have that extra butter kettle corn you like. We can break the news to the kids together." "Stacey are you sure?" Monique questioned. "Of course!" Stacey spoke with enthusiasm. "What time should I come?" "Whatever time you feel like getting here." Monique agreed, and they ended the call.

Stacey felt butterflies in his stomach as he hung up the phone. He hadn't felt this excited about anything since he got the number of a sexy little girl he would woo and later marry. He felt a little ping in his heart as he thought about the memory of the day he first met Raven. Raven had stolen his heart the instant she walked past him all those many years ago. Stacey knew in his heart that he would always love Raven, but he also knew that he had to move past that to be happy. As he lay back against the bed the realization made a smile appear across his face. He had the moment when you realize you can actually move pass the person you thought you would love forever. The poignant moment caused a tear to fall down the side of his face.

Monique dropped the phone on the side of her on the bed. Her heart told her to run as fast as she could to get her man. However, the experienced woman she was told her to make him wait. She couldn't help but be happy everything was coming together. She laid there for a while mentally picturing what mouthwatering ensemble she could put together. The phone dinged and it snapped Monique back to her senses. Picking up the phone she notices she has a Facebook notification. Monique clicked on the button and a horoscope appeared on the screen. The horoscope said: Today you feel like you're on top of the world but beware of Karma! It comes quick and fast. Monique rolled her eyes and dropped the phone back down on the bed.

Tonya grabbed Raven by the throat causing her head to hit the wall in the process. The sound of Raven's head hitting the wall had some kind of effect of Tonya. A euphoric feeling came over her and she continued pushing her head into the wall over and over again. "What the fuck bitch! You thought I was just gonna let you play me! You thought you could have your dick and eat some pussy too. I'll kill you before I let him have you! Do you understand me!" Tonya relentlessly belittled Raven as her grip on her throat grew tighter. At first Raven just stood there letting her do whatever she wanted to her. Throughout the year she had learned not to fight back because it only infuriated Tonya more. This time was different she felt in her heart Tonya would kill her. In her mind she knew she had to do something to defuse this situation or she wouldn't make it out of this.

Raven knew she couldn't make it out the door and if she ran it would piss Tonya off even more than she was now. Even though the pain was increasing in her head Raven had to focus on how to get out of this. With one quick movement Raven punched upward striking Tonya in the throat. The unforeseen blow caused Tonya to drop to her knees as she gasped for breath. Tonya's reaction time was mere seconds and she was back on her feet. The seconds were enough time for Raven to grab the cell phone off the floor and run into the closet and lock it. "Open this fucking door bitch!" Tonya yelled as she punched and kicked the closet door from the outside. Raven's hands were trembling so bad she dropped the phone. She clumsily searched for it on the floor but with every hit on the door she thought Tonya would break it down. Remembering the light hanging just above her head Raven jumped to her feet. As she franticly reached for the pull string she knocked several boxes to the floor. Raven clicked the light on and started throwing things everywhere to locate the phone that she had dropped. You have to get a hold of yourself Raven yelled. She forced herself to focus on trying to find the phone.

Tonya kicked the door with everything she had making it crack up the middle. This made Raven crash to the floor and move to the back of the closet. As she scooted her hands brushed against something cold and hard. Pulling her hands up toward her face Raven realized she was holding Tonya's gun. She must have knocked the box with Tonya's things from work on the floor when she was grabbing for the light. The cracking of the closet door snapped the world back into focus. "Tonya please I'm begging you! I'm scared all I want to do is leave." "The only way you're leaving me is in a body bag!" Tonya replied. Using her legs and back Raven pushed herself off the floor until she was standing.

Holding Tonya's black Glock 9-millimeter in her shaking hands she demanded her enraged spouse to move away from the door. Huge tears formed and began to fall down her face. Disregarding what Raven was saying Tonya continued to hammer away at the door until she succeeded in breaking it down. For a moment there was nothing no sound or movement from either one of them. Then out of nowhere Tonya hurled herself at Raven and the world around them began to move in slow motion. Raven shut her eyes and squeezed the trigger of the gun. The bang from the gun was so loud that it left Raven's ears ringing. The swelling of her face and the puffiness of her eyes made it almost impossible for Raven to see. She stood motionless with her arms still extended. "Tonya!" Raven called from the midst of the clothes in the closet. When she received no response from beyond the closet Raven slowly eased herself toward the entrance. As she walked towards the door she felt her foot kick the phone and she bent down to pick it up. "What is that?" she asked trying to hear pass the ringing in her ears. There was an unrecognizable sound coming from somewhere in the room. Raven peered out the door to see if she could see anything before she left the safety of the closet. "Tonya?" Raven called again as she looked around the edge of the closet door. That's when she saw Tonya's feet coming from the other side of the bed.

"Oh my God!" Raven screamed as she rushed to her lover's side. The sound Raven was hearing was Tonya struggling to breathe through the blood that erupted out her mouth. There was one single gunshot wound center mass in the middle of Tonya chest. Pressing down as hard as she could Raven tried to apply as much pressure as she could on the open wound. Tonya tried desperately to speak. "I'm sorry! Don't leave me!" Raven pleaded. Raven tried to open the phone but when she would move her hand the blood would squirt out harder. Tonya looked up at Raven and with her last breath she mouthed "I love you." "Tonya NO!" Raven screamed. It was too late Tonya had accepted the light and crossed over.

Stacey, Monique, and the kids sat on the plush sofa watching TV and eating popcorn. Stacey's phone began to ring. He looked down at the caller ID seeing that it was Raven he pressed ignore. I'll call her back later he said to himself. He didn't want to ruin the moment between him and Monique. Before he could put the phone back down she was calling again. Stacey looked at Monique his eyes were saying what you want me to do. "It's ok Stacey answer it, I'll just run to the kitchen to refill the popcorn and soda for everyone." The biggest smile appeared across his face. "Thank you" he said kissing her forehead before she walked away. "Hey Raven!" Stacey spoke in to the phone. "Hello? Raven?" The concern in his voice made Monique stop in her tracks. "Stacey Tonya's dead!" Raven said through the sobs. "What!" Stacey yelled as he jumped off the sofa. "Tonya's dead! I shot her!" "What the fuck? Did you call the police?" The question hit Raven like a ton of bricks. Everything happened so fast she didn't even have a chance to call the authorities. "No! She attacked me, and I shot her!" Raven screamed into the phone. "Raven listen to me hang up the fucking phone and call the police right now! I'm on my way!" Stacey clicked the phone without giving Raven a chance to protest. He stood there in shock he didn't know what to do next.

"Stacey what wrong?" Monique asked. He was about to speak but then he noticed the kids staring at him with concern on their face. "Daddy is momma ok?" Omari inquired. He didn't know what he was gonna tell his kids. "It was just an accident. Let me talk to Monique and then we'll go check on mommy." Stacey led Monique into the kitchen near the back wall as so to be far enough out of the kids' ear shot. "Tonya's dead." he said. The words felt like acid coming out of his mouth. Monique couldn't move a muscle she felt glued to the floor. "What happened?" She managed to get out. "She attacked Raven and Raven shot her." No sooner had the words left Stacey's mouth the contents of Monique's stomach lurched forward, and she had to dash to the sink. Monique collapsed to the floor the words of her horoscope burned in her head. "Baby you gotta get up. I gotta go check on Raven." Stacey helped Monique to her feet then dashed quick to grab his wallet and keys. Monique refused to stay behind so Stacey packed everyone up and headed to Raven's house.

Stacey arrived at Raven's house parking down the street, so the kids wouldn't be subjected to anything to traumatic. "Daddy why the police and things here?" The kids kept asking. "I want mommy" Kelly began to weep as she laid her head against the back seat. "It's ok kids stay here with Monique while I go check on mommy." They agreed, and Stacey jumped out the car then sprinted toward the house. The officers outside saw Stacey running toward the house and they grabbed their guns. Hey! They yelled in unison. "Do you know they people in this house?" One of the officers asked. "Yes, this is my ex-wife's house!" Stacey yelled. "We have children together!" "Are the children supposed to be here now?" Another officer asked. "No, I have them with me." he replied. "Can I go in or are you gonna continue to catechize me here on the lawn?" "I'm sorry sir but you can't go in this is a crime scene." "Please Officer is Raven ok?" The officer looked at Stacey then let out his breath. "Let me go get someone to talk to you." He said before he walked off in the direction of the other officers.

The officer returned to where he had left Stacey standing. "Sir," he said as he stood in front of Stacey "Ms. Raven Alexander is not the deceased. However, she has been very badly beat up. They are currently speaking with her and then she will be taken to the hospital." While Stacey and the officer talked an enormous screech came from inside the house. Everyone bolted to the door including Stacey. They found Raven clinging to the body bag that held the remains of Tonya Hakeem. The coroners tried to remove the body, but Raven wouldn't be moved. Stacey was stunned, and his eyes couldn't believe what he was seeing. Raven was drenched in blood, her face so swollen that she looked disfigured, and her hair was matted to her head with thick dry clotted blood.

"Raven," Stacey said as he walked toward her. One of the officers tried to grab him but the officer who was outside with Stacey took hold of the officer's arm. Shaking his head, he said "no let him help her." Hearing the familiar voice Raven looked up toward the direction it came from. Seeing Stacey gave her the strength to release Tonya and she was carried out the house into the awaiting van. "Oh Lord Stacey! I didn't mean it! I didn't know what else to do!" Raven managed through her engorged bloody lips. Stacey wrapped his body around Raven and hoisted her up into his arms. "Is she being place under arrest?" he asked not even taking his eyes off of her. "I still have a few more questions a young detective asked." "I'm sure if you need any other information you can locate Ms. Alexander at the hospital." Stacey turned and carried Raven out the door to the awaiting ambulance.

23

Why Does Love Hurt?

Nashunta

Detective Moss arrived at her office bright and early feeling refreshed. Coffee in hand she was ready to take on the world. Before her butt even hit the chair, she was on the phone checking on the APB she put out on Lameka's car. Even though she knew what to expect it was a letdown when she learned that nothing had opened up for her. Detective Moss had half the force out looking for Nashunta and Lameka. She secretly hoped that the two of them had run off to start a life together. Sitting back in her chair she brought the cup of steaming hot elixir to her lips. Everything about the case ran thru her head. She just couldn't put her hands around what she was feeling. If Nashunta still wanted Lameka then why had Lameka sent those cut up things to her? Moss put her cup down on the desk, it just didn't make sense to her. A realization popped in her head. Wait didn't Nathan say Nashunta had broken up with Lameka right before she was last seen? Seeing how petit and helpless Mrs. Rogers was, she let her mind sway from seeing Lameka as a cold-blooded killer. That was a mistake she couldn't afford to make.

Katrina stood over the bed watching the woman she loved sleep soundly away. Katrina had been helplessly in love with her best friend since they had first met. She never had the courage to come out publicly like her friend. Terrified by the consequences if she told how she felt out loud. Despite the complex feelings she had Katrina still couldn't help admiring the curvature of Montana's hips and thighs. The supple breasts that peek from under the cover sent moisture that drenched the fabric between her legs.

Touching her own lips wishing they were being brushed by her secret crush's lips. Her chest began to rapidly rise and fall as her ON button flipped pass being turned on to please fuck me now. Katrina was seconds from letting her fingers slide inside her satin, lace, low cut bikini underwear when the phone next to Montana started to ring. Montana jumped up out her sleep the phone scared the crap outta her. Taking that as her cue Katrina chimed in with a loud "morning sunshine." "Morning beautiful!" Montana replied to her as she picked up the phone to answer it.

"Hello!" The still groggy Montana said into the phone. "Good Morning Ms. Santiago. The all too familiar voice said on the other end. "Detective Moss what a pleasant surprise" Montana said putting extra emphasis on pleasant. Katrina dropped her head hearing the woman she loved flirt with another woman chipped away at her heart. Silently she took her wounded spirit and left the room. She could still hear Montana sweetly giggling as she walked down the hall.

"My call is a pleasant surprise huh?" Moss asked as she twirled a pencil in her fingers. "Sure!" Montana elated. "What person in their right mind wouldn't want to get a wakeup call from an extremely beautiful woman?" "Extremely beautiful I think I might like the sound of that." Moss replied as she let the words slide down her lips. Shaking her head Moss jumped up in her chair. She couldn't allow this lady to corrupt her train of thought. Montana just oozed with sexuality, she could see how anybody who came in contact with her would fall under her spell. How did she let Lameka rule over her? A flash of Montana danced across her frontal lobe. That girl can have anybody gay or straight that she wants. "I really just wanted to check on you to see if you were ok." "Well if I wasn't I'm feeling great now." Montana teased. Moss let a tiny laugh escape her lips. This girl gave her butterflies she thought. "How's your friend Katrina doing?" The detective asked as to remove the spotlight off of herself. "Oh, she's great, she's probably waiting on me to get up, so we can eat breakfast together." "Is that right?" Moss asked sarcastically. "She really cares about you huh?" "Of course she does she's my best friend!" Montana proclaimed. "I'm sure!" Detective Moss said. "Well anyway I just wanted to say thank you again for your help and to make sure you guys were alright." "Yes, ma'am we're A OK!" Montana replied. "Thanks for the check up and don't forget to call me when you bring Nashunta home safely." "Sure thing!" Moss replied but in the back of her mind she held her doubts about her come back at all.

After she ended her call Montana made her way to the kitchen. Katrina was busy arranging food on plates. "I'm glad you finally decided to grace me with your presence. I thought I was gonna have to starve this morning." "Well you really didn't have to wait for me." Montana said as she grabbed a strawberry off the counter and placed it to her lips. Katrina turned around only to find Montana nude except for pink and black polka dot undies and eating a strawberry. Letting her eyes linger a little long then she should Katrina memorized every inch of Montana's frame. "So, can I have my plate?" Montana joked grabbing her plate out of Katrina's hand. Following Montana to the table Katrina tried to get her thoughts under control. She sat with her head bowed focusing way too hard on her on her food.

"So, what did Detective Moss have to say?" Katrina asked before she shoveled scrambled eggs in mouth. "Nothing really, she just wanted to check on us and see how we were doing." Even though Katrina had her eyes parallel to her plate Montana noticed the look on her friend's face. "What? She asked about you too?" "Yeah, I'm sure!" Katrina smirked. "Funny she said the same thing." They both look at each other and the room was consumed with laughter.

Nathan sat staring into the air as he wondered what he could have done different about his last conversation with Nashunta. He couldn't let her go every time his eyes closed he would see her. See her always standing there waiting on him to find her. He decided to take a leave of absence from school because it had been weeks since Nashunta's disappearance and he couldn't bring himself to leave. He dialed her number faithfully every day in hopes that this time she would pick up. The world around Nathan began to grow distant as he spent all his time searching for his friend. The TV clicked on as the timer was set for 8'o clock so he wouldn't miss the news. This time the TV didn't have his attention and Nathan got up to retrieve the phone. Grabbing the card out his wallet he dialed Detective Moss. He hadn't talked to her since the press conference and he wanted to know if she had any new leads.

Moss stood moments from walking into a meeting at the police station to speak on Nashunta's case. She wanted to make sure every car and every officer had an eye out for Lameka's missing car. The vibration of her phone caught her of guard. "Moss!" she said into the phone as she put it to her ear. "Hey Detective Moss, it's Nathan. Do you remember me from the press conference?" "Of course, I do! How are you holding up?" "I'm good I really wanted to talk to you about Nashunta's case." "I would love to speak to you about the case but I'm heading into a meeting." "Would it be alright if I called you a little later?" Nathan agreed the call was ended and Detective Moss walked in the room to start the meeting.

Officer Hicks grabbed some coffee and took his seat before the meeting started. He had heard about the Nashunta Jones case from other officers, but this was the first meeting they had at his precinct. The meeting began, and officer Hicks sat back in his chair and listened intently. Having a daughter of his own the case struck close to home. He had to wipe away a few tears as he thought about what he would do if it was his daughter. He said a quick prayer thanking God for his family and that they find Nashunta safe. After the meeting Officer Hicks waited in line with the other officers to exit the room. He shook hands with the Detective and thanked her for coming. Then he grabbed a flyer off the table and headed to his squad car.

Officer Hicks could not take the information about the case off his mind. The thoughts ran through his mind even as he did his routine check of his car before he left. Before he left the precinct to start his shift he taped the flyer to his dashboard and silently prayed again that the Lord would guide them to swiftly find the young lady and safely bring her home. The morning was going by so slowly there was nothing going on. Officer Hicks decided to park on the side of the Chevron and wait until he received a call. Officer Hicks was laid back in his car when an hour later the radio in his car came to life. There was a domestic dispute 3 blocks from where he was so he grabs the radio to let them know he was in route.

Pulling up at the address Hicks sees that two other officers have gotten there before him. He said the prayer he says every time he gets a call. Lord please let me make it home safe to my family. Officer Hicks said Amen then he exited his vehicle. Hey guys! Hicks said as he walked up to the officers standing outside with the lady of the house. "Apparently, the neighbors are having one of their weekly altercations." one of the officers said looking back at Officer Hicks. So, after talking to the neighbor the next hour was spent tryna sort everything out with the couple who were actually fighting. Nobody wanted to cooperate with them it was becoming more hassle then it was worth.

In the end since there were no physical bruises and there were no other witnesses to the fight besides the neighbor. It was really nothing they could do. So, the couple was given a verbal warning. If we have to come back, we are taking everybody to jail. The lead officer said. They agreed and closed the door. As the officers walked back to their cars the lead officer let out a short laugh. I wonder how long the truce with them will last before it starts all over again. Both the other Officer and Hicks looked up and they all started laughing. According to the neighbors Officer Hicks stated about a week.

Back in the car Officer Hicks once again patrolled the streets to keep them safe. The time passed by so slowly nothing interesting had happened at all this shift. Looking down at his watch his stomach guessed what time it was before his head could catch up. "Lunchtime" he said out loud to nobody but himself. Letting every restaurant in the area run through his mind Officer Hicks finally decided on Captain D's. Well I better make one more ride around before I take lunch. Officer Hicks said as he pulled up to the red light.

So, he wouldn't feel guilty he rode around for another half an hour making sure everything was as it should be. Officer Hicks then chose to take the back road instead of the regular street way. Turn after turn nothing but trees, trash covered abandoned properties, and condemned houses. Officer Hicks was about to turn his cruiser around when something a little further up the way caught his eye. The reflection from the sun made it impossible to see past the brightness. What the hell, was his reaction as he tried to shield his face in order to see beyond the gleam. Slowly proceeding forward Officer Hicks pulls up to what looks like an abandoned car.

Officer Hicks looked at the license plate and for some reason it ringed familiar. He could not remember where he had seen it before. Then suddenly he wanted to slap himself across the face. Officer Hicks snatched down the paper he had taped to his dashboard this morning. No fucking way! He said as he searched the paper for the tag number of the missing car. He spotted the tag number then looked up for verification. Hicks was excited about this being the car they were searching for. That was until reality kicked him in the stomach. If the car has been left out here, then where were the girls? He called in to dispatch to check the tag to make sure. Once he had a positive identification of the car he asked for backup and requested that Detective Moss be contacted.

Anticipation bubbled up inside him as he waited for his back up to arrive. He wanted to rush in guns blazing and save the day, but he knew he had to do things by the books or a killer could go free. "Fuck this" Officer Hicks yelled as he got out of his car. He was about to go snooping around when he spotted the first car of back up high tailing it up the way.

Three cars of back up arrived and Hicks brought everyone up to speed about what he wanted to do. They divided themselves into three groups and proceeded to search the property around where the car was parked. The rest of the search party busied themselves with the search, but Officer Hicks was determined to check out the old shed that stood in the back of the property. As he drew closer he swore he heard voices. He turned down his radio, so he could listen intensely. He made eye contact with his search partner to signal he had something. They moved in to circle the shed. Upon reaching the window Officer Hicks noticed a light was on inside. "Why would the power be on in the place?" he asked his partner. As they continued to listen they realized they were not hearing voices, but it was actually the radio that was on. "Do you think the girls have been living here?" the other officer asked Hicks. "I don't know but if they are I don't want to terrify them and make them do something stupid. Ok this is what we finna do, you go around the front and enter that way. Ima give you a twenty count from the time you bend the corner them Ima knock on this door. That way if they run you can head them off." The officer agreed then started around the shed.

Officer Hicks waited until he could no longer see the officer until started his count down from twenty. The sweat from his brow blinded him as he sat crouched with his back against the wall. Ten one thousand, nine one thousand, Officer Hicks counted under his breath. Six one thousand, five one thousand, he began to rise to standing position in front of the door. Just as soon as one one thousand left his lips his knuckles hit the door. "Police!" Officer Hicks yelled as he struck the door again. He made one more attempt to identify himself then using his shoulder forcefully pushed the door end.

Moss was completely exhausted by the time she made it back to the office. Her morning was consumed by meeting after meeting with its endless array handshakes and greeting. Her palms were tender, and her voice nearly spent. Once off the elevator Moss made sure she walked with her head down as she made the lonely trek to her desk, so no one would speak in her direction. Half way down the hall she could hear the phone on her desk ringing. Her mind willed her to rush forward to catch it, but her legs did not follow through with the thought. Her mind got the message they'll call back she thought to herself.

Pushing open the door to her office Moss barely made it thru the threshold before the phone was ringing again. "Moss" she said into the phone her normal greeting gone with the onset of hunger and fatigued. "Davis this better be good you're coming in between me and a much-needed lunch break. What?" She yelled into the phone. "Where? I'm one my way!" Moss replied. Moss was out the door and back in her car so fast she could've made her own head spin. The signs of stress and fatigued were obliviated from her thoughts. By the time Officer Hicks and his search partner were heading to investigate the shed Detective Moss was charging, lights flashing, siren blaring to the area.

Speeding in and out of traffic Detective Moss could almost feel her heart in her throat. The pounding grew louder and louder with each beat until nothing else was audible. Her foot never left the accelerator until she was sliding into park behind the other government cars at the scene. Moss was off and running before the engine stopped spinning. Half running and sprinting she caught up to the first officer she saw. "Hey!" She said then as quickly as she could Moss identified herself. The officer sensing the urgency told her that a couple of officers had found a shed up ahead and went to investigate it. "Thanks," she yelled over her shoulder as she struck out running toward the direction of the shed. Detective Moss was coming up on a clearing the looked to be the back of the shed when she heard a loud banging noise. Unknowingly to her it was Officer Hicks knocking in the door to the shed up ahead.

Detective Moss stopped her stride long enough to unhook her shoulder strap. She removed the safety as she ran full force up the clearing and to the back door of the shed. Moss ducked inside the door, but she could see nothing until her eyes adjusted to the room. She put her arm up in front of her in an attempt to feel her way, but she was knocked back by something in front of her. The force knocked her back out the door and on to her ass in the dirt. Raising her gun in the preparation to defend herself she jumped to her feet. After blinking her eyes several times Moss realized that it was an officer that stood with his back to her at the door. "Hey!" Moss yelled in an effort to get his attention, but the officer was too focused on whatever it was in front of him. In the back of her mind she knew there was a person with a gun in front of him and he knocked her to shield her. Detective Moss stood with her back pressed as flat as she could manage to the side of the wall. Officer Hicks slowly backed out of the shed oblivious to the world behind him. He hadn't even felt the impact of the Detective as she crashed in to him. Waiting like a predator for its prey, she remained still until Officer Hicks was far enough away from the door before she charged in. "Freeze!" were the last words that rang out through the air.

24

I Love You to Death

Nashunta

N ashunta looked nervously at Lameka as they drove down the street. "Lameka I know we've had some pretty tough times." Nashunta tried to start off but Lameka cut her off. "Not now! We can talk once we get to where we are going." "And where is that?" Nashunta inquired. "Dang Nashunta why all the questions? You act as if you've never been anywhere with me before." Nashunta didn't know how to feel she had major butterflies in her stomach. Giving up she just sat back against the seat. Lameka said nothing she just kept her eyes glued straight at the road like nothing else mattered.

The quietness from the car and the purring of the engine had Nashunta dozing off. She tried to keep her eyes open, but sleep won out. When she opened her eyes, she saw that they were pulling in at Lameka's house. "I need to grab something" Lameka said, "come on get out." Nashunta opened the door and reluctantly followed Lameka. "You can have a seat Nashunta I'm not gonna bite you. Would you like something to drink? We have those little cherry pops you like." For some reason Lameka was being way too nice, Nashunta thought. "Sure, I'll take one," she agreed, she wanted this talk to go as smoothly as possible. Better yet she wouldn't tell her it was really over until she was safely back home.

Lameka knew Nashunta couldn't resist the cherry pop and her plan was working perfectly. I know she still loves me and I'm gonna make her realize it. Grabbing a glass out of the cabinet she placed it on the countertop. Lameka pulls out a little plastic bag that held the pills she had crushed down earlier. Pouring a minute amount of pop in the glass she let the pills become completely absorbed before she poured in the remainder. She placed some cut up fruit pieces and a few ice cubes before turning to take the concoction to Nashunta. "Wow! That looks great," Nashunta said as she took the glass and downed half of it before Lameka even put her hand down. "Let me go grab this and we can bounce alright?" Lameka said as she turned to go up the stairs. Moments later she crept back down to watch Nashunta without notice.

Time ticked away and Nashunta started to get worried. "Are we leaving soon?" she asked into thin air. "Lameka! Are we leaving soon?" What the hell is she doing Nashunta asked to herself. Nashunta stood to her feet but when she bent down to put her empty glass on the table she felt light headed. Quickly she tried to straighten back up, but it only made it worse. Nashunta found that she had to grab hold of the sofa for support.

"You really should sit back down or you're gonna end up hurting yourself." Lameka replied as she walked from behind the wall. "Just relax the more you fight it the sicker you're gonna be." "What the fuck did you do!" Nashunta yelled. The world swirled in a circular motion inside Nashunta's head and she thought she would vomit. She tried desperately to stay on her feet, but they became wobbly and she crashed back down against the sofa. Seeing that her body no longer worked she used the only thing left that could. Nashunta used every last fiber of her being and she started yelling at the top of her voice. "Help! Help me please!" Lameka anticipated this move so before Nashunta could get the third help me out a large piece of duct tape was slapped across her lips. With all her energy spent Nashunta's head hit the couch as she lost consciousness.

"Finally!" Lameka said as she quickly jumped up to get everything together. Using the same tape, she quickly constrained Nashunta's hands and feet. Lameka pulled her car in the garage making sure to secure it tightly so she wouldn't be seen. She then half carried half dragged Nashunta's catatonic frame thru the living room, dining room, and kitchen to the awaiting car in the garage. Placing her gently on the back seat Lameka covered her with a blanket then placed boxes on top to conceal everything. Stopping long enough to catch her breath she hurried back in to the house to clean things up. After things were back in their original place Lameka grabbed her bag, jumped inside her car, and off she drove.

The cold water hit Nashunta's face and she groggily opened her eyes. It took her a minute, but she managed to see through the fogginess of her head to get her bearings. She tried to move but found that she was tied to a chair. A blurry figure came in focus as Lameka walked closer to her. Lameka straddled Nashunta on the chair, she was so close Nashunta could feel the warmth of her breath. "Now if I take that off your gonna listen and not scream right?" With tears streaming down her face the helpless Nashunta shook her head yes. Lameka carefully but quickly snatched the tape from Nashunta's lips. "Why have you done this?" Nashunta whispered. "Shut up!" Lameka snapped. "I brought you here to listen not to talk."

"I tried everything to make you see how much I loved you. I gave up everything to prove to you that you were the one. I can't let you leave me! I can't deal with the hurt and the pain of being without you." "What is it you want from me Lameka?" "I want you to understand!" She yelled back at Nashunta. "Understand what! That you're fucking crazy!" Nashunta replied. The moment the words left her mouth she knew it was a mistake, but it was too late as Lameka's hand came firmly down across her face.

"You're making me do this, I didn't bring you here to hurt you." Lameka spoke looking inside Nashunta's eyes. "Fuck you!" Nashunta replied right before she spit blood and saliva into Lameka's face. Lameka stood up in front of Nashunta and wiped the bloody spit away. "We can do this the easy way or the hard way." With the same hand she used on her face Lameka balled a fist and punched Nashunta as hard as she could striking her in the nose. "How about I leave you to rot here" she yelled over her shoulder. Lameka grabbed the small radio that her grandpa kept there and placed it on the table. She turned it on and walked back over to Nashunta. "To keep you company while I'm gone." "Lameka please don't leave me here!" Nashunta yelled. "You leave me no choice! You said you would be good but instead you spit in my face! Ima give you some time to think about what you wanna do." Lameka turn and walked out the door.

"No! Please don't leave me here!" Nashunta screamed at the top of her lungs. "Help! Help!" Lameka had no intentions in leaving her lover she just had to break her. She had to be made to understand that she was in charge. She sat against the bottom steps lit a Newport and laughed at the futile attempts at her captive to get help. Finally, the screams and shouts were no longer heard from inside the shed. Taking her sweet time, she slowly smoked another Newport before she picked herself up off the step.

"Are you done with your tantrums?" Lameka asked as she stood in the doorway. The tears cascaded down Nashunta's face as she shook her head yes. "Are you hungry?" "Yes." Nashunta replied. Lameka pulled the table over to Nashunta. She had it laid out with two box dinners from Church's chicken. "Look at you," Lameka said as she grabbed some wet naps off the table and started wiping Nashunta's face. "Thank you" Nashunta said when she was done. "I do love you and yes, I know you love me. I couldn't be without you anymore," Nashunta continued. "That's why I wanted to talk to you. My friend Nathan was gonna help me run away I was gonna ask you to come with me." "Really!" Lameka said baiting herself on the hook Nashunta dangled for her. She wanted so much for Nashunta to love her again Lameka was ready to believe anything.

Taking a wet nap and cleaning off her own hands Lameka began fixing the food to serve Nashunta. "I'm sorry I made you mad. I know I can do better you just have to show me." Nashunta said between bits of chicken. "Lameka," Nashunta called her name in the sweetest tone she could muster. "Do you think I can feed myself? I promise I'm gonna behave. I was just frightened before, but I know you won't hurt me." Lameka thought about it for a second but quickly dismissed it. "Sure, but if you act out Ima tie you back down and lunchtime will be over." Using the plastic knife from the food Lameka cut the tape from around Nashunta's wrists. Nashunta rubbed her wrists to increase the circulation and regain feeling. Lameka watched her captive apprehensively as she pulled a chair up to the table next to her. They talked as they finished the rest of their meal.

Nashunta tried to get her game plan together before she made a move. Once she freed herself she would try to knock Lameka out. After that she would grab the keys off the stand by the door and run. She let the scenario run through her head over and over again. Every now and then Nashunta tried working at the tape that still held her tight to the chair. "Fuck!" she said under her breath. She couldn't get the tape loose with her hands. The plastic knife on the table came to mind but before she could get a hold to it, Lameka cleared everything off and dumped it into the trash. Anger took hold of every cell in her body. She didn't care what it took she wanted out of this situation.

"I knew you would see thing my way once you had time to think about our love." Nashunta continued to let Lameka think she had the upper hand as she wrestled with the tape around her ankles. Words mingled thru the air but Nashunta heard none of it. She pulled, and she dug until she freed both of her legs from the chair, but she didn't move. Lameka had no idea she was loose. "You know something?" She asked her capturer. "What?" Lameka replied. "I've been here all this time, and not once did you kiss me. And you call yourself in love with me." A spark glazed over Lameka's eyes as she walked over to her lady love. Lowering her body, she moved in slowly to place her lips seductively on Nashunta. Lameka let her body melt, she had longed to taste of these lips for seemed like an eternity. A massive blow to the head caught Lameka off guard causing her to fall to the floor. Nashunta leaps up and darts full steam towards the door. Hands extended the doorknob was right within her grasp. A blinding force struck Nashunta in the back of the head causing her to surge forward hitting the door. That in turn knocked her back and she fell on top of the very object that had caused the tumble in the beginning. What Nashunta didn't take into account was Lameka's quick reflexes. Yes, her powerful whack across the head caused Lameka to drop. However, within seconds she was back on her feet and hurling the folding chair thru the air.

Nashunta lay helplessly on the floor atop the chair. Her legs made temporarily useless from the blow. Looking puzzled Lameka walked over to Nashunta. "What the hell you hit me for!" "Fuck you Lameka! You think you can kidnap someone and get away with it!" The words stung as they hit Lameka square across the face. Anger and rage rumbled its way from deep inside until it seeps out her very core. Nashunta continued to spit verbal fire as she struggled to her feet. Using the wall for support Nashunta tried to regain her equilibrium. The room around her was spinning and her ears were ringing.

Grabbing Nashunta without warning Lameka pinned her captive against the wall by the throat. "All I ever did was love you! I went against everything I ever believed in just to be with you!" The more she poured her feelings out the more enraged it made Nashunta. "What!" Nashunta replied. "The only person you ever loved was yourself!" Something inside of Lameka snapped. The world around her darkened and looked as though it was moving in slow motion. She could feel the arms of Nashunta striking against her in defense, but it only felt like vague memories of a pass life.

Nashunta didn't know that the moment the words left her lips it would be the last mistake she ever made. The grip Lameka had on her throat tightened and her air supply became nonexistent. She scratched and clawed at Lameka's hands in an attempt to free herself from her grasp. When that failed Nashunta began and all-out assault sending massive blows upside Lameka's cranium. Nothing she attempted seemed to faze Lameka. The expression on her face was like she was there but gone. Nashunta continued her struggle until her body was so weak she could no longer lift her arms to strike.

The world around Nashunta seemed as if it were a movie theater preparing for the main attraction. At first it was Lameka's stone features, but it quickly changed in to an early childhood memory. Each apparition was a different time in her life, some made her laugh others made her cry. In her heart Nashunta knew she was dying but she was helpless against what was happing to her. There was no longer any pain or worry surrounding her. What was that? She began reaching for it before she knew it she was standing and walking to investigate the image she saw in front of her. The closer she got to the image the clearer it became. "Grandma!" Nashunta screamed as she ran into the waiting arms of her loving Grandma. Taking her hand Nashunta left this world and crossed over to the next.

Lameka stood frozen over Nashunta's lifeless body with her hands still clasped around her neck. She was oblivious to the fact that the love of her life was no longer with her. Once the heat of the moment wore off and she slowly came back to her senses Lameka quickly snatched her hands back. "Babe!" She shrieked. "Babe!" Lameka grabbed hold and shook Nashunta's motionless frame in an effort to wake her from her trance. It wasn't until she checked for a pulse did Lameka came to grips with what she had done.

There was no panic or frantic running around to hide the body as you see on the TV. There was nothing, no void of emotions, just simply numbness that came over her. Lameka stood up, gently picked up the dead body of her murdered love and walked her to the sofa. With tearful eyes she laid Nashunta on the sofa with her head resting on the armrest. Lameka cleaned the blood from her face and folded her arms across her chest. In her mind she looked just like Snow White awaiting her prince charming. Even though Lameka thought she would have no use for it she went and retrieved the hand gun she had securely tucked in the inside pocket of her duffel bag. Without having any paper, she tore off the lid from the discarded Church's box out the trash. On the lid she wrote in big letters. "I AM SORRY! MY FLOWER HAS DIED AND SO SHALL I!" Lameka placed the chair in front of the sofa facing the love of her life. Unlike Nashunta there were no loving images of lifelong memories only darkness as Lameka pulled the trigger ending her life. Nashunta and Lameka were long dead before their mothers even knew they were missing.

25

Predator or Prey

Mercedes

As Mercedes lay unconscious sprawled out across the floor, Hakeem instructed Monea to rummaged through the drawers to find something to tie herself up with. She found some duct tape and Hakeem taped her hands, and then placed some tape across her mouth. He told her he wasn't there for her and if she remained calm everything for her would be ok. Monea used the wall to slide down to the floor and she sat there staring at her lifeless lover on the floor. Hakeem walked over to where Mercedes lay on the floor and kicked her feet. "See the problem is she belongs to me, every part of her!" He starred Monea dead in her eye as he lowered himself down beside Mercedes on the floor. He placed his hands on both sides of her light denim leggings and pulled them and her underwear slowly down until they were completely off. Monea watch horrified as he positioned himself between Mercedes lifeless legs. "Let me show you what you are supposed to do with pussy, and if you like what you see I'll give you a taste to." Hakeem without taking his eyes off Monea, undid his pants and forced his erect penis inside Mercedes.

Mercedes traveled in the darkness from reality into nightmare. There was nothing no noise, no light, nothing. She was yanked out of the darkness by Hakeem as he snatched her up out of what looks like a she had been sitting in. She was confused was this real or was this dream. Mercedes screamed them she jumped up and ran to the room. Mercedes tried to dress as fast as she could before Hakeem burst through the door. She only managed to get her shirt over her head before he burst in the door. Grabbing Mercedes by the hair Hakeem threw her into the wall. In her mind as this was happening, she realized she was playing back the last time she was with him. She felt the pain in her face as her head made contact with the wall and then again darkness.

Hakeem tried several failed attempts to call Mercedes to make sure she was ok. He was so terrified after she didn't respond when he knocked her into the wall that he bolted from the apartment with Twon trailing close behind. There was no fucking way he was going back to jail especially not for murder.

Mercedes awakened on the floor of her room. Stars swam around her head she slowly sat up. Making her way to the bathroom Mercedes had to make a survey of the damage to her face. There was a huge hand print across the side of her face, a bloody knot at the back of her head, and some superficial scratches on her cheeks. Mercedes downed two pain pills then made her way to the living room to find her smokes. Once she reached the table where she had left them there was only an empty pack left in its place.

Mercedes put on her shoes and she left the house walking to the store. She prayed and cried the whole way to the store. Do you know what happens when prayers go up? Of course, you do. Blessings come down! Sometimes it's not the answers that we seek but it's the answers that we need. Mercedes walked in the store and purchased her pack of Newport's. She turned and started to head out the door, but something caught her eye. The picture on the newspaper looked familiar from a distance. As she got closer and the headlines were visible for her to read she dropped everything from her hands. Keys, cell phone, money, cigarettes, lighter, and ID all went crashing to the ground as she raced for the newspaper.

The newspaper headline read as followed: **Nashunta Jones and Lameka Rogers Both Found Dead in an Abandoned Shack From What Appears to be a Murder Suicide.** Mercedes stood there in disbelief. The store clerk came around the counter, picked up her things, and handled them to her. Grabbing her things, she paid for the paper raced out the door and ran to the house. Blessed the house was still empty she knew she had moments before the kids got home. With one hand across her mouth she read what the papers had to say about this young girl whose life was taken away. At the end of the article Nashunta's mom made a tearful plead to anyone in an abusive relationship to get out while there was still a chance. The newspaper picture of the sobbing Mrs. Jones caused Mercedes heart to ache. Is this what I'm gonna subject my mother to go thru when Hakeem goes too far one of these days. Mercedes thought to herself and then she flashed back to waking up on the floor alone after he had thrown her into the wall.

"My daughter did not deserve to die like this and neither do you. Please don't make the mistake of thinking what you are going through is love. If I couldn't save my child I'm gonna make it my mission to save someone else's." Mrs. Jones words continued to ring in Mercedes' head. Mercedes felt like a failure no matter what Hakeem did to her she couldn't bring her feet to move. She wanted so desperately to leave! Where would she go? What would she do? Something inside her clicked Mercedes picked up the phone and start dialing. It was like the Heavenly Father took control of her for a moment. She had no clue of who was on the other end until the voice rang out Hello. "Dee Dee?" Mercedes said sounding a bit confused. "Umm yeah! Who else number did you dial? You ok sista girl?" Dee Dee asked. "Not really!" Mercedes replied. "Hey if I need to move in a hurry could I come there?" The silence from the other end made a nauseating feeling rise from her stomach to her throat. "Are you in some kinda trouble?" came the response. "Define trouble!" Mercedes tried to joke. "We're kinda tight over here but I'm sure we can make room for y'all. When you need to come?" Dee Dee asked. "I'm not sure if I'm coming or not just wanted to make sure if I need to come I can." Mercedes replied. "Hey, let me call you right back." Mercedes quickly stated. "Ok!" Her sister answered before the call abruptly ended. As she walked to the bathroom to relieve herself, her mind was so preoccupied that she had momentarily forgotten about her appearance. Leaning over the sink to wash her hands Mercedes looked up into the mirror and reality took its turn to slap her in the face. Seeing her battered and bruised face was the last straw for her.

Mercedes grabbed the roll of gigantic lawn trash bags she kept under her kitchen sink and started tossing things inside. While she was doing this, she was dialing Dee Dee's number on the phone. The sound of her sister's voice rang out in her ear causing an eruption of emotions to come flowing from her. After the crying stopped and even before Mercedes had a chance to explain her sister spoke. "What time are you coming?"

By the time the kids came home Mercedes had packed up half the house. She yelled directions at the kids and they jumped into action. After everything they could take was packed on the back of the pickup truck she borrowed, Mercedes pulled her kids to the side. "Things are gonna get tough for us but as long as we're together everything is gonna work out fine." They embraced each other in a huge group hug then turned to leave the house. Mercedes cut off the light and locked the door. She rounded the truck once making sure her cargo was secure then they loaded up in the cab of the truck. Starting the engine Mercedes said goodbye to Hakeem and living a life of misery. At least that's what she thought until she came face to face with him standing in her doorway.

The sound of Hakeem's voice could be heard from somewhere over her. Mercedes' brain tried to reboot itself as she slowly regained consciousness. Her brain sent awareness to her body one area at a time. The burning between her thighs was felt long before her brain sent word to open her eyes. Hakeem lay atop her half naked frame savagely raping her body. Once her senses awaken Mercedes realized she was pinned with her legs up in Hakeem's arms as he angrily drove his penis deep inside her in rapid succession. There was the sound of clapping as their bodies made contact with each stroke. Mercedes wanted to scream but her airway was restricted, and she could barely breathe. She prayed that death would claim her to save her from further torment. But before she could think clearly Hakeem released her legs. With one movement he flipped her over, pinned her head down and was back inside her forceful pounding her from the back. She could feel her vaginal lips swollen so tight that every time he slammed into her it felt like sandpaper ripping layers of flesh from her private area.

Mercedes looked up and saw a terrified Monea huddled, crying in the corner. It wasn't until then that she realized this was reality and she started crying. Mercedes made the mistake of letting her cries be heard. At that moment he knew he was hurting her. Hakeem reached his hand down and forcefully jabbed three fingers in her tight anal cavity. Her screams excited him and went to work madly digging into her with his hand and his penis simultaneously. Moments later Hakeem exploded inside Mercedes sending his seed shooting up into her body.

Crashing back against the floor Hakeem's body separated from hers. Mercedes unable to move her legs, she felt like her lower region was on fire. "Fucking bitch!" Hakeem yelled at her. Lifting her head, she was just in time to catch a glimpse of bottom of Hakeem's foot. He kicked her in the face sending her cascading across the floor. Fearful of another attack she lay frozen in the spot on the floor. Mercedes lay there for what felt like an eternity until she heard the sounds of snoring coming from behind her. Mercedes sat upright on the floor, but she had to quickly wrap her hand across her swollen lips because the move sent pain shooting from every direction of her body. Mercedes knew she only had moments before Hakeem's eyes would pop open and he would be on her again, or worst hurt Monea.

Without making a sound she mouths to Monea, "are you hurt?" Monea shook her head no. Mercedes was trying to figure out what to do next then it dawned on her. She tried to stand but her legs wouldn't move, so she half slid, and half crawled in to the kitchen. Monea did not know what was happening, where was she going, she wanted to shout but she knew that would awaken the crazy man that was holding them hostage. Mercedes wasn't in the kitchen for long and when she returned this time she was standing, and she had a small black bag under her arm like a purse. She motioned for Monea to come to her, but Hakeem's leg was resting on top of hers. Mercedes then put her hand next to her face in attempt to ask Monea where her phone was. She shrugged her shoulders and motioned towards their captor. They had to get out of there fast, Mercedes thought. Mercedes threw on her pants as fast as she could without making a peep. She was now running off pure adrenaline, she felt no pain.

While she was putting on her pants neither of them noticed that Hakeem was no longer snoring. He just laid there like a cat waiting on the right time to snatch a mouse. Mercedes was easing her way toward Monea when suddenly Hakeem's leg shifted on Monea as if he was about to move it. Mercedes and Monea both held their breath, the only sound she heard was the thumping of her heart in her ears. But instead of moving it off he raised it and came down forcefully on Monea's legs causing her to scream out in pain.

Mercedes watched as Hakeem kicked Monea over and over again. Before Mercedes could move in an attempt to help her Hakeem had his gun pointed directly at her. "She has nothing to do with this Hakeem, let her go." Mercedes said. Hakeem stood there looking around from her back to Monea as if he couldn't decide what to do. It was then that Hakeem started to lose grip on reality. It was like a light just clicked on and he could fully see the severity of what he had done. He started pacing back and forth hitting himself in the head with the gun and saying how he wasn't going back to jail. Mercedes knew she had to calm him down if she wanted to get them out of this alive.

"You still have time to leave Hakeem, no one is hurt, you can leave if you want." Mercedes said in an effort to offer him an out. Hakeem said nothing in return, it was like he was battling with himself and they weren't even there. While Hakeem mind was occupied somewhere else Mercedes slowly move the black bag from under her arm to behind her back. She pulled the small gun from the bag, letting the bag fall behind her down the wall to the floor. Once she realized he hadn't noticed any of that, she used her free hand to locate and removed the safety on the weapon. She stood there watching a man she once love disintegrate mentally before her face and she prayed this wouldn't be her last move, then she coughed loudly as she gently cocked the gun back.

The sound of the loud cough brought Monea's focus toward her, as she motioned for her to slowly start moving towards her. Monea moved as cautious as she could possibly move as she pushed her way up the wall in a standing position. By the time she reached her feet Hakeem swung around to face them. As he moved closer to them, Mercedes moved closer to Monea. "You can't have her!" Hakeem yelled as he pulled the hammer back on the gun and raised his hand towards Monea. Mercedes put herself between the gun and Monea and at that moment Hakeem pulled the trigger. Even though things were moving in slow motion for her, it took was mere seconds for Mercedes to realize that Hakeem's gun had jammed, and he stood in front of her with a total look of shock. She whips the gun from behind her back and points it directly at Hakeem's chest. "Drop the gun Hakeem! Please Don't make me kill you!" Without warning Hakeem leaped toward Mercedes and she just closed her eyes and pulled the trigger. Hakeem was struck in the midsection and the force of the shot sent him tumbling over the side of the couch. Mercedes ran over to Hakeem, she kicked the gun back towards Monea. Monea seeing that Hakeem was down, pulled the tape from her mouth and quickly bit through the tape around her hands. She then quickly picked the gun up off the floor and while Mercedes stood with the gun still on Hakeem she searched him for a phone. As Monea dug inside Hakeem's pocket he grabbed her arm, and Mercedes hit him in the stomach as hard as she could with the butt of her gun. He let go and Monea was able to pull the phone free from his pocket. She stumbled back a little but got to her feet quickly and dialed 911. They both stood frozen in time until help came for them.

The sirens could be heard in the distance, then the footsteps in the hall, and finally there came the pounding on the door. Monea rushed to the door, unlocking it as fast as she could. The policed rushed in guns drawn all pointing at Mercedes because she was the one standing there armed. "Drop the weapon!" they all screamed in unison. Mercedes dropped the gun and stepped back. One police officer grabbed Mercedes and started telling her the Maranda Rights as he began placing handcuffs on. "No!" Monea screamed as she rushed to Mercedes' side. "She's not the one, it's him, he's the one who attacked us!" Monea yelled as she tried to pull Mercedes' arm from the arresting officer. Mercedes felt her knees start to buckle and her head started spinning. Her overwhelming emotions, the rush of the chaotic scene around the, coupled with her multitude of injuries became too much for her and she collapsed down to the floor. The last thing she remembers hearing was the voice of Monea screaming for her as everything faded to into darkness.

For the first time in a long time there was no nightmares in the darkness. There was just darkness, peaceful and calm. At first Mercedes didn't know if she was dead or alive, because the darkness was so welcoming. Then in the darkness she heard it, a low steady beeping. After she heard the beeping she became aware of how stiff and sore her body was everywhere. "So, I guess I'm not dead." Mercedes thought she had spoken it in her mind, but she had said it out loud. "She's awake!" yelled several different voices at once. She couldn't make out the voices just yet and she was unable to lift her eyelids. She slowly opened her eyes, but her vision was blurry, and she had to wait for things to come into focus. Her mouth was dry, and her lips were chapped. They felt as though they would split open if she tried to move them. Within minutes nurses were surrounding her poking, prodding and asking her questions like 'did she know where she was?' By process of elimination she decided that she was in the hospital. It was then that she learned the amount of damage she had suffered at the hands of Hakeem. Amidst the countless bruises, she had a concussion, seven stiches to her head right above her right eye which was also red on the inside and black on the outside, a busted lip, bruising on her inner thighs and pubic area, and anal tearing which required stiches. As she set there listening she felt herself losing control of her emotions. She was so careful, she always watched her back. How did it come to this? How did he find her? So many questioned filled her head all at once.

The softest touch grazed across her hand, and her heart began to beat madly, which increased the beeping sound of the machine. "You didn't think you could run me off that easily?" Monea asked. The sound of her voice was enough for Mercedes to momentarily forget the pain she felt throughout her body. "I'm so sorry!" Mercedes blurted out as tears traveled down her cheeks. "This was the situation I needed to talk to you about." She then told Monea everything there was to tell about her life with Hakeem. Mercedes talked about the love they once shared, the abuse she experienced at his hands, and most importantly the day she left. Mercedes also talked about the first moment she laid eyes on her, and the moment she knew she loved her. She then told Monea when she started back receiving calls and threatening messages from Hakeem again, and why she chose to push her away.

"What made you decide to call me again?" Monea asked as she held on to her lover's hand. Mercedes lifted Monea's hand to her lips and kissed it gently. "I remembered why I chose to leave Hakeem in the first place. I wanted to live a life where I wasn't scared anymore. Me choosing to be in love and to love who I want felt like I was finally breaking away from him. Please believe me I would never have put you in any danger, I didn't know he knew where I was. I still don't know how he found me, I thought I was being so careful. What did I do wrong?" "You did nothing wrong. From this moment forward we are not living in fear of Hakeem. We are going to walk out of here, we are going to heal, and we will move forward," Monea spoke with so much passion, Mercedes knew in that moment she wanted to spend the rest of her life with her. And that is exactly what they did, but that's another story.

About the Author

Was born in March of 77, she currently lives in Georgia with her family. She is an author and an advocate, who's passion is to assist victims of domestic/partner violence in the LGBTQ community. Her mission is to help victims of domestic/partner violence understand they are not alone. Everyone needs to know that there is someone in their corner during a dark time. For this reason, she founded Mercedes' Closet which is a nonprofit geared to offering support and resources in the LGBTQ community for not only victims of domestic/partner violence but also victims of other violent crimes such as rape, hate crimes, as well as trans-violence, which is due to officially launch in the beginning of 2020.

April Jackson-Hunter received a Master of Art in Forensic Psychology from Argosy University. A Bachelor of Science in Business Administration from Herzing University. She has a love for a plethora of things, but books and literature has always been her passion. Her story isn't different from anyone else's, she took a portion of her life that wouldn't be forgotten and harnessed it. Her life is filled with family and memories that would get her through some long, rough, and sleepless nights. She experienced violence at the hands of someone who was supposed to love her. For many years after this she battled fear, guilt, and shame until she couldn't mentally handle it anymore.

After seeking help for what she thought were mental instabilities, she received some game changing advice. A counselor suggested that she start a journal in an attempt to help with reoccurring nightmares and insomnia issues.

The journal she started turned into the literary work of art you see in front of you today.

To Find out about April's upcoming events and organization go to

www.MercedesCloset.com